Memories of No One

Jaclyn Titterington

Dedication

To Mike, for telling me to become better.

Contents

Contents

Part I: Nothing but Flashes

"If you wish to live, then don't rely on the supposed kindness of others."

—Amon Ballory

Prologue

Even in this world that I was forced to grow up in, there was just one piece of advice or more of a truth that stuck with me. The more a sovereign is allowed to take, the more he is going to want to take. A bridge of ice is what a select few of us walked on from the day we were born, and surrounded by an ever growing chasm. If a man tried to please one sovereign, he would find it difficult; if he tried to please two, it would be almost impossible. Seven sovereigns would be considered a death sentence, for all.

   This story had to be recorded in secret, for it would have been considered treason if it were ever found out. It was dangerous to know the truth, and those who knew would disappear, or even be executed on a false charge.

   If you were to ask people how they thought the end of the world happened, you would get the usual answers. War, resources were used up, the environment continually rotting made the world collapse on itself, or there wasn't a place to go found in time. But, no one ever guessed the reason that really happened; the extensive genetic engineering of trees. If I was around for the end of the world, I would have said it was war; the constant fighting and bloodshed would have just brought fire raining down on the world. But, I wasn't even close.

Chapter 1

Elena

I didn't have long to get from my house to the Justice Building. Having to rush annoyed me, for I would forget something vital and with what I was going to be doing…things could go from bad to deadly in just a few seconds. I also had to get to the building before my father, or anyone with an officer rank, made it there. It was easier for me to sneak around those who hadn't had the years of training and experience.

Lacing up my boots outside, Enrik, the family wolf, came up to me and licked my face. "I can't take you with me; it's not easy to hide you from those with guns."

"And you think it's easy for you to hide in there? I don't think so." I looked up to see my twin brother, Selig, holding an axe over his shoulder. He was covered in sweat and currently mopping up his face with his shirt; the various scars on his torso seemed to be screaming at me to stare at them.

"Why do I get the feeling you're going to be doing something that will irritate dad?"

"What makes you think that what you're going to do won't make him want to smack you?" Selig cocked his head to the side, raising an eyebrow. I had always been a little jealous that I've never been able to do that before. "Besides, it'll be more believable if we both go." He put the axe against the house and walked into the house. At the most, he was just going to change clothes and wipe off the sweat. Water was a very precious resource; too valuable to use for an everyday bath. We were all used to having some dirt on our skin or sweat on our faces for a week or two before we actually found it necessary to bathe.

Selig came back out a minute later wearing the same dark pants, but with a different shirt. He had chosen the cream colored shirt our mother had made him last year. He was pulling on his brown jacket, the article of clothing he never went anywhere without. I snapped my fingers and pointed at the house, sending Enrik back inside. "Keep it up and you're going to have to have mom patch up the jacket again."

● ● ●

We didn't start on our way until Selig latched the door shut behind Enrik. Normally Enrik went everywhere with us, but for what we were about to do, it was better that he stayed home. There didn't need to be any accidental bloodshed on property that was owned by the Royal Province of Arcadia.

The last thing we wanted was to draw attention to ourselves, so we took separate paths to the Justice Building. Selig went through the market square and I took the more abstract route of going through nature and the forgotten paths.

The war had been broken down and was now just being called a thorn in the previous King's side; which was inherited by the new King. But, those who it still effected called it the Soli Rebellion, or just a campaign for false hope. The rebellion had happened over a hundred years ago, and my brother and I had grown up in this lifestyle that was thrust upon those who survived the slaughter. The once vibrant city of Ragnar was now nothing but a broken shadow. I had seen some decaying photographs of the city that the elderly held onto from previous generations. We had a few things in a lockbox, but no one ever looked at the photographs. We all knew it would just bring on unnecessary feelings. Too much of a burden. Even though we couldn't seem to get rid of them, maybe we all just needed something to hold onto.

I stuck to the outer limits of the area that was considered livable, holding lost or abandoned houses which were slowly degrading into nothing. Even the stone foundations that once would have withstood the fall of man had been wilting away. I shook my head and continued on; the brief conversation Selig and I had ate up more time than I realized.

Selig had beaten me to the Justice Building, which meant only one thing. The love of his life wasn't in the market square, at least not at this time. He was waiting outside, acting as nonchalant as he could. More like, as he cared to. He knew what I was going to be doing in a matter of minutes and didn't approve of it. Though, he knew, like me, it was the only way.

He just looked at me with a bored look on his face. "You don't have a lot of time."

"Are you here to help or hinder me?" I asked, fighting the urge to roll my eyes. We had enough time to get what I needed to do done.

Selig opened the main doors. "I'm going with a little bit of both." Walking inside, we went left, the way to the high officer offices.

Selig and I had been in the Justice Building more times than either of us cared to keep track of. When we were younger, it was because our father would bring us by with him if he had something to sign. As we stared to get older, we would be dragged in for getting into trouble.

Being second in command, Captain Carter Hawthorne's office was easy to find. Selig tried the door and found it was unlocked. "That's weird," he said, and we both looked at each other. The office was always locked, even when our father was in his office. The only way to unlock the door was with a one-of-a-kind key held only by the officer or the scanner on the underside of the desk, customized to the officer's handprint.

"You know, you two really need to work on your reconnaissance skills." We turned to see CROSS Second Class Lieutenant Amon Ballory standing there. He held up a silver key in his hand.

"Lieutenant…" said Selig.

Ballory was our father's personal assistant, and he also dealt with the demolitions for CROSS. He was dressed in the CROSS fatigues of black cargo pants, a charcoal grey colored sleeveless shirt, and a black tank top over it. His short, dark hair was all tasseled showing he had either finished exercising or he was training the newest recruits. For all we knew, he was practicing making stuff that would blow up when someone breathed wrong. He tossed me the key. "Carry on. Oh and, Elena…be more careful next time, you didn't get that key from me." Without another word, he walked away, not looking back at us.

"Think he's known the whole time?"

"Ballory wouldn't have stolen the key from dad if he didn't know." I ushered him inside and closed the door behind us. I used the same key to unlock the desk drawer and stopped. It had been awhile since either of us had been in the office for longer than a minute. I looked around the office, wondering if his sense of personal touches had changed at all. They hadn't. The office was bare, as it was since the day he was given this place. The only thing that made it his office was the handprint reader on the underside of the desk and the House animals that were burned into the walls.

Ragnar is located within the Blackwater Province which has the mascot of a Master Wolf. I was told the term master came from a specific breed of wolf that bore only Alpha wolves. Arcadia, where the Capitol, Ashtan, resides, has a bird known as the Raptor as their mascot. The Raptor is a massive blood-red bird favoring only the flesh of a certain kind of human. The House Animal of Aion is a Grand Stag. A mighty creature that those who are truly a part of Aion could ride, or so the rumor says. The Grand Stag is more dangerous than the Master Wolf and the Raptor.

Kouros' mascot is an Ophidian, or a rather dangerous snake which I've only seen drawings of. The Xing Province uses a Sea Dragon, or Kraken, and Banorae has a Black Scorpion as their House Animal. Solanum, the last of the seven provinces, stands proudly with a Sand Fox.

Seeing the images of each animal burned into our father's office wall has always been a little strange to me. Yes, at the moment, the provinces are at peace, but it is a forced peace. "Burning up time, Elena," Selig said, bringing me back to reality.

Using the same key we unlocked the door with, I opened the desk. We gathered everything we needed and I snatched the key from his desk drawer, locking it back. As we leave, I get the feeling that Ballory was how we had gotten into our father's office before. Right now, I have no idea if it was good for me to be in his debt or not.

Outside the Justice Building, I toss Selig the key. I was about to go break some rules and, as far as I knew, Selig was not. He frowned and pocketed the office key. I knew exactly where he was going. I would have wished him luck, but I found it strange to wish my twin brother luck when he is going to see his girlfriend. "Watch your back," he said.

"Same to you."

● ● ●

Selig and I went our separate ways. A moment later, I spot our father walking toward the building. Running late, I picked up my pace and started to run. I made my way through a forgotten path, shaving two minutes off my time.

++++

Sindri was already there when I arrived. He gave me a simple nod before going back to concentrating on what he was doing. "Where's the other one?" I asked, pulling out the pack that I kept hidden from under the brush. The citizens of Ragnar City were subject to random searches. Carrying something you weren't supposed to have fell under the same authority code as stealing or walking around the square in broad daylight armed. Which was why I never carried my most prized possession around, my three-inch, serrated-blade hunting knife.

"He should be on his way back from disabling the sensors by now," Sindri grunted as he gave up on the metal wheel that kept the restricted door shut and locked at all times. He bent over, leaning on his knees, and breathing heavily. "I think this thing has rusted shut," he stated in between breaths.

I held up the key, amused at his effort. "Sindri..."

He looked up at me and groaned. "You always have this stupid door unlocked before I get here."

"I got caught up with something," I say, deciding that telling him Ballory knew exactly what we were doing wouldn't be the smartest thing to do.

"Father, brother, sister, mother, or wolf?"

"Wolf," I say, noting that Selig had been helping me.

He took the key and unlocked the door. After tossing it back to me, I watched him do his part.

Rotating his shoulders, he gripped the wheel and started to turn. He was the only one would could do this. It took three people to get where we were going and we all had a specific job. There wasn't any need to overlap where it wasn't necessary.

"We're racing all the way to the bottom this time," Sindri said, giving me his charming grin. "Get ready to be left behind."

• • •

"Only in your dreams." I pulled my hair back into a messy knot. "I mean, there was that one time I had to save your ass."

Sindri gave me a playful shove. "I know you can. Having a father in charge of keeping order, all you'll get is a slap on the wrist." He was still grinning. I knew he only said it to get a rise out of me, and it was working. My father's position had gotten us out of a harsher sentence once or twice before.

Sindri Anton and I have been best friends for as long as I can remember. We were about as different as it gets, but it works for us. I am from the northern part of Ragnar City, also known as the Northern Wall, and Sindri is from the southern part of the city. Like night and day, the city is split in a definitive half. Laborers and impoverish citizens reside in the north, whereas nobles and merchants lived in the south. The differences didn't stop with the societal classification, the north and south also differed in culture and appearance, like separate provinces mashed into one.

Sindri, aside from living at the furthest northern point of the south, looked very southern with his light colored hair, grey eyes, and pale skin. I, on the other hand, had the northern look of dark hair, blue eyes, and olive tone skin. We also live along the invisible line of distinction. My mother is from the south whereas my father is from the north. Unlike my sister and twin brother who take after my mother in appearance, I look like my father.

Even though Sindri had an easier life than I did being a merchant's only son, I respected him. He rarely went without food on the table, but he was out here with me breaking one of the most sacred rules; stealing water from the reservoir.

"If we're going, now is the time."

We looked up to see Mihkel Tiitus standing there in all his self-inspired glory. Mihkel was a close friend of Sindri's, but he and I weren't that close. When we first met six years ago, sparks flew. Though, not in the way one would think. If I had my way, I would haven't anything to do with him. Unfortunately, he was essential for us to get to the bottom of the reservoir for the city. Like it was essential for me to steal a key from my father and Sindri to have the strength from being the masonry merchant's son. Mihkel knew how to deactivate the sensors, something he refused to tell Sindri or myself how to do.

Sindri tossed Mihkel a black strap made of animal's skin.

"How much time do we have?"

"Fifteen minutes at the most," Mihkel said, tying the strap around his left wrist. He took the strap off his right wrist and handed it to Sindri. "How long have we been exchanging these things?"

"Ever since you saved me from falling to my death."

I remembered that night like it was yesterday. We had made the decision to come up here at night, which was stupid. It had rained earlier, making the rocks, metal, and tree roots slick. It was almost impossible to get a grip on anything. We used to climb down into the reservoir relying on our own strength, but last year, Sindri lost his grip and fell about eighteen feet. He managed to grab hold of a cable, saving himself from a deadly plummet. His hand was broken in four places, but he was alive. Mihkel got to him before I did and wrapped the leather strap he always had around his arm, around his wrist, giving Sindri something hold onto. Ever since, they've been trading the strap. Since that incident, we began taking more precautions. Our families depend on us, death is not an option. To help our cause, we pull on fingerless gloves, allowing for a better grip.

My brother, Selig, was handy to have around the house, but our skills differed. Each equally important, but also equally necessary. He could build and repair things with the little material available to him. The house we lived in was small, but it wasn't a poor excuse of a house. Anything broken, Selig had it repaired within a day or two. I remembered him building a small shed that held what tools he was able to acquire over the years and doubled as a place Enrik would sleep. The catch, he had to work with supplies around him. Which meant the trees. The trees that looked to be a hundred years old when they were only a year old. The trees that had bark so solid, it took the sharpest tools and the strongest diligence to make a dent. Luckily, one tree was enough lumber to last the family for a few years. Growing up, we had to use everything sparingly, so using the wood only when we truly needed it wasn't anything new. Whereas with me, I mastered scaling heights and tree jumping, one of the more dangerous activities done in the city surrounded by the massive trees.

"I'll go down first," I said, tightening my gloves to prevent them from coming loose.

Volunteering to check the sensors meant I got to pick the easiest way down, through the trees. The trees around the reservoir were so giant, it was a battle to see which ones would survive in the area. Oak trees swallowed up the sky when the leaves were alive, making it almost impossible to know whether it was night or day. The willows with branches so dense, they kept the rain off one's shoulders. Pines with needles so razor sharp, you didn't realize you were cut until a part of you was covered in blood. If you could handle the pain, then the trees became an irreplaceable ally; as they had for me. I was the best at climbing trees; I was the lightest and it was something my father had taught me how to do. I taught myself tree jumping, an essential skill to have in today's world.

I took one last look at Sindri and Mihkel. They were moving toward the other ways of getting down to the water. Sindri had chosen to go by the cables which were put in by CROSS so they had an easier time accessing the water. The problem with this route were the leftover ruined buildings. The previous world had mastered the art of stable buildings which is why they're still disintegrating. While the trees could be someone's greatest ally, they could also be their biggest enemy. Some of the tree roots have grown through the buildings, keeping the buildings in place. With Sindri choosing the industrial path, that left Mihkel with the rocks and tree roots. The Eastern wall was a mix of clay, rock, and random hollowed spots where precious gems were mined out long ago. Because of the hollow spots, I found that route to be random stepping stones. It was the hardest route, not only because you have to have an advanced knowledge of the ever changing layout, but also because the sensors started up there again.

I took a deep breath and let it out slowly. Relaxing my body, I jumped. I reached my hand out to the nearest branch, finding myself coming up short. I had to grab it. Missing the jump would mean marks, bruises, possible broken bones. The gloves prevented my hands from tearing, an indicator my father would surely catch onto, but, if I couldn't land the jump, my father would definitely know what we were doing today.

I felt my fingertips brush the branch and I immediately threw my other arm forward, managing to grab hold of the branch with my left hand. I swung there for a couple of seconds, strengthening my hold on the branch. I started to pull myself up and froze. I was face to face with a tree climber snake. It was flicking its tongue out at me, preparing to rear back and strike my face. I closed my eyes for a moment, grounding myself for my next move, when a short burst of air and whir of sound flew by my face. I immediately opened my eyes, finding the snake pinned to the tree by an arrow.

Turning, I saw Mihkel holding the black bow that had once been my great-grandfather's. He had seen the snake, too. Mihkel's handle and skill with the bow was phenomenal, which is why I had given it to him in the first place. He was much more agile than I was and rarely missed his target.

Sindri and Mihkel didn't break their gaze until I pulled myself up onto the branch. I took out my treasured hunting knife and worked the arrow out of the tree. The arrow was one of blacksmith's secret projects; it was sharper than any knife he was allowed to make and sell to Ragnar citizens. Stuffing the snake and the arrow inside my pack, I was ready to go again. There were a few in Ragnar City who wasted game, I wasn't one of them. Food and supplies were hard to come by for someone living in the Northern region. Most of what my family called food was traded for by Selig selling his skills to the merchants. There were some people who could grow vegetables in the dry soil we had to work with, but along with the lack of water, most people gave up trying to grow food. It cost money, time, water, and space they just didn't have. Mihkel was one of around five who had the equipment to hunt. Sindri went with him most times to help set up traps while I went with hopes of learning how to hunt. I spent most of my time gathering up edible plants and, once in a while, fishing with a net Sindri had made out of willow tree vines. The snake Mihkel had just killed wasn't ideal for human consumption, I knew from personal experience. The meat wasn't cooked enough, making the poison the snake carried rather strong. Too little heat and the poison could be lethal; too

● ● ●

17

much heat and the meat dissolved before one could eat it. Just enough heat, made the snake a meal. It was rare to get just the right amount of heat when all you had was fire. In the end, I would give the snake to Enrik. His stomach would be able to handle the snake without any issues. We also couldn't leave any evidence behind. We were already breaking too many rules just by being here.

A soft mechanical, beeping noise sounded next to my ear. It was time to move or get caught. I signaled to the others that the sensors would be back up in ten minutes or less and gathered my bearings for the next jump.

"See you at the bottom," I muttered to myself.

I had gotten halfway done the tree when I noticed that Mihkel had caught up with me. We didn't stop as we looked at each other. Sindri wasn't far behind. Due to his hand, he had to move much slower. After the incident, Mihkel had to set his hand and it had never healed quite right.

I reach out to latch onto another branch. I had five left to maneuver before we were in the clear. Suddenly, my vision flashes white and I am no longer in the trees.

My vision is blurry. I look around, blinking, trying to find any indicator of where I am. It's white. Everything is white. I sit up abruptly only to have my neck jerk back. I scream, the pain that suddenly shoots through my body unbearable. The pain subsides and my pulse quickens, my hands shaking. I reach up, trying to find the offensive object that hindered me from moving when the pain starts again. Sharp, pulsating pain shooting through my neck and down my spine renders me useless. I can't move, my body stiffening and contracting. Flashes of memory play through my head like a video reel. Wires attached to my head, a stark white room with nothing in it. I scream again, the pain getting worse. I can feel my adrenaline soar in compensation for the pain. I can't fight the terror taking over my body.

There are branches around me again, my vision coming back. I let out a scream at the jarring images that just flashed through my head and frantically reach for the branch. My hand brushes just short and I'm falling.

"Elena!" they both yell.

Twisting my body around, I see that I am closer to the water than I realized. I manage to take my pack off and put it in front of my face, attempting to lessen the impact. It was going to hurt when I hit the water, but this gave me a chance at surviving.

I landed in the water, my muscles tightening from the impact, the air knocked out of my lungs.

I shot out of the water, gasping for air. My lungs contracted and retracted, each breath painful to suck in. I mentally assessed for any damage. Nothing feels broken. I try to calm my breathing, forcing myself to take deep breaths. I watch as Sindri dives into the water, Mihkel following suit. There was something different about his dive. He was graceful, avoiding any and all debris as he came into the water. He came up to the surface and looked at the two of us.

"What?" he asked.

"You sure you aren't from the Royal Province?" asked Sindri, climbing out of the water. He pulled himself onto the metal island, a broken down building that had been sinking in the water for the past hundred years.

"Only those from the east would have the time to perfect something like that," he continued.

"You should know by now that I am truly a miner's son," Mihkel grunted. It was true, he had dark hair and dark eyes similar to mine, but his hair has a permanent tone of grey mixed in, a significant trait of a miner. Like a permanent layer of dust passed on through their families.

"Lay off," I said. I didn't care that Sindri was questioning Mihkel, we were just running out of time.

Mihkel checked his watch. "We have five minutes."

"All right then," Sindri stated, opening up his pack.

We took out our containers and started to fill them up with water. I filled up the first one and quickly proceeded to the second container. This wasn't a foolproof plan. We could each only carry a few gallons, but this was how it had to be now. We had tried coming down more than once a day, but it ended...unpleasantly. Mihkel couldn't disable the sensors more than once every few days without the authorities taking notice. That is, if they haven't already. Ballory was one of the kinder officers in CROSS, but that didn't mean he wouldn't turn us in.

● ● ●

As I finished filling up the second container, Mihkel's watch beeped. "We need to get out of here. Before CROSS, or even GUARD, comes," Sindri stated, gathering up his pack.

As we started to put the containers up, we heard a familiar sound.

"That's not good..." Mihkel whispered.

We slowly looked up, locking eyes with about twenty men in CROSS uniforms. They all had their guns drawn and pointed at us. "Go!" Sindri yelled. "Go!"

We dove into the water, hoping they hadn't closed the underwater gate. I hadn't gotten five feet when I felt a sharp pain in my side. I tried to push forward, but felt myself being tugged back as the pain intensified.

Being ripped from the water, I hung in the air with a metal claw clamped in my side. All I could do was watch as my blood seeped out of my wounds and dripped into the water, immediately disappearing. My pack had fallen off, sinking to bottom of the reservoir with the weight held inside. I looked around, searching for Sindri and Mihkel. We had all been caught. Sindri was hanging by his ankle. From the look on his face, it was broken. Mihkel was hanging perfectly still, the claw clamped around his collarbone. One slight move, his neck would be broken. "Well, well, well... this is an odd place for you three to be," a man with a familiar voice said.

I had to wait until the cord turned enough to see his face. With water in my eyes, my vision was blurry. The black military boots, black pants, and matching vest of the CROSS uniform stood out to me. The white and blue sash tied around the waist signified that of a higher ranked officer. With the over jacket and white button down shirt, I had always thought the combat uniforms were a little showy. But, I've seen my father in action and it never seemed to hinder their movement. So, I wasn't one to point out my opinions. Especially not to the twenty armed men that looked rather angered right now.

Finally, the water cleared from my eyes, my vision becoming normal once more. Dragan Sayers. My father's partner, friend, and third in command of CROSS. "You three better have one hell of an explanation for why you're out here."

Chapter 2

The three of us were separated. I didn't recognize the CROSS member who took Sindri away, but the one who took Mihkel away was one I never wanted to anger. CROSS Second Class Lieutenant Nazar. A man who enjoyed the part of interrogating more than anything else. Did Ballory turn us in or did we miss something? It was at that moment I was wishing my father, the second in command, was in charge of interrogations. He typically didn't enforce too much punishment on those he thought didn't deserve it. But, I had the misfortune of being Sayers's first victim.

Ballory escorted me to Sayers's office without a word. As he unlocked the door, I looked at him. "Did you turn us in?" I asked, not attempting to hide the anger in my voice.

He didn't say anything as he shoved me into the office, kicking the door closed behind us. "Sit down," he said.

"I'm not going to do anything until you tell me—" Ballory shoved me against the wall, placing his hand over my mouth.

"Elena, you need to be quiet. Give me the key." I felt my muscles tense up as his body pressed up against mine, his permanent five o'clock shadow millimeters from my face. His grey eyes showed an intensity I had never seen before.

Without a second thought, I reached for my knife. Just as Ballory started to relax, I swiped it at him, cutting him on his neck and under his right eye. He clutched at his neck and spun me around, wrapping his free arm around my neck. "You're getting pretty good with that knife." He sent me back to the wall, my knife in his hand. "Remember what I taught you?" He raised the knife to be level with my collarbone.

Ballory had taught me a few things, none of which I wanted to discuss. Right now, I wanted was my knife back in my hand. "You know how I feel about personal space," I breathed.

Flipping the knife around so the handle was facing me, he held it out to me. "Every cut is a lesson, every lesson makes us better." He checked his lower lip for blood, sighing when his fingers came away smeared with it. "Give me the key. I need to return it to your father's office."

● ● ●

Slowly, I took out the key that I had stolen not even an hour ago and put it into Ballory's hand, trading him for the knife. He slipped the key in his jacket and smiled.

"You're getting very good. Keep it up and you'll be able to hold your own against someone like your father. Now, sit down. Captains Sayers will be here any second."

I sat down in the chair Ballory motioned to and slipped my knife back into my boot. Sayers wouldn't be able to see it unless he was looking for it or searched me. I watched as Ballory touched his neck and cheekbone.

"I'm going to have to arm myself next time. I'm going to need stitches."

"Told you that I wouldn't be a disappointment."

"Still. Keep in mind—if you wish to live, don't rely on the supposed kindness of others."

Ballory touched the side of his head. "Not bad, Elena. But, remember."

"Not today."

"Or any day."

Our conversation was interrupted by the door opening and Captain Sayers walking in. The sounds of someone screaming broke the barrier, quickly fading off as he shut the door behind him. He had a file in his hand and continued to read it as he walked over to his desk, acting as though he was more interested in the contents instead of interrogating me.

"So, tell me something, Elena Hawthorne. Why should I allow you to leave here alive?"

I just stared at him, not knowing how to answer the question. More so, not knowing if he wanted an answer. Sayers motioned to Ballory's face. "You do that to my Lieutenant?"

"Captain…" Ballory started.

"I don't want to hear excuses or any covering up for her," snapped Sayers.

"Go make sure Nazar doesn't get too carried away with the miner's kid."

Ballory rushed out of the room. Not because he was afraid of Sayers, but because once Nazar got going on an interrogation, it was hard to stop him. The scar Sayers hid with his collar was a souvenir from Nazar. Along with the abdomen

● ● ●

scars my brother carried. I turned to look at Sayers. He placed the file down and took his glasses off, pinching the bridge of his nose. "Elena, when are you going to learn?"

++++

The force of his hand knocked me to the floor. I felt dizzy as my head hit the stone. I had to close my eyes and focus on breathing, the too familiar metallic taste of blood coating my mouth.

"What the hell were you thinking?" Sayers shouted, putting his boot on my neck.

"Do you know how lucky you are it was me that showed up and not Captain Bogdan from GUARD? He would have issued your kill order on sight. He doesn't care that your father is second in command. That only means something to the officers and soldiers in CROSS."

I had to fight not to bring up how much it bothered Sayers that he was only third in command and had to answer to my father. I probably would have ended up with a broken nose for that comment.

"W-We ne-needed the w-water," I managed to whisper, Sayers' boot unrelenting on my throat. It was true. We did need the water. We were a family of five, struggling with normal rations. That, and my younger sister has Stigma disease. Hydration is a big part of keeping her remotely healthy.

"Your father was handling it," said Sayers, removing his boot from my neck and coming to stand in front of me. The front of his boot wasn't even three centimeters from my face. I knew he was doing it on purpose. While my father chose to apply physical pain, that wasn't Sayers's style. He liked interrogating through scare tactics, showing people just how much control he had over them before inflicting pain.

"It would have taken too long." I slowly blinked once and looked up at him from the floor. "You know I'm right. The CROSS badge doesn't mean much to the higher authority figures.

Sayers didn't say anything as he lifted me up to my feet and put two fingers under my chin, forcing me to look at him. "I can't keep saving you and your friends. Your father can't either,

• • •

sooner or later you will be taken to the Arcadian Capitol by GUARD. When that happens, we can't do anything for you."

Law enforcement in Ragnar City was handled by CROSS. It was also the law enforcement all over the livable parts of the world. And, it was run by three men. CROSS First Class Captain Dragan Sayers, CROSS First Class Captain Carter Hawthorne, and General Elias Nolan. From the little bit of history my father was willing to give us, my father grew up with the two in the Royal Province before they were transferred to Ragnar City. For what, I had no idea. They probably broke some rules. But, being the exceptional team that they are, the King couldn't bear to part with them. GUARD was the military force that resided over CROSS in Arcadia with the same layout. I've never met any of the men in charge of GUARD, for which I am thankful.

"Captain Sayers," another member of CROSS came into the office. It was Lieutenant Solomon Cried, also known as CROSS Second Class. "You're needed in the holding room. Nazar has that look in his eyes again and the miner's kid has lost some blood."

Sayers groaned and ran a hand through his hair. He picked up his glasses from the desk and slipped them on. "Get her checked out in the medical bay and let them know there's a possible emergency coming. The last thing I need is to have Craig Tiitus in an uproar," he commanded before running out of the office.

Solomon kept the door open, acting like he was waiting for me to stand up and walk out. After a minute or so, he stuck his head out into the hallway and then closed the door behind him. He walked over to me and took a couple seconds to look at my face. His face was so close to mine, his sandy colored hair grazed my cheek. He put his arm around my waist to keep me steady. He knew I would fight him if he tried to carry me, so he decided to just forgo it. There was already enough of my blood on the stone floor, neither of us saw any reason to add anymore.

As he walked and I stumbled along, Solomon kept me from falling. My head started to spin and I hoped I wasn't going to be sick. I managed to get through the door with his arm around my waist. As he was locking the door behind us, he looked at me. "What happened this time?" he asked.

"My family needs water," I said. "Normally gathering rain water gets us the water we need, but it hasn't rained in over a hundred days."

Solomon suddenly pulled me into an empty office and shut the door, not caring that I was leaving a trail of blood with every step I took. He turned and kissed me lightly. The familiar warmth of his lips against mine was stronger than normal. His scent was masked by the almost sickly sweet scent of the overpriced specialty soap sold in the market square. Something the majority of people could never afford. I felt a numb spot at the base of my neck. I broke the kiss and he looked at the side of my face and cringed slightly. "Who did this to you?"

It being actually the mix of Ballory giving me a random lesson and Sayers being Sayers… "Sayers," I said simply. It wasn't the first time I had been hit, it was how my father disciplined Selig and me at home. He never overdid it. One slap with the back of his hand, usually gloved, and then we were safe for a week or two. Of course, he never hit our mother or our little sister. Selig and I were exactly like our father, so he knew how we would respond to discipline.

Solomon was only a few years older than me, but he was from what people considered the nobility in this city. Becoming a Lieutenant was easy for him. He took something out of his pocket and put it in my hand. "These will help, just don't overdo it."

He had put a generous amount of hydration tablets in my hand. A person could take one of these and their body would be hydrated for twenty-four hours. They're used for military personnel and only meant to be used in emergency situations. They aren't a total replacement for water, but they would do in a bind. "I suggest you come to me before breaking the rules again."

"Thank you," I said, slowly pulling myself up on my toes and grabbing onto his jacket, using it to keep my balance. I held my breath as I gave him a chaste kiss, the warmth from his lips gone. He returned the kiss before breaking it.

"I'll escort you to medical bay."

* * *

I opened my mouth to protest, but a wave of dizziness and nausea overcame me. I clutched his jacket to keep from falling. He wrapped his arms around me, keeping me steady once more. Knowing my luck, Sayers probably gave me a concussion. Ballory's ambush hadn't helped much either.

++++

Medical Bay was the hospital for CROSS, GUARD, and the nobility of Ragnar City. Common people like my family had no hope of getting the proper medical attention. While my father receives medical attention as a favor from the doctor, it's only because of the favor. My father was supposed to marry a woman from a noble family from the Royal Province, but he married my mother instead. Yes, she was a Southerner from Ragnar City, but she wasn't from a noble family. I think those in the Arcadian Capitol still frowned on his choice of a wife.

I sat there on the examination table, barefoot and in my underwear. The flimsy gown the nurse made me put on was the only thing covering me and I was freezing. The dizziness and nausea had gone away by the time the doctor came in.

Damien Aryen was the head doctor in the hospital. Though, he didn't look like the traditional doctor. He had long, dark hair kept back in a low ponytail with his bangs free and always had stubble on his chin. He was also usually seen with a cigarette in his mouth. He wasn't much for appearances, but he did keep his glasses immaculately clean. Sighing, he looked at me through his glasses. "Do I even want to know what happened?"

"My face met Sayers's hand," I said. "Then my head hit the floor."

"Do I want to know what you were doing before this happened?" Damien pulled on gloves. He gently touched the swelling cut on my cheek. "You don't need stitches, but you'll have a scar."

I was used to scarring, I had quite a few of them and didn't feel like they were a huge deal. Most of them from tree jumping and scaling down to the water reservoir. There were also the ones from getting hit by my father or another member of

• • •

CROSS. Then, a few from skinning and cleaning game that Sindri would bring to my house.

Damien put a couple butterfly bandages on my cheek and moved to the cut on my head. "It's just a scrape," he said as he started to clean up the cut.

"I had some dizziness and nausea when I hit the ground."

"How long did it last?"

"Maybe two minutes, at most."

Damien didn't say anything as he looked at the cuts in my side from the metal claw that grabbed me this morning. He cleaned those quickly and turned his back to me. He came back around and my throat tightened at seeing he had the items needed for stitching. "I don't want to hear one word," he said sternly. "You're lucky that you're getting this much treatment."

He had a point. Damien had the medical technology to begin the healing process almost immediately, but, like everything else, it was off-limits to the regular citizens of the Blackwater Province.

As Damien was stitching up the cuts on my side, he sighed again. "Why do you keep doing this?"

"You know why."

"As much as I enjoy seeing you...I would rather not be the one that declares your cause of death to your parents."

We remained silent as he finished stitching up my cuts, only stopping when I started to hold my breath. I had to force him to stop when a very strong wave of nausea came over me.

As I tried to stand up, my legs went weak underneath my weight and I collapsed in Damien's arms. "Easy, Elena," he said, helping me back on the examination table. "You've lost more blood than you realized."

I kept my eyes closed and laid down on my good side. I jumped slightly when I felt a cool gel on my side. The pain started to melt away. "That will keep the pain away for at least twelve hours."

Damien stripped his gloves off and went over to the sink. As he was washing his hands, I could tell he had something on his mind. "How's Ally doing?"

Ally, or Allison, was my younger sister. "She's okay. Well, as much as she can be," I said.

● ● ●

"Keeping her hydrated?"

"It's kind of hard when we have little to no water."

Damien frowned and dried his hands. He picked up a small notepad that had his name and rank on it and wrote something down. Tearing the piece of paper off, he handed it to me. "This is to get some water. Give it to your father the next time you see him and he'll know what to do with it."

"Thank you."

"When I get the chance, I will come by to check on your sister." He picked up a syringe and filled it with a light green liquid. "This will kill any infection you might get." He injected it into my arm.

"Aren't you afraid of being exposed to my blood? I mean, Ally has Stigma and I've been exposed to it every day."

"I have immunity to Stigma, just as you do, Elena."

++++

Damien had left so I could get dressed. I was pulling on my black t-shirt when there was a knock on the door. Since I had already pulled my pants on, everything was covered. "It's open," I said.

Ballory came into the room with a grim look on his face. My heart went in my throat when I saw he was covered in blood. "What the hell happened?" Damien asked moving over to Ballory.

"It's not my blood, its Nazar's. He's…gotten carried away again."

"Who is it?"

"Mihkel Tiitus."

"Bring him in here." Damien pulled on a new pair of gloves and gave me a pair. "Elena, this will be your life in a matter of days, so I suggest you get used to it." What he said had meaning to it. In a matter of days I would be eighteen and that meant I would have to choose a profession. I was pretty adamant about not going into CROSS, but I had to pick something. My mother had pushed me toward becoming a healer, which is what she had once done. Although, I wasn't like her; I didn't have a gift for this. Everyone else's pain made me freeze, the sight of a stranger's blood made me feel sick, and the smell of burning flesh sent me running. Damien had already signed off on me training under him, as a favor to my parents. So, I didn't have much of a choice.

As I fumbled to pull the gloves on, Ballory and Sayers brought in a very weak looking Mihkel. They laid him on the table. Just as Sayers was about to leave, Ballory grabbed his arm with a blood hand. I couldn't hear what they were saying, but I had a feeling I knew what it was about. Sayers took out his sidearm and checked it. Not even attempting to conceal the gun, he walked out of the room, letting the door slam shut behind him.

"What's going on?" I asked.

Ballory didn't answer as he helped Damien rip the blood soaked clothes off of Mihkel's torso. "What in the Gods...?" Damien asked. Unable to look away, I saw what gave Damien the look of horror on his face. Mihkel's body, usually the olive tone skin color like mine, was now pale. Even as Ballory tried to wipe off the blood of the multiple cuts, fresh blood replaced it seconds later. Nazar had taken a knife to Mihkel as if he was a piece of wood. While Mihkel had numerous scars like myself, these cuts wouldn't just be the thin lines that we acquired on almost a day-to-day basis. These would be deep, jagged, and it would be almost impossible to hide them.

"How long did you leave that bloodthirsty monster alone with him?" Damien continued.

"I don't even think he asked a question, he just started in on him," Ballory said. "Sayers gave him a shot of emergency coagulant and medical adrenaline."

"It's a good thing he did." Damien filled up a syringe with a black liquid. "Nazar caught an artery, probably more than one. I can't tell. Who cleared him to receive this medical care?"

"Captain Sayers and myself."

I did a double take at Mihkel's face. He was staring at me. "Elena," he whispered.

Not knowing what to do, I went over to him and held his hand. "Mihkel," Damien said. "I'm going to inject you with this medicine to slow the bleeding. Then, I'll start the process of

• • •

closing up your wounds. It's going to hurt like nothing you've ever experienced. Once I start, I can't stop it."

Mihkel just closed his eyes and squeezed my hand, hard enough his knuckles went white, as did mine. Ballory picked up a piece of thick leather and put it in Mihkel's mouth. "Bite down on this."

"You can't give him something for the pain?" I asked.

"He was cleared for treatment, but that doesn't mean it would be a pleasant experience for him," Ballory snapped.

"Mihkel, I need you to breathe," Damien said, ignoring me.

I held onto Mihkel's hand and Ballory leaned over Mihkel's legs with his torso to help keep him still. Damien stabbed Mihkel in his chest, injecting the medicine. I don't know if Mihkel screamed from the needle going into his heart, the black medicine coursing through his body, or both.

When Mihkel passed out from the pain, Damien checked his pulse and breathing. "He's going to make it, just needs to sleep off this nightmare," he said with a relieved look on his face. "Nice job, Elena."

"I didn't do anything," I said with raised eyebrows.

"You kept him calm despite what happened. I have a feeling if you weren't here, this would have been a lot harder." Damien pressed a button on the wall and waited.

The next thing I knew, I was being hustled into another room where a nurse instructed me to get undressed and get cleaned up. She pointed to a shower and motioned for me to undress. "The water will automatically start and you'll have five minutes to get clean. Then, it will shut off whether you want it to or not. When the water starts to sputter, you have one minute left. Now, hurry up and undress, I'm going to clean those for you."

Hastily, I undressed, attempting not to get Mihkel's blood everywhere. "Come now! The place will be spotless after you're done." The nurse clapped her hands a couple of times, trying to get me to go faster. Just as I pulled off my bra and underwear, the nurse snatched them from me, gathered up the rest of my clothes, and left.

• • •

I stepped into the shower stall. The water instantly turned on, the perfect temperature cascading over me. I undid my hair and started to comb my fingers through it, savoring the hot water. I saw there was soap and shampoo and swiftly began lathering my hair, wanting to get it as clean as I could. It was probably going to be a couple of weeks, at least, before I got to wash my hair again. Rinsing the shampoo out, I grabbed the bottle of liquid soap and started to scrub. Soon, I smelled like a mix of rare citrus fruit.

I had finished rinsing off just as the water started to sputter. Since there wasn't a valve to turn the water off, I stood under the water until it turned itself off. Stepping out, I picked up a thick, white towel and started to dry myself off. Wrapping the towel around my torso, I looked around, wondering what the hell I was going to do without my clothes.

++++

My clothes had never been cleaner. I pulled them on with the pleasant surprise that they were still warm. As I was pulling on my underwear, I stopped when I realized my stitches had gotten wet. Looking down to check them, my heart skipped a beat. They were gone, and so were the cuts that made them necessary. I didn't know why I was so surprised. I knew Damien had access to this medical technology, but I had never seen it work like this.

Finishing getting dressed, I combed my fingers through my wet hair and pulled it back into a messy knot. I wanted to see if Sindri and Mihkel were doing okay, but I had a feeling I would need an escort.

Walking out of the room, I saw Solomon had a pair of clear looking glasses on. He was currently in the middle of something. When he saw me, he smiled and took the glasses off. I realized they were the HUD glasses that all CROSS and GUARD member's wore. Each pair was personalized to each soldier and they acted like a lifeline for the soldiers. People like Sayers and Ballory typically had theirs on all the time. My father took his off when he was off the clock, but I had never seen them on Solomon.

• • •

Solomon looked relieved when I walked up to him. "The doc says you're good to go, I'll walk you home."

"I want to see how Sindri and Mihkel are doing," I said.

"Anton was already released. It was implied that he better get home before minds were changed. Tiitus is recovering still," he said, using their last names as if it were an annoyance for him to have to talk about them.

"I want to see Mihkel," I repeated.

Solomon fought not to roll his eyes and motioned for me to follow him. "Since you're going to go off on your own to find him, come on."

We walked down the hall and I saw we were going back in the examination room that I had been in. Solomon motioned for me to walk through the door and I did so with hesitation, making me wish I had knocked first.

Mihkel was completely naked aside from a small cloth around his waist. He had been cleaned up and the color was coming back to his face. As both of us blushed, I turned my head, a feeble attempt to hide my embarrassment. "Sorry," I said.

"Nothing you haven't seen before," Mihkel replied. "Could you hand me those clothes?"

I reached for the pile of clothes to see they were CROSS fatigues with a pair of thick black socks and black underwear on top. I felt heat rise up on my face once again. I handed him his clothes and turned my back to him. "You look good for an almost dead guy."

"Doc Aryen snuck in some higher medical attention when there weren't any witnesses. I'm going to have more scars than you now, but I guess I'm pretty lucky."

Mihkel was lucky. Few survived Nazar when he got a knife in his hand. I waited as I heard Mihkel struggle to get dressed. "This might be a strange request, but could you help me with my shirt?" he asked.

Carefully, I turned, catching a clear view of Nazar's work on his newest canvas. Mihkel had several linear cuts that looked randomly placed all over his torso and back, though, we both knew those cuts were placed there specifically. I picked up the sleeveless shirt and gently pulled it over Mihkel's head. Helping him work his arms through the shirt, I had to fight to

• • •

keep the heat from rushing to my face again. I helped with his tank top and he had managed to get the pants and socks on.

As I started to take a step back, Mihkel put his arm around my lower back and pulled me to him. Before I could tell him to stop, he kissed me. Unable to do anything, I just stood there. The familiar feeling of him touching me, brought the memories back of that time years ago, where we planned our days around seeing each other. He opened his eyes to see mine were filled with shock, causing him to break the kiss. "Sorry. I figured since I almost died, I should cheat death once more today."

Shoving his arm off me, I moved back and walked out of the room.

++++

"You know you were incredibly lucky this time," Solomon crossed his arms over his chest. I could see the cloth from his shirt tighten as his arm muscles expanded. "Just some advice, don't go to the reservoir again. Next time you won't be so lucky."

"What are you saying? Let my family die from dehydration?" I asked without looking at him. My lips were still tingling from the familiar touch of Mihkel and, against my better judgment, my head welcomed the familiarity.

"No, I'm saying you should be willing to ask for help from more than just the two people you do ask. Relying on people isn't a bad thing."

I knew he meant Sindri and Damien Aryen. Sindri was my best friend and I could be myself around him. I could be myself around Mihkel, but our personalities clashed. Damien was an old friend of my fathers and he brought my siblings and me into the world. My mother had also worked for him in the hospital before she met my father, so the three of them were close. I could ask Damien for help, he had proven himself to be incredibly reliable.

"I'm already weak enough with having to rely on other people," I said. I trusted Sindri, the doctor, and even Mihkel with the well-being of my family if anything ever happened to me, but

• • •

I hated it. I hated the fact that I couldn't take care of them all on my own.

"What's it going to take for me to be let in here?" Solomon asked, placing his fingers to my chest, over my heart.

I wasn't in the mood for this conversation. I moved away from his hand. I knew where this was going. This…relationship was pursued by Solomon, and yes, I used Solomon sometimes. I had to choke down the guilt that I felt from time to time for doing this to him. "You of all people should remember the piece of advice my father gives to people."

"What's that?"

"Only the fools believe their fantasy can become reality," I said and walked away.

Chapter 3

I had to put my hand up to shield my eyes from the sunlight. I half expected for Solomon to chase after me, but he didn't. This was fine with me at the moment. I wanted to be left alone. "I see the doctor has pulled a favor for you," a familiar voice said. Sayers stood next to me, smoking a cigarette. He was wearing his HUD glasses.

"What do you mean?"

"You hit that floor hard when I smacked you. Even if you weren't feeling anything from it, you would be recovering for a week or so. He gave you something so you would be on your feet in no time."

"Does it matter?"

"No, not right now." Sayers took a drag of his cigarette, letting the smoke escape through his partially opened mouth.

Frowning at his sudden one-hundred and eighty degree personality change, I motioned to his jacket. "You missed a spot."

Sayers looked down at the blood spot on his uniform. He sighed and brushed at the dried blood. I started to walk down the steps of the Justice Building when I felt a hand on my shoulder. "You should be aware that your father can't and won't protect you that much longer. You may want to start thinking about obeying the rules." He had a point, I was turning eighteen in a matter of days.

"I'll keep that in mind," I said, turning back to Sayers. He was holding my pack with an outstretched hand. I took it, felt that it was considerably lighter, and slipped it on over my shoulders.

++++

A large, charcoal grey wolf was lying outside the house when I finally made it home. The swelling on my cheek had already started to bruise and it was going to look bad for a week or two.

Enrik was the wolf cub my brother, Selig, had found when he was roaming through the city one day. He had a broken leg and his mother was probably killed by someone in CROSS or

GUARD. I remember that day like it was yesterday. Our father was at work and our mother was out. Ally fell in love with the pup immediately, but I wasn't cast under the spell of his eyes right away. When our mother came home, she made a splint for his leg and Enrik became more loyal than a dog ever could be.

"Hey, Enrik." I stuck my hand out and he licked it. I knelt down and put my pack on the ground. I took the snake that Mihkel had killed and set it on the ground. Removing my knife from my boot, I cut the head off; didn't want the wolf to ingest poison, my siblings would accuse me of doing it on purpose.

I left Enrik outside eating the carcass and went inside. The house was small for two people. It was crowded for three and impossible for five and a rather large wolf. I wasn't sure where my sister was going to sleep when she got too big to sleep in the bed we shared.

I first saw my mother sitting in a rocking chair my father had built for her when Ally was born. Selig and I were six years old, having already started to harden from the life we were forced to survive in. Our father had worked on the chair whenever he wasn't working, forbidding Selig and I to go anywhere near the chair.

My mother looked tired. She was more than likely up all night again watching Ally. I slowly walked over to her and set my pack down. "Hey, Mom," I greeted.

"Hey there, small world." She hadn't used that nickname in years. She sat up and rubbed her eyes. "Did I fall asleep?"

"Yes." I knelt down and squeezed her hand. "Why don't you go lie down and get some sleep? You're running on no energy."

My mother gently touched my swollen cheek, automatically knowing what happened. "I wish you wouldn't risk your life going to the reservoir. Your father is going to want answers from you and his superiors will want answers from him," she warned. She was never mean or threatening, just informative. She was grateful for the risks I took with Sindri and Mihkel, but she worried about what could, and probably will, happen to us again.

I watch as my mother's golden hair falls past her shoulders. I had always found her to be beautiful, finding myself

• • •

upset long ago over looking like my father instead of my mother. I took out the thin, black box Solomon had given me. "Take one of these, it'll make you feel better." I took a hydration tablet out of the box and held it up to her.

"No." She tried to push the tablet out of my hand. "Your sister needs it more than I do."

"Mom, please," I pleaded with her. "They're hydration tablets. What would happen if you collapsed from exhaustion and dehydration?"

"How many do you have?"

Counting the tablets, we had twenty of them. Everyone would be able to take one. The rest I would use to create more water. The only problem was you needed water to create more water and we had very little at the moment. Especially since Sayers kept the water I gathered today. "Twenty. Take it, please?"

She slowly took it out of my hand and swallowed it. Almost instantly, her color came back into her cheeks. Now, if she would eat something, she would be fine for a while. "Where's Selig?" I asked, hoping he wasn't out doing the one stupid thing he liked to keep from our parents.

"He's outside."

"I'm going to go give him one, then I'll give one to Ally." I stood up and walked out the back door.

Selig was out back working on chopping our wood supply for the upcoming winter. Like everything else, we'd have to use it sparingly. It was one of the reasons I shared a bed with my sister, Ally, and Selig shared the smallest one with Enrik. We had to use each other's body heat to keep warm during the colder nights.

He stopped chopping the wood and looked at me. "Was that dad or Sayers?" he asked, leaning the axe against the wall of the house and motioning to my swollen cheek.

"Sayers," I answered.

Selig picked up his shirt, wiping his face and neck dry with it. His blonde hair was slick with sweat, but he didn't try to dry it. "Dad's going to be angry."

"I know." I took out a hydration tablet. "Take it, you need it."

"What is it?" He took the tablet and then looked back at me when he saw the marking on it. "Where did you get this? Not even dad could get you out of this. Or the General, it doesn't matter if his father is the regent of Blackwater."

I couldn't help but cringe slightly. Regent Renner Nolan was the most powerful man in Blackwater Province and was also the most dangerous. With the connections he had, I was surprised that Sindri, Mihkel, and I hadn't been dragged to Arcadia yet.

When I didn't say anything, he made a face and sighed. Like Sindri, he wasn't a fan of whatever it was I had with Solomon. Of course my father wouldn't be either if he knew about it. He started to give it back to me when I pushed his hand closed. "Take it," I repeated. "What would happen if you got sick?"

I knew that would make him reconsider the tablet. Selig was like me, always wanting to stay strong from the family.

He took the tablet and swallowed it down. Turning his back to me, he picked up the axe and went back to chopping the wood. "Dad is going to be home tonight," he said over his shoulder. Great. That meant I was going to be disciplined.

"How is Ally doing?" I asked, leaning against the house and crossing my arms.

"The stigma is spreading," he said without stopping what he was doing. "The medicine Doc gave her isn't working."

Stigma was a disease that at least one-third of population of Ragnar City had. Its origins are unknown, but it seems that people in poorer conditions contract the disease quicker than anyone in the Royal Province. The symptoms were headaches, nosebleeds, high fever, and painful black marks on the skin that oozed pus and blood. It was highly contagious. Once one member of a family was sick, the rest were usually soon to follow.

It was unusual that no one else in the family was sick. As far as I knew, I was the only one in the family with immunity to it.

I walked back into the house and went into the bedroom, which held three twin beds. Ally was curled up in our bed with bandages covering her black marks. I sat down on the bed and

* * *

gently shook her awake. "Hey, little one," I said. "I have something for you."

Ally rolled over and blinked with her good eye. "What is it?" she asked trying to sit up. I helped her up and placed the hydration tablet in her hand. "This will make you feel better."

Taking it without hesitation, she looked at me. "A hydration tablet, where did you get it? I thought those were only for CROSS and GUARD?"

"Solomon gave me some," I said. "I'm going to use the rest to make us some water."

She took hold of my hand. "What happened to you?" We both knew she already knew the answer. My family was aware that I went to the reservoir when we needed water. This was just one of the few times that Sindri, Mihkel, and I had actually been caught.

Chapter 4

I laid with Ally until she fell back asleep, then made my way into the kitchen. Our mother was cutting up a small pile of vegetables for vegetable soup. If we were careful, we could make it last a couple of days. I would have gone gathering with Mihkel or Sindri but we had to lay low for a day or two.

I started to mash up the rest of the hydration tablets with the handle of my knife, leaving out three; one for me, Enrik, and my father. "You think we have enough water for those?" Selig asked, coming into the house. His sweat-soaked shirt was draped over his shoulder. I couldn't help but stare at the scars on his abdomen. When Selig and I were fifteen, we broke through a fence where prairie hens were kept for the CROSS soldiers. He was caught by Nazar and Sayers wasn't informed until Nazar had already given him about five of the seven scars. Selig noticed and raised his eyebrows at me. He never blamed me for what happened, but from then on, I was in charge of putting food on the table. I didn't want to put him through that pain again.

"I hope we do," I said quickly. Which in truth, we didn't.

"Ironic, isn't it?" Selig pulled his shirt on.

"What?"

"Blackwater Province is the water source for this world and yet the last time we had running water was when we were, what? One? Well, according to dad anyway." Neither one of us took our father at his word when it came to the history or stories of this place.

Selig had a point. The main water reservoir was in Blackwater Province, right in the middle of the city. It was a mile wide and around a mile deep. The reservoir fed into the other provinces through underground canals parallel to the train tracks above ground.

We had taken what water we had left and put it in a large pot, heating it up to a boil. I gathered up the powder and stirred it into the water. Selig had set a container down on the ground to catch the water.

Just as the powder was causing the water to rise, there was a knock on the door. I undid the plug in the top of the pot

• • •

with my knife so the water wouldn't overflow. "Keep any eye on it. When it starts to foam, the powder is used up."

"Hey, I need you to back me up on something that is going to infuriate dad."

"Dare I ask what?" I responded, already knowing the answer.

"I wouldn't at this moment."

I walked over to the door and opened it. Sindri was standing a few feet back, holding a burlap sack over his shoulder. He saw the bruise and cut on my cheek. He had one similar under his right eye. "Here," he said simply, holding out the sack.

Taking the sack, I opened it. Inside were two squirrels and a prairie hen. The squirrels he would have hunted for with Mihkel, but the prairie hen he would have stolen from the off-limits CROSS barracks. I closed the bag and looked at him. Letting him inside, I smiled slightly. "Thank you. How's your ankle?"

"It's fine. The claw didn't break the bone, it was just digging into a nerve. It's just a little sore. Sayers do that to you?"

"Yes, he do that to you?"

Sindri raised his hand and gingerly touched the welt under his eye. "Yes. Mihkel got the worst of it though."

"Have you seen him?"

"No, I was ushered out of the Justice Building after I was done being questioned. But, from the screams I heard…"

Mihkel was the one who disabled the sensors, so he got the torture. "I think he's at home recovering now."

"Depending on how hurt he is…his father will probably make him feel worse. You know how Craig gets when he's angry."

Craig Tiitus was the head miner and a hard man. Like my father, he used the physical aspect of discipline, but he was willing to cause more pain to his son than my father was to his two oldest. But, then, Mihkel had a higher tolerance for pain than I did, being a miner's son and also doing most of the physical labor around his house. Mihkel once said his father had a lot of frustration due to his mother having the Stigma, and he needed to take it out on someone.

• • •

Sindri only has his father, Robert, and his younger sister, Kara. His mother had died giving birth to his sister. So, Sindri had taken over caring for his sister, as I did with my family when my father was away. Though, I had my brother to help out with everything that needed to be done.

My mother had finished chopping up the vegetables when I brought in the burlap sack. She gave me a small smile, but it faded when she saw Sindri. "Hello, Sindri. I see you were disciplined as well."

"Mrs. Hawthorne," said Sindri. "How is Ally doing?"

"The same," my mother replied.

I handed her the sack and she opened it. "Prairie hen? Where did you get this? If your father finds out that you've stolen from GUARD..."

Selig looked at Sindri and myself, but didn't say anything. We were interrupted by Ally crying for our mother. She hurried into the bedroom, slamming the door behind her. Sindri rubbed his mouth. "She's getting worse isn't she?"

"Yes," said Selig.

"Could you cut up the squirrel or the hen for the stew?" I asked my brother.

"Yeah..." He took the bag from the counter and pulled out the prairie hen. Sindri had already gutted and cleaned it. "Sindri, you mind waiting outside? I want a word with my sister."

Sindri didn't respond. He walked out of the house, closing the door behind him. "Selig—" I started.

"What the hell are you doing?" Selig asked, slamming the knife down. "How long is this going to go on? You were just caught stealing water from the reservoir, the most sacred law, and now Sindri shows up with illegally hunted game? Something that only CROSS, GUARD, or the wealthiest of citizens are able to have. Are you trying to get all of us killed?"

"I'm trying to keep our family alive," I said. "Our dad may be second in command of CROSS, but that doesn't mean anything when it comes to the wellbeing of our family. The only clout he has is keeping us from getting into a lot of trouble. Both of us would be dead a few times over if he didn't step in."

• • •

Selig slammed his fist on the counter. "Ever wonder why he doesn't come home? It's because of us!"

Our mother suddenly came into the kitchen with a furious look on her face. "What in the Gods' names is going on here?" She walked over to Selig and slapped him. She then turned to me and did the same. Neither of us moved, our mother has never laid a hand on us. I could see tears forming in Selig's eyes, feel them welling up in mine as well. "You two will stop being so selfish about everything that you do." "Selfish?" Selig snapped. "Everything that I or Elena do is for Ally, for you!"

"No, you two are being selfish. Thinking that if you do everything, you won't have to deal with what is happening in this family! I will not stand for it anymore. From now on, nothing illegal is going to be brought into this house. Get rid of the squirrel and the prairie hen. Both of you are turning eighteen in a couple of days, which means you will be adults and your father won't be getting you out of trouble unscathed. Selig, you want to help this family, you get an apprentice job with one of the merchants. I don't want you working in the mines. Elena, Damien will teach you how to run an apothecary or you can work for him directly. I will not...bury all three...of my children." With that, she went back into the bedroom, closing the door behind her.

Selig didn't say anything. He shoved the meat back into the sack and tossed it to me. "Give it to Enrik or back to your friend." He went back outside where he would spend the next half hour chopping wood or breaking rocks. It was how he got rid of his rage, the rage he inherited from our father.

I walked outside to where Sindri was, letting Enrik go in the house before I shut the door. "I want you and Mihkel to teach me how to hunt," I said.

Sindri raised an eyebrow. "You serious?"

"Yes." I couldn't continue to rely on those two to go out hunting food for my family. "I need to be able to provide for my family completely."

"Did I just dream that fight you, your brother, and mother had? Something tells me she's worse than your dad when he's pissed off at the world."

"Are you going to or not?" I asked. "If you don't, I will go out there on my own."

Sindri sighed and looked at me. "All right, I'll go back and check on Mihkel, see if he's up for it in the morning. If not, in a couple of days," Sindri said. "But, don't tell your boyfriend."

I gave him a shove and he left with the same grin on his face he had earlier. I honestly didn't know what was between Solomon and me. I liked him, but I didn't know how serious my feelings were for him and I didn't know where he stood. For all I knew, he could be like Captain Sayers; a man of fictional honor.

Chapter 5

We were just sitting down to eat when the door opened and two pairs of footsteps came through. It was my father and Captain Sayers. "Sorry I'm late," he said, greeting my mother with a kiss. She instantly brightened up when my father came into the house. Selig took the opportunity to sneak a piece of turnip from his stew to Enrik, who swallowed it whole.

My father said something in Sayers' ear. He nodded and then left. Something must have happened or was happening if they were walking home in pairs. My father didn't say anything about the bruise or cut on my face. He just took out his gun and set it on the small side table by the door before walking into the bedroom.

"Think he's going to be able to do anything for Ally?" Selig asked.

"I hope so," our mother said, taking a bite of stew.

"I doubt it." I hated always having to be the cynic in the family, but I was better at facing the truths of reality. "There isn't a cure for Stigma. We all know that."

"That's optimistic of you." Selig shot a look at me. I returned it by kicking him under the table.

I put my spoon down. "I'm just being realistic. If they can't find a cure in the Royal Province, then there isn't one." I wasn't a fan of Arcadia, but their citizens had the best chance at surviving the Stigma disease. Unfortunately, they were dying just like everyone else.

We were interrupted by our mother standing up. "Stop it, the both of you. Stop talking about how your sister is going to die." She walked into the bedroom and closed the door, locking it behind her.

Selig sighed and put his utensil down, a guilty look on his face. We both knew that he agreed with me on this, but it also came with dangerous consequences. Having the family stay together was something that was very important to our parents, mainly our father.

He stood up and went back outside. He always retreated to physical labor when he was upset about something. I remembered he once said he was going to work in the mines, for the rage he carried inside was permanent. The pay wasn't as good as it was for merchant apprentices, but it was easier to get work in the mines. Selig and Mihkel weren't best friends, but they had gotten along since we were young. Because of this, Selig already had a spot saved by Craig Tiitus. My brother was one of the few people that openly enjoyed physical labor and usually kept his thoughts and emotions to himself.

I got up and started to clear the table just as my father came out of the bedroom. He kept quiet until he heard the door latch shut. "What the hell were you thinking?" he asked in his naturally deep, raspy voice.

I didn't answer him, continuing to gather the dishes.

"What the hell were you thinking?" he asked again, hitting the wall with his fist. "Do you have any idea what could have happened to you? Do you think I like coming home to see your face the way it is? Are you aware of just how lucky you are that Sayers and Ballory found you? If it was GUARD, you would have been taken to Arcadia or shot on the spot. How am I supposed to protect my family when you keep breaking the rules?"

"We need the damn water," I said, irritated. Taking out the piece of paper Damien gave me, I put it to his chest. "You know what the doctor keeps saying. Keep Ally hydrated and make sure she gets enough protein. She'll be more comfortable with whatever time she has left!"

He raised his hand and slapped me, the contact harder than usual. I went flying to the wall, hitting it hard. Sinking to the ground, I looked up at him. I knew the look on my face was daring him to do it again. "You say you're nothing like men in GUARD…when will you stop lying to everyone?"

"What did you just say to me?" he asked.

"You inflict pain before you ask questions and there is a man under your command that has to be restrained when he's interrogating a prisoner so he doesn't kill him."

"Watch your tone with me, or a nosebleed will be the least of your problems."

I raised my hand up to my nose, my fingers coming away smeared with blood. He started to reach for me and I moved out of his reach. "Don't touch me," I said.

• • •

"Have you had any more of those?"

I hesitated before I answered him, "No." He glares at me in response.

"Elena, don't lie to me," he snapped.

"It's nothing. Just...whenever I go to the reservoir I get a nosebleed," I lied. I had a feeling the nosebleeds had something to do with whatever the flash of the white room was. But, I wasn't about to tell my father that. If he was going to defend Nazar's actions, I was done with him. He was a man who followed protocol when it came to certain parts of his job. I was willing to bet a month of my food rations that he would go to the Royal Province with it. After all, I had just admitted earlier that the Arcadian Capitol, Ashton, had the best chance of finding a cure for the Stigma disease. Of course they would have the best bet of finding out what the hell was going on inside my head. But, I wasn't about to leave my family. I won't let them take me from them.

My father sighed and looked at me. "Suit yourself."

He knew I was lying but he was either too tired to get the truth out of me or he didn't care. Either way, he thought it wasn't worth it at the moment. "I suggest you stay away from the reservoir from now on. If you can't...then you can find a new place to live. I'm tired of being stuck in this shithole." With that, he picked up a bowl, filled it with some stew, and went back inside the bedroom. I didn't have to stay in the kitchen to know he was going to shut the door.

I walked outside to see my brother was breaking up rocks. "You want to know something about mom and dad?" he asked when he noticed I was outside.

"What?"

"We could be living in Arcadia right now. Hell, we could be living in the wealthiest part of Ashtan right now," said Selig, tossing the sledge hammer to the ground. "You know how he was supposed to marry a woman from a very noble family right?"

I nodded.

"Apparently our mother was part of the staff to the house."

I groaned. "So, he just blamed me for his bad choices?"

* * *

"What do you mean?"

"Our dad just told me that I either shape up or get out. He didn't want to live in this shithole anymore."

Selig started laughing as he tore a piece of his shirt off and handed it to me. I wiped the blood off my face and looked at my brother. "He turned down the offer of heading GUARD to be second in command of CROSS? He just couldn't live with ruining mom's life with him not being able to be with one woman. Grandfather raised him with strange morals..."

"So, you would rather live as bastard children? Just so we could live in the Ashton Capitol? You want to live like they do? Everything handed to them, not have to work for a thing in their lives?"

"You think that's a bad thing? We wouldn't have to ration water, food, oil...anything. Ally wouldn't have gotten sick. You wouldn't have to break the rules to get water or food. You wouldn't come home looking like someone used you as a punching bag. I wouldn't be...doing what I've been doing to make sure the house doesn't fall down around us."

I raised my eyebrows at his last comment. The look on his face told me I wasn't going to get an answer for that one. "But, you're okay with risking your life in the mines for little pay? What about Willow? You would be willing to leave and never see her again? What about all those hours I helped you pickpocket coins from nobles to get that necklace for her? I seem to remember that you want to marry her as soon as you turn eighteen."

Willow, the daughter of Regent Nolan and younger sister to the General; my relationship was frowned upon, but Selig was playing with fire. It wasn't against the law for someone from a noble family to get involved with a commoner, but typically the nobles stayed within the nobles. Regent Nolan would just exile Selig, but the General would most likely kill him; especially when they find out they're engaged to be married.

"What about the baby?" I asked.

Selig's muscles instantly tightened. "You leave them out of this. I will be there for my family."

• • •

"Not if you get shot for impregnating the Regent's only daughter. I wouldn't be surprised if she were shot as well."

Both of us stayed silent after that. I knew Selig had a point, just as he knew I had one. But, Selig was more like our mother than our father. I was more like our father. We both now knew the true reason why our father turned down the head of GUARD. It wasn't because he didn't want to answer directly to someone in Arcadia. It wasn't because he had been exiled due to something he did. It was because he couldn't live with himself because he fell for a woman who wasn't supposed to become his wife. He sacrificed everything for this rotten life because he wouldn't be able to live with the guilt of changing the life of Elise Sonje, now Elise Hawthorne.

Chapter 6

Later that night, I was staring up at the ceiling unable to sleep. The pain serum Damien had given me was starting to wear off and too much had happened for me to calm my mind down enough to get a couple of hours. I had my back to my sister when I felt her start to shiver. Rolling over, I put my arm around her to help warm her up. Listening to her steady breathing, I heard my father get up and leave. No doubt, CROSS business. I wouldn't be surprised if we didn't see him for a few days, maybe even a few weeks. I waited around five minutes to make sure he was gone before I got up.

I pulled on my clothes and was picking up my boots and jacket when Ally woke up. "Where are you going?" she asked, rubbing her eye that wasn't covered by a thick bandage.

"Go back to sleep, I'll be back in a little bit," I whispered.

"Take Enrik with you."

I sighed. I knew if I didn't comply with her request she would wake our mother. That, and I would be in more trouble than I already was. "I will bring Enrik with me if you go back to bed and not tell mom that I left in the middle of the night."

"Where's dad?"

"He had to go back to work." I kissed Ally on top of her head without hesitation. I did this because it made her feel better about having Stigma. She had been sick with Stigma for half a year and I hadn't contracted it from her. I was one of the lucky ones who were immune to the disease, which is how I was still sleeping in the same bed as her. A blood test had proven it, but I was the only one who carried the disease already in my bloodstream. The rest of my family wasn't immune, so they had to have regular blood tests. Luckily, no one else has gotten sick. It was hard enough getting the help Ally needs. It would be impossible if someone else were to become sick. No amount of hunting and trading would get us the money we needed for the medicine. My father wouldn't be able to do anything, but get us separated. He may be second in command, but that didn't matter to the Royal Province. Like everyone else, he was expendable so we have to be careful. The only reason I wasn't taken to the

Capitol when my blood test came back showing I was immune was because Damien didn't report it.

I pulled on my jacket, went into the kitchen, and sat down. As I was lacing up my boots, Enrik came into the kitchen. "Hey there," I said scratching him behind his ears. "Want to go for a run?" I picked up his collar and slipped it around his neck.

++++

I left the house and started down the road with Enrik staying beside me. Starting off at a mid-paced jog, I quickly moved up to my normal pace. Enrik, of course, had no problem keeping up with me. He was right beside me watching me about every other ten steps I took.

We made it to the wall on the outskirts of town that kept the city barricaded from the rest of the world.

The wall was made up of stone, concrete, and wood. Sindri, Mihkel, and I had long since found a path that made climbing and descending the wall much easier. As I made it to the top of the wall, I decided to take a different way down. The trees would be the fastest way down and they would also offer better cover to keep me hidden.

Gathering my bearings, I scanned the area and found a suitable branch that would sustain the impact of my weight landing on it. I reached into my pockets for my grip gloves. Empty. Crap. Tree jumping without those gloves is dangerous. Not only would I have to explain why hands were torn up, I also risked losing hold of a tree. I needed to make a decision, time was running out.

There was going to be a sweep of the area. This meant if I wasn't in the trees or on the ground and out of the range of the camera, I would be caught. That would mean I would be back in the Justice Building where not only Sayers would be able to smack me around some more, someone from GUARD would have a turn. Then, I would be taken to Arcadia. That would be the end of my life. I would never see my family again. I would never see anyone again. Being taken to the capitol didn't necessarily mean an automatic death sentence, but it was close. The two times I had been to the Capitol, I had gotten the feeling of something…heavy. My father had the same look in his eyes as I did.

Emptiness.

With even less time now, I decided to go through the trees. My hands would be paying the price, but it was better than the alternative.

I jumped.

As the sweep started, I wrapped my fingers around the branch and swung. I let go of the branch and grabbed another. Just as I wrapped my hands around the branch, it broke. I started to fall. Scrambling, I tried to grab another branch like I had yesterday. Only this time, I didn't have a very deep pool of water under me. There were only branches after branches.

My vision is blurry again. Just like it was yesterday. The blinding white light is back. The pain, and paralysis is back. Every single one of my nerves is on fire, I am unable to scream. I watch helplessly as the wires have a life of their own, making their way into my body, sending my nerves into overdrive. As flashes of memory play through my head again, I try to focus on the shadow. This memory of no one is the only thing keeping me from passing out.

It was then I hit a branch on the side where the hook had sunk into me, the pain was almost unbearable. As my vision went from blurry to clear with a shade of red, a wave of nausea came. I must have hit another branch. I wasn't falling.

I remained still, waiting for the nausea to pass. It didn't. I managed to turn my head just in time for the vomit that came up not to choke me. I heard barking from the ground, it was Enrik. He had waited for me.

My vision slowly came back into focus, with the red hue dissolving, and the sick feeling in my stomach started to dissipate. As soon as I was able to see clearly, I forced myself to sit up. Warm liquid slid down my arm and back. Checking out my arm, I saw that I was bleeding freely. Mercifully, the cut wasn't too deep. I reached behind with my good arm and felt the cut on my back. It was more like a gash. Below me, Enrik was barking incessantly while resting on his hind legs, trying to get my attention.

• • •

Looking at my hands, I saw just how torn up they were. I was going to need stitches in at least three of the cuts. I also wasn't going to be able to do much of anything with my hands in this state.

I struggled out of my jacket and laid it over the branch. Pulling my t-shirt off over my head, I used my teeth to tear it into strips. First, I wrapped my hands as best as I could and then I wrapped up my arm. The pain was slowly spreading through my body as I tried to figure out how to take care of the cut on my back. I was still bleeding freely and tried to stop it. I decided to just wrap what was left of my shirt around my torso and hope that I was able to make it back within the city without drawing too much attention.

After I was done, I noticed that I was shivering. Winter was getting closer, so the air felt almost frozen. The days were cold, the nights even colder.

Pulling on my jacket, I zipped it up to my chin and started to climb down the tree. I had to bite my lower lip to distract myself from the pain in my hands.

As I lowered myself, I saw that I was close enough to the ground. I let go of the branch and trunk, landing on the ground safely. Enrik came up to me and tugged on the hem of my jacket. "We're going home," I said to him. "Don't give me that look."

Chapter 7

We had to take the long way home; a route that I had only taken once before with my father. He had shown me the route in case something every happened. I asked what could possibly make things worse than they already are and it took him two full days to come up with an answer. 'When the birds stop singing that is when the damned show their faces.' In my seventeen, almost eighteen years of life, I have only heard the bird stop singing once and that was in a dream. I still remember the feeling of waking up in a cold sweat and not being able to sleep for the next two days.

We had traveled maybe about a quarter of a mile when Enrik suddenly stopped and pricked his ears up. The fur at the base of his neck stood on end. I started to take out my hunting knife when I noticed I was about two steps away from a snare.

Only my eyes moving, I spotted where it was tied to a tree. "Stay…" I said, holding out my hand to Enrik. He responded by licking my fingertips.

I walked over to the base of the tree and twirled my knife around in my hand a couple of times, getting within reach of the wire holding up the snare. I put the blade to the wire when I heard a twig snap. "I wouldn't do that if I were you," a man's voice said. "Give me the knife. Slowly."

I held up the knife and felt the rough hands of the man take it from me. "Who are you?" I asked. "What are you doing out here?"

"I could ask you the same question, girl," he said, patting me down. He stopped when he felt my blood on his hands. "Turn around."

Slowly, I did what I was told with my hands up. He looked at me, my knife in one hand and a gun in the other. It was a standard issue to CROSS, around five years ago.

The man looked to be a couple years younger than my father and was wearing the tattered remains of a CROSS uniform. He had uneven, white hair combed back with fingers and matching facial hair. It was his white hair that made me the most curious, but that changed when I saw the color of his eyes.

● ● ●

54

They were the same color as mine. He noticed the similarity between us and began to lower his gun.

"Wait a minute…" he said in a raspy voice similar to my father's. "You're Carter Hawthorne's girl, aren't you?"

"Depends, who are you?" I didn't dare to take my eyes away from his.

"Crispin Frost," the man said. "CROSS First Class. Or, I used to be anyway…"

"Frost?" I had heard that name before, my father talking to Sayers about the Frost brothers a couple times last year.

"Yes, Frost. Your turn," he said, aiming the gun steadily between my eyes.

"Elena," I said. "Elena Hawthorne."

Frost cocked his head to the side slightly and lowered his gun. "You just confirmed what I already knew. What are you doing out here, past the wall? It's dangerous."

When I didn't say anything, Frost simply smirked and held out his hand to Enrik. "How do you manage to pass him off as a dog?"

"We don't," I said. "My dad is second in command of CROSS."

"You say that like it's something important. It's not." Frost knelt down and reached a tentative hand out for Enrik to sniff. When Enrik relaxed, he began scratching him behind his ears. "He's merely a lapdog for GUARD and the Royal Capitol of Ashtan." He had a point. Selig and I had once pressed the issue with our mother, but that earned us a lecture from her and a beating from our father.

He stood up and looked at me. "Are you going to tell me why you're bleeding?"

"I fell," I said quickly. I wasn't about to tell Crispin Frost what caused me to fall. I didn't know him and I certainly didn't trust him. I trusted my mother. I trusted Solomon, Sindri, Mihkel, Selig, and Ally. However, I wasn't even going to tell them about whatever the hell was going on in my head. It was dangerous to have something unusual happen to you in Ragnar City.

As soon as I said that, we both knew I was lying. Fortunately, Frost didn't push it. "If you trust me enough to

* * *

follow me, I'll stop the bleeding and fix up your hands. I'll also give you a shirt to wear."

Having forgotten that I was only wearing a black bra and my jacket, I checked the zipper to see it was still up around my chin. "Easy girl," said Frost. "I took a guess by seeing the black cloth wrapped around your hands. If you're coming with me, then come on. A storm is coming and I don't want to be out in the open when it starts."

Enrik was acting like Frost was an old friend he hadn't seen in a while, so I decided to go with Frost. Enrik was a good judge of character.

Chapter 8

Five minutes into our walk, Frost stopped suddenly and turned to look at me. "What are you doing out here, Elena?" he asked, holding my knife up between two fingers. "I may be presumed dead for over two years, but I know the rules have not changed. Leaving the city without proper clearance? That's punishable by death. But, then, there are a lot of things punishable by death in this life."

"I needed to clear my head," I said. "I was climbing up the wall when an unexpected sweep started. So, I got into the trees but I…" I trailed off, trying to think of some way to describe what happened.

In this world, you didn't trust anyone but your family. And some people didn't even have that luxury. After the first time I saw what my father did for a living, it took over five years for me to start trusting him again. After all that time had passed, I still didn't completely trust him. Not sure I would ever be able to trust him again.

"Forget I asked," Frost said. "I should have known you'd respond the same way your father would."

This was at least the second time he had brought up my father without any pushing from me. "How do you know my dad?"

"Carter Hawthorne—he was my boss until about three years ago," said Frost. "Do you remember what happened three years ago?"

I didn't even have to think about it. Three years ago was when the Stigma disease surfaced. I remembered my father was quarantined for six months. The story was the Capitol was trying to find a cure for Stigma, but they never did. I honestly had no idea how hard they tried and my father wouldn't speak a word about it. "Stigma came out of nowhere," I said.

"Wrong," said Frost. "I don't know the origins of the disease, but I do know how it spread so quickly throughout this world."

"How?"

● ● ●

Frost opened his mouth to answer, but hesitated when he looked at me. "How about I doctor you up before I tell you the details? You're looking a little pale."

"Tell me now."

He put two fingers to my lips. "You look a little dead on your feet. I may hate your father but that doesn't mean I have anything against his family."

I pushed his hand away. "Why do you hate my dad? Everything he does is to help the people in Ragnar City."

"That is where you're wrong," Frost snapped at me. "Now, either shut up and follow me, or you're on your own to get back to the city." He continued to walk into a meadow.

I didn't follow him until he was about seven steps in front of me. Enrik stayed by my side, which I was grateful for. He was my bodyguard when I went out beyond the wall, especially at night. I really needed to learn how to use a bow and arrow. I could defend myself with a knife, but there were some animals in these woods that would look at my hunting knife and laugh.

We walked through the meadow and didn't stop until we came to a medium sized pond. Frost knelt down and stuck his hands in the water. I stood a couple steps behind him and waited for him to drink his fill. To my surprise, he simply splashed some water on his face, stood up, and kept walking.

++++

Fifty feet later, we came to an old stone hut covered in thick vines. It was small, looked to be only one room, and the wood door was mostly rotted. Frost took out my knife again and checked something on the door. When he was satisfied, he opened the door and walked inside. "Come on. You don't want to be out in the open when the storm starts."

I looked up in the sky and felt something I hadn't felt in a long time, a raindrop. I wanted to stand out in the rain, but Frost pulled me inside. "I don't think I should be here."

"You're not going anywhere when you're bleeding the way you are. And, we need to talk about something concerning your father. So, unless you want to drown, I would stay here."

"Why do you want to talk about my dad?"

Frost lit some candles and I saw just how small the hut really was. It only took three candles to light the entire room. There was a chair, a small fireplace, and a makeshift bed. "You live here?" I asked.

"Yes," said Frost walking over to the fireplace and taking a couple pieces of wood out of his pack. "When you're trained in CROSS, you don't need a whole lot to survive on."

"That pond back there, the water is clean enough to drink?"

He motioned for me to sit in front of the fire. "Yes."

I did as he told. Enrik came over and lied down next to me, resting his head on my leg. I started to turn when Frost came over and knelt beside me. "You are going to have to take your jacket off."

I hesitated long enough that Frost took my jacket off for me. He checked the cut on my back. "This is pretty deep. I'll have to stitch it up."

Immediately, I felt my muscles tighten. I've had stitches before, but never in this situation. Any stitches that I've had done were by Damien's hands. I didn't mask my discomfort at the thought of more stitches. "Not a fan of needles?"

"Not a fan of stitches."

"I have something that will numb the area," he said, taking a small handful of leaves out of a piece of white cloth.

"Leaves?"

Frost snapped the thick, triangle shaped leaves at the base and started to apply the liquid that came out from the base. The coolness from the liquid transferred to a cool numbing, as if it were spreading through my veins. "How long does it last?"

"Not that long, but I don't need more than a couple minutes to stitch this up," Frost answered, snapping the base of another leaf off.

I sat there, only barely feeling the slightest amount of pressure of Frost's working fingers. It was only when I felt the texture of a bandage that I knew the numbness was gone. "Now your arm," he commanded.

Frost put his hands on my shoulders and turned me ninety degrees with ease. As he started to clean up my arm, I

• • •

heard the rain turn into a downpour. "I have to get out of here." I started to stand up when Frost forced me to sit back down.

"You will lose the arm if you let the wound fester. You haven't realized it yet, have you?"

"What?"

Frost picked up a discarded leaf and showed me the base of it. It was dead; the rest of the leaf slowly dying in front of our eyes. "Black tip poison…"

"Now, would you let me finish? As much as your father and I clash, the last thing I want is for him to lose both of his daughters."

That made my heart skip a beat. Just the mentioning of my sister made me want to go home. Even though I was quite sure that I wasn't welcome there anymore. "How do you know about my sister?"

"Ally?" Frost stood up, stripped down to just his pants, and turned around in a circle once.

Slowly, I stood up and reached my hand out. He grabbed my wrist. "Do you want to get infected with Stigma?"

"I have immunity to it," I said but that didn't make Frost let go of my wrist.

"Let's not test that theory out more than we already are." Frost let go of my wrist and picked up his shirt. Pulling it on, he motioned to my arm. "If you let me finish doctoring you, I will get you home and the only punishment you'll have to endure is from your father."

"I think he disowned me today…" I muttered. "Why help me? You don't even know me."

"As I said before, I knew your father. We used to…work together."

"You're one of the leaves on the wall of the Justice Building. One of the few that have died for the Blackwater Province and are actually being honored."

The leaves were about half the size of my palm and made up of a metal compound that is only available to the military and law enforcement of the new world. I remembered the first time that I saw the monument to the fallen. My father had taken my brother and I after a friend of his had died

* * *

'defending the honor.' He explained how it was a great honor to have a leaf up on the wall.

"You are Carter's daughter," Frost said as he yanked his jacket on.

"Why do you keep bringing him up?"

Frost sighed and scratched Enrik behind his ears. "There are things you need to know about him. Things that will change the way you view him for the rest of your life."

I knew my father had a past with the Ashtan Capitol, and it was dark; darker than any of those stories that I knew were hidden in the files in the Justice Building. "I know my father has done things that he would never want anyone in his family to learn about. But, he's a good man...to a certain degree."

"Would a good man knowingly infect hundreds to thousands of people with a disease that would never have a cure?"

I just stared at Frost, not knowing what to think or how to feel. My father was the man who made sure people got some form of medicine when they needed it. He was the reason no one had starved to death in over two years. People still went hungry, hell, my family went hungry, but no one without some ration of food, no matter how small. Sayers and Solomon called him a 'humanitarian with a gun'.

"I don't believe you."

"Believe me or not, ever wonder why your father always has his right hand gloved? Even when he's home?"

I knew my father wore a black leather glove on his right hand, but I never gave it a second thought. I just figured it was because he had hurt his hand and was covering up the scars for his family's sake. Or, at least for the sake of his wife and youngest daughter. Selig and I had more scars combined than our father did, and he had quite a lot of them.

"I have to go home." I stood up and Enrik followed me.

It took all of five seconds for my clothes to be completely soaked through. I couldn't remember the last time it rained this hard. My night vision was shot the second I stepped outside. The fire had completely ruined it. Enrik stayed by my side, allowing me to keep my hand on his neck as he guided me away from the hut.

* * *

"You know with a wolf as your guide in a storm, you still won't make it very far…" someone whispered in my ear.

I jumped and Enrik started growling. The rain was becoming a solid mass as it continued to fall. "Tell me why!"

"Would you come back inside? Just because you can hold your own out in the woods, doesn't mean you can in a storm. It's only going to get worse," Frost said. "Come back inside. I won't be responsible for your death."

++++

I was in nothing but a thick blanket wrapped tightly around my body, shivering by the fire. Enrik was curled up in a ball beside me, half asleep with steady breathing. Frost had changed clothes and hung ours up to dry.

"Let me apologize," Frost said, handing me a piece of stale bread. "I didn't think."

"How could he hurt innocent people? He—"

"That's only slightly true. He never wanted to hurt innocent people, but he didn't have a choice. None of us did," Frost said. "There are a few of us who had contracted Stigma on purpose, thinking it was an immunization protecting us from contracting Stigma."

"So, you knew of Stigma before it spread?"

"I didn't know, wasn't high enough in rank at CROSS to know all the details. Only two men knew everything."

I took a bite of stale bread but didn't chew it. General Nolan and my father, they would know. They got the privilege to know everything as long as they didn't abuse it. Then, it hit me. Both my father and General Nolan had a black leather glove on their hands. "They spread the Stigma disease around…that bastard got my sister sick on purpose."

Our conversation was interrupted by a loud thunder clap. Enrik was instantly on his feet and I had to quickly rewrap the blanket around me after I jumped. "The storm is at its full capacity," Frost said, taking the blanket he was wearing and wrapping it around me. "If you'll allow me, I want to show you something."

"Okay…?"

"Give me your hand."

"Cautiously, I put my hand in his outstretched hand."

I feel a sudden weakness in my legs as I am standing next to Frost. Instead of both of us soaking wet, we're in dry clothes and he is still holding my hand. Only, he has a death grip on it. This isn't the strangest thing though: it is that Frost and I aren't in the crumbling stone hut anymore. We seem to be in the Justice Building, and my father looks at least five years younger. I can't believe how I barely recognize him, but then again it is unreal how much someone changes in a short period of time in the Blackwater Province.

My father is in the CROSS uniform, like he usually is, but he has a beard and his hair is long enough, I see it has a slight wave to it. Like mine. There is something different about him, he doesn't have the permanent tired look to him and he is smiling. I haven't seen him smile in years.

Sayers is next to him, and the two are having a lively conversation. This, too, is weird for me; looking away, I see Frost standing next to me. "What's going on?"

"*I'm showing you something that you need to see.*"

"How?"

"*That is a long story that I won't start the avalanche of.*"

"Bringing us to the past isn't starting an avalanche?"

Frost doesn't say anything. He just motions for me to look back at the man I barely recognize. The familiar pain is creeping up on me. I won't be able to stand this much longer. The visions or memory flashes are taking their toll on me. A light breeze seems to encircle us. My upper lip feels the breeze the most, making me check to see my fingers come away with blood on them. I'm already getting a nosebleed, meaning my body isn't taking the transitions well. Or whatever they were.

Captain Carter Hawthorne; there is something else that is different about him. He's wearing a wedding ring. Even though everyone knew he married Elise Sonje, he never wore a ring. Back before they had my siblings and me, the salary he took home was more than enough for the two to live on.

"*Carter…what's going on? You are the last person that should be keeping secrets from me,*" *Sayers asks with a hint of* urgency in his voice. *"After everything we've been through? After what I did to make sure you got back to Elise?"*

The mentioning of my mother sends a sharp pain through me, making my nerves feel like they're on fire.

"Dragan…this isn't something you want on your conscience. Trust me on this." My father's voice is low and raspy. *"Let it go, or there will be consequences."* My father starts to walk away and without thinking about it, I start to follow.

Sayers grabs his arm. *"Are you threatening me, Carter?"*

"No. I'm telling you the absolute." He just stares at Sayers until his arm is released and he walks away. Again, my legs start moving when Frost stops me.

"What was that?" I ask.

"We're not done, come on. Stay right next to me," Frost says as he starts to walk. I follow, not wanting to know what happens if I stray.

The next thing I know, we are standing in my father's office. Frost is leaning against the wall with his hands in his pockets. *"He can't see us?"*

"No. Listen to this."

I turn to see General Nolan coming into the office and closing the door. He takes a vial of red liquid from his pocket and tosses it to my father. *"This is it?"* My father asks, looking at the vial. My chest tightens, making my heart feel like it's going to be smashed in a matter of seconds.

"Yes. That's enough to infect those in your team who will survive the duration," the General said, sitting down.

My father sighs and looks at the vial. *"We're sure this is the way to go?"*

"Getting cold feet, Carter?"

"More like he's getting bored with his role in all this," snaps Frost.

"General…a lot of innocents will die because of this. In case you haven't realized, we're still paying for the last attempt of trying to save the human population."

"Keep talking like that, and everything will be blown." The General sighs. *"It's already been tested, it won't harm the environment. Or, the environment won't retaliate against us…again."*

● ● ●

"Just the already struggling human population…" Frost takes the vial from my father.

"Careful Lieutenant." The General narrows his eyes at Frost. "Keep in mind, I can order you to do this or I can give you incentives to do this. Your wife? That merchant's daughter you're sweet on?"

Frost and I watch as my father pulls off his gloves and holds out his hand for the vial.

The Frost in the memory tosses it to him, and my father opens the vial. "There have only been two times I wished I had died during the rebellion. This moment is now number three." He put a drop of the rather thick liquid on his ungloved hand. A sharp pain below my stomach explodes as I watch his skin soak up the red. "If I end up on the fatal end of this…I will take her with me."

"If you end up dying from this, I will take her away before you can do anything," the General says and holds out his hand.

I can't take anymore. The pain overwhelms me as I collapse to my knees with Frost trying to keep me on my feet.

I took in a sharp, fast breath as Frost let go of my hand. "Elena, you need to calm down or you're going to hyperventilate." He put his rough hands on my face. "Elena, look at me. Follow my breathing, breathe with me."

"I…can't…stay…here," I managed to get out.

"Elena, I will get you home, but it will have to be after the storm."

To be honest, I didn't want to go home. Frost was right. I would never be able to look at my father in the same way ever again. "I can't go home."

"You're going to have to at some point. Even if it's just to gather up your things."

I was starting to feel very sluggish. "What's going on?" I asked, getting the feeling this was brought on by the something besides the trip back in time.

"It's the poison," Frost said, picking me up. He carried me over to his bed and laid me down. Bringing over a candle, he lifted up my arm. "This poison is spreading farther than it should be."

I started shivering uncontrollably, unable to control the way my body was reacting. The last thing that went through my head before my consciousness slipped away was how what Frost just showed me probably had everything to do with the flashes.

++++

Waking up to an unfamiliar ceiling was one of the worst feelings. I was still wrapped up in the blankets, but my bandages were soaking up fresh blood. Enrik was next to the bed on the floor, fast asleep. Making sure the blanket was wrapped tightly around my torso, I sat up to see Frost was sleep on the floor by the smoldering ashes. There was something unusual about him. He was sleeping in a manner that was similar to Enrik; curled up in a ball, like a wolf.

Watching him for a couple of seconds, I noticed that his eyes were moving under his eyelids. He was dreaming. Carefully, I picked up the second blanket off the makeshift bed and started to carry it over to Frost. As I laid it over to him, his eyes suddenly opened, making me jump. His eyes looked almost identical to Enrik's, except they had the same emptiness my father carried in his eyes.

I started to back away, my eyes still focused on his. Without watching where I was going, I stepped on something sharp. Without putting weight on my injured foot, I managed to get back on the bed without embarrassing myself any further.

Frost picked up the blanket I had dropped and wrapped it around his waist. He came over and knelt down in front of me. "I didn't mean to scare you." He looked at my foot and then back to me. "It's not very deep."

"What did I step on?"

Frost held up the object I stepped on. "Is that a tooth?" I asked.

"More like a wolf's fang…" Frost wrapped up my foot with what was left of the bandages. "The storm should be over by now."

"I have to get home. I was never supposed to be gone this long." It wasn't that I wanted to go home, per say. I just wanted to let someone know I was still alive.

Frost went outside with Enrik following him as I got dressed. I pulled on my clothes as quickly as I could, which was proving difficult due to my injuries. My shirt was destroyed, so I just pulled my jacket on and zipped it up all the way. Pulling the hair tie out of my hair, I pulled it back into a messy knot and left the hut.

As I was walking up to Frost and Enrik, I stopped when I saw my reflection in the pond. I looked even worse than I did after Sayers was done with me. Turning, I shielded my eyes from the morning sun and saw something I hadn't seen in a long time. The world was covered in raindrops. It was beautiful.

It was about an hour past dawn by the time we had gotten to the wall. I was feeling a little sluggish from the amount of sleep I had gotten before I left the house. But, then it could also be a side effect of the poison or the maelstrom Frost put me through.

I didn't recognize the area Frost was leading me to. I had never been to this part of the wall. It must have been around the merchant part of the city, where Sindri and his family lived.

Frost stopped walking when we hit the southernmost part of the wall. "The one true blind spot on the wall, the only problem is...you have a long way to go to get back to your house. You'll have to go past the Justice Building."

I was supposed to meet up with Sindri to see if we were going to go hunting in a day or two. So, it wouldn't matter. "I can just act like I woke up early."

"Okay..." Frost had a look on his face like he wanted to ask me a question but decided against it. He took out my knife and held it out to me, handle first. "This is a good knife, your father teach you how to use this?"

I took my knife from him, shaking my head. "My...dad taught me how to climb trees and evade the sweeps."

"What about tree jumping?"

"I kind of taught myself that."

Frost started to smile when he suddenly clutched his neck. My heart skipped a beat when I saw he pulled out a dart from his neck. "Damnit, Alek..." He suddenly clutched his head and collapsed to his knees.

* * *

"Frost?" I asked, going to my knees, afraid to touch him. "Frost? What's wrong?"

"Get…away…from…me…" he managed to whisper through clenched teeth.

"Let me help you, what's going on?"

He suddenly put his hand around my neck, causing the air to escape from my throat. Enrik sunk his teeth into Frost's wrist. My lungs screamed for air as his fingers tightened around my neck. As my vision was going in and out, I looked in his eyes. They were different. Instead of the blue color that we shared, or even the split second when they were identical to Enrik's, they were a jade green. "Get away from me," he said, releasing me.

I collapsed to the ground, massaging my throat. My sight slowly became clearer and I managed to get air back into my lungs. I raised my head to look at Frost. He was clutching his head, his head bleeding steadily. I started to reach for him when he looked at me with green eyes. "Get away!" he yelled.

Chapter 9

Enrik paced himself to match my speed. I had no idea which way I was going; all I knew was I had to get away from Frost. Not because of what he did, but because of that look of emptiness and hate in his eyes. They were so cold, so empty, a maelstrom forming behind his eyes.

As I was making my way through the woods, I felt countless branches and thorns scrape across my skin. I only stopped once when one of the thorns got caught in the bruise on my face. Staggering with my hand to my face, I tripped over a fallen branch and landed hard on something.

I carefully started to force myself to stand up when I felt a sharp pain in my leg. Looking down, I saw there was a piece of branch stuck in my leg. Managing to drag myself over to the nearest tree, I leaned against it to survey the damage. It was a through and through, with little blood. Either, it wasn't deep or it was deep and the bleeding was being blocked by the branch.

Taking a closer look at my leg, I saw that it wasn't deep, the sharp point just barely under my skin. But, it still hurt. I started to pull it out when Enrik began to growl. I looked up, locking my eyes with a very large, white wolf not even a foot away from me.

The wolf was larger than Enrik. He stood there, baring his teeth and growling at me. All I had was my hunting knife. That wasn't going to save me when it came to this beast. A branch snapped, causing the wolf to look up, disappearing not even a moment later. I looked up to see my father standing there, holding a rifle like it was part of his body. Sayers and Solomon were also with him, "Elena? What the hell are you doing out here? Do you have any idea how worried your mother has been?" He stopped when he saw the state I was in. He slung his rifle over his shoulder and knelt down next to me. "What the hell happened to you? It looks like you had a personal visit from Fenrir himself."

Hearing my father reference the one religion Arcadia allowed meant I did look bad. To someone untrained, I most likely looked like I was going to die.

* * *

I didn't get a chance to answer when we heard rustling behind us. My father took hold of his gun again and stood up. Frost came stumbling out into view, his clothes more ragged than they were before. My heart skipped a beat when I saw he had fangs, canine fangs. "Frost?" my father asked, keeping his gun steady. "That can't be you."

"Carter Hawthorne…" Frost said, keeping himself steady against a tree. "Never thought I'd see you again. Dragan Sayers, I had hoped to never see you again."

"You and me both," Sayers said, holstering his gun and taking out restraints.

"Lieutenant Creid," my father said. "Take my daughter to the doc and then make sure she gets home."

"What are you going to do with Frost?" I asked.

"Creid, take her to see the doc," my father repeated. "Now."

Solomon holstered his gun and walked over to me. "You really have a knack for getting into trouble. Can you walk?"

"Yes," I said, even though my leg felt like it was on fire. I ignored the hand he held out to me and stood myself up. "Enrik…" I called.

Enrik looked at me and nudged my hand with his wet nose. I scratched him behind his ears and looked at Solomon. "Did you walk here?"

"Airship," Solomon responded. "But, you and I will be going back in the jeep."

I raised my eyebrows. I had never been in one of the CROSS vehicles. I had been in an airship a couple of times, but, other than that, I relied on my own two feet to get myself places.

I could stand without much issue, but I couldn't walk very well. I had to steady myself on Solomon's arm as we walked back. "What's going to happen to Frost?"

"It depends," Solomon said without looking at me. He was helping me walk with one hand while the other held his gun, making sure nothing came charging at us. I wasn't in any state to defend myself at the moment, so I was grateful for it.

"Depends on what?"

Solomon sighed heavily and stopped walking. "It depends on what happened. Something tells me you didn't do any of this to yourself on purpose." His fingertips grazed my neck where bruises were already beginning to form. The blood from my nosebleed had dried, though I hadn't bothered to wipe it away. The nosebleeds were becoming more and more frequent and lasting longer and longer. At this rate, I was going to die by exsanguination from a nosebleed.

"It was an accident," I countered.

"He accidentally grabbed you and tried to kill you? For some reason, I don't believe that."

I pushed him away from me and leaned against a nearby tree. "Don't treat me like a child."

"Then stop acting like one. You think you're constant breaking of the rules doesn't have repercussions on your father? If you actually did what you were supposed to do, then your father would actually have time to be a father."

"What is that supposed to mean?"

"He's always working, keeping you and your friends alive," snapped Solomon. The way he said *friends* gave me the feeling if it were up to him, he'd have them in front of a firing squad. "Come on, I have my orders."

Solomon was starting to anger me. I wrapped my hand around the branch stuck in my leg and pulled. The dull pain that was there went away, but a new pain came along with blood. "Damnit, Elena!" Solomon tore off his gloves and looked at the wound. "It's not that deep. You didn't hit an artery or anything…" He took out a handkerchief and wiped his hands off. He then took out some bandages and wrapped them quickly around my leg. "So you don't bleed out," his tone was thick with sarcasm.

"You're so considerate," I muttered.

By the time we started to walk again, my father and Sayers had caught up to us. Sayers was sporting a cut above his right eyebrow, and my father looked like he had a broken nose. Frost was in hand restraints with a collar around his neck. He looked a mix of scared, nervous, and angry. "Why don't you just kill me now? I'd rather this not drag out at all," he said, trying to keep his voice level.

"Creid, when I give you an order, I expect you to follow it," my father barked.

"Your daughter has a death wish which I don't even think the Gods would challenge," replied Solomon.

"That shouldn't be news to anyone here." My father shot me a look. "You two, take him on board the airship. I need a word with my daughter."

My father waited until Sayers and Solomon had started to take the struggling Frost on the airship before he grabbed my arm and jerked me out of sight from the others. He smacked me out of the blue, sending me to the ground. He knelt down and dragged me to my feet, raising his hand to hit me again when he hesitated. "Are you trying to get yourself killed? At this rate, you will. Keep it up and I won't be able to protect you anymore."

"What are you going to do with Frost?"

"That's confidential."

"That's a lie if I've ever heard one." I was betting Frost was going to be deemed a traitor and then publicly executed. The Royal Province loved to show off their power around the different provinces.

"You're telling me exactly what happened when we get back to the Justice Building," my father said. The look in his eyes revealed the restraint he was using to not hit me again. "Stop trying to get yourself killed, I'm not losing a daughter."

"Don't you mean both daughters?" I asked as we started to walk back to the airship. More like my father walked back and dragged me along with him.

My father stood and looked at me. "Ally isn't going to die."

"Yes, she is. She doesn't have the medicine she needs! No one in the city has it and you're the reason for it!"

I had done it. The look on my father's face was pure fury. If he didn't kill me here, I was definitely not allowed to live at home anymore. At this point, I was no longer his daughter. "What did you just say to me?" My father clenched his hands into tight fists.

"I know what you and General Nolan did five years ago."

The man who had spent most of my life trying to make the quality of life in Ragnar City better just stood there, a look of defeat in his eyes.

• • •

Chapter 10

A medic of CROSS had started immediately treating the wounds. When he got to my back, an impressed expression took hold of his face. "That's very impressive. I've never seen this type of stitching before. It will leave a scar, but you don't seem to mind that," he said, eyeing the various other scars I carried with me.

Without another word, he finished doctoring me up with quick and efficient work of his fingers. I was feeling better by the time we arrived, which was around thirty minutes from when we took off. The bruises were still going to be there in the morning, but most of the pain was going to be gone.

My neck started to feel tight when we landed. I gingerly touched the spot where Frost had grabbed me. It was still tender. I could see myself in the window, the bruises almost black. I jumped when I felt someone's hand on my shoulder. "You'll be escorted home after the doc finishes checking your wounds." It was Sayers. "Where you will stay until you and your father actually get a real conversation in."

I snuck a look at my father. He appeared to be sleeping, sitting next to Frost with his head down and his arms crossed. But, I knew he wasn't. He was going to stay away from me. Not because I hurt him, but because he would more than likely lash out more than usual before he could stop himself.

"He's not going to want to speak to me again."

Sayers sat down next to me and put two fingers under my chin, looking at the damage to my face. "You'll heal up alright."

"I always do."

++++

"Look at what the cat dragged in...again," Damien said pulling on gloves. "Someone try to kill you or did you try to kill yourself?"

"It was an accident."

Damien first looked at the cut on my arm. "You were beyond the wall, black tip poison. I'm surprised the flesh around the cut isn't dead."

* * *

"Frost," I said. "He used some leaf to slow the poison."

"That actually only stops the poison from spreading, but it doesn't stop the decaying of flesh," Damien said picking up a syringe and filling it with a clear liquid. "This will help stop the decaying of your skin around the cuts."

"What stops it completely?"

Damien simply looked at me before turning his attention back to the syringe he had in his hand. "The antidote. I don't have any in stock because it's manufactured in the Ashtan Capitol. But, I assure you, you will not die from this. Crispin Frost made sure of that."

That made me stop, I looked at him as he injected my arm and then back to the syringe. "You know him?"

"He used to be in CROSS, as was his older brother."

"Why did they leave?"

"Well, his brother left after everyone thought Crispin was dead. As far as I know, Roiben Frost is dead as well."

"Where did he go after he left CROSS?"

Damien sighed and started to take off the bandages the CROSS medic had put on my arm and back. "Your father came by before he, Sayers, and Creid went out into the forest."

"Do you know why they went out beyond the wall in the first place?"

"Nothing that I can talk about with a civilian, why were you out past the wall?"

I took in a breath. "We're not being monitored in here, if that's what you're worried about. If we were, I wouldn't be making conversation with you," Damien said, giving me a reassuring smile.

Damien has been part of my family for as long as I can remember. When I was around ten, my parents told Selig and me that if anything ever happened to them, Damien would be taking us in.

"Last night, I just needed to clear my head. I went for a run and ended up past the wall."

"What aren't you telling me?"

"Nothing important."

"At the moment anyway," Damien said with a raised eyebrow. "I will say this—your father is using up more good will than anyone else in CROSS. His status doesn't matter, GUARD will kill him by the order of the King or his advisor Dorian."

Cyrille Dorian, the worst kind of person. He was the personal advisor to the King known for dribbling poison from his words into the King's ear. At least, that's what I've heard my father say to my mother under the roof of our own house when they thought none of their children were listening or asleep.

I didn't say anything as he finished redressing my wounds. My jacket had seen better days, but it was still the only jacket I had and I could get more mileage out of it. Having to take it off so Damien could dress my wounds, I was once again in nothing but a bra.

As soon as Damien finished, he went into his office and came out with an oversized white t-shirt. It was better than nothing. As I was pulling it on, I heard water running. A rare thing to hear. I pulled the shirt down over my head to see Damien holding a glass of water in front of me. "Drink this, you're probably dehydrated."

"How? I had a hydration tablet yesterday."

"The poison has been in your bloodstream for quite some time. One of the symptoms of the poison is dehydration. Drink."

I did as I was told. The water tasted clearer than I was used to. It was also cold, not the room temperature our water was at this time of year. I drained the glass and he refilled it. "Again."

I slowed down on this glass for the cold temperature was giving me a headache. "I need to talk to you about what symptoms you're going to experience until the antidote gets here."

"How bad is it going to be?"

"You'll be dehydrated, your core body temperature will rise to fever level, and you may experience some hallucinations."

"What kind of hallucinations?"

"Those who have been poisoned experience the hallucinations differently." Damien took my empty glass from me and filled it up again. "I only know one person who remembers the episodes after the antidote was administered."

"It's not my dad, is it?"

"No. It's Crispin Frost."

. . .

75

I left the clinic after Damien forced two more glasses of water in me. The sun was high in the sky, meaning I spent half the day waiting for my punishment from my father. I still had no idea what it was. Selig had once told me he hated receiving the punishment. Well, I hated waiting to find out what it was going to be.

"You look a little worse for wear."

Turning, I saw my father's boss and head of CROSS standing there. General Elias Nolan wasn't much older than my father, but he looked older. His short hair which used to be brown had gone mostly grey, as did his facial hair. He always had a tired look to him, but he always dressed professionally. "It was a long night and morning."

"Normally you would be facing disciplinary charges for going past the wall, but, due to you breaking the rules, you have allowed CROSS to bring in a wanted man."

I felt the blood drain from my face. "Do you mean Frost?"

"Yes," Nolan said as if it weren't a big deal. "I suggest you go straight home before I change my mind."

Nolan stood there, watching me until I went in the direction of my home. Just thinking about Sayers or my father questioning Frost made me break out in a cold sweat.

Walking through the streets, I could feel the air getting colder as I made my way north. It was also a sign that winter was coming; it was going to be a ruthless one.

Rubbing my arms, I concentrated on trying to warm myself up when I walked into someone. "Sorry," I whispered.

"Elena what are you doing in the mining district?"

I looked up to see Craig Tiitus covered in mining dust. "I was just on my way home."

Craig had what used to be a red bandana over his head to help catch the sweat. He pulled it off his head and wiped his hands with it. "I'm not even going to ask what happened to you." He had accepted whatever game his son brought home for food, but he didn't like the method of how it was obtained, just like my mother. Craig was responsible for the welfare of what went on in the mines and it was speculated if Mihkel broke a rule, then Craig would have a harder time getting what was needed in the mines. It wasn't like we broke the rules to get water and food because we liked to, we did it in order to survive.

"I'll tell my dad you said hello."

"My son is inside if you would like to see him," Craig said. "Just keep it brief, he has chores. That, and his mother is trying to get some rest."

I walked inside the house and closed the door behind me. The house was almost identical to mine. Except, three people lived here, not five.

"Elena," Mihkel said. "You look like hell."

"Not as much as you," I shot back.

I saw that he had several cuts and bruises, some stitches under his lower lip, and his left hand was heavily bandaged. I was willing to bet his torso was covered in stitches as well.

His normally wavy hair had been cut close to his head due to the couple of cuts Nazar had given him. Damien must have shaved his hair after I had left. His dark hair, almost matching my own had a natural shine to it, as did his blue eyes. When he turned his head, I saw the permanent coal grey color was still there, even after the haircut. The short hair suited him. I liked it better like this. He usually let his hair grow out until his mother forced him to sit still long enough to cut it.

Mihkel turned slightly and I saw there was a welt that went from his neck and disappeared under his shirt. Craig must have struck him with his belt a few times. I also noticed he had a bandage wrapped around the bend of his right arm. "Doc Aryen took some blood to see if I had contracted Stigma yet. I haven't, but my father is showing signs in his blood."

That was one of the worst things someone in the family would hear. When the majority of the family comes down with Stigma, death for the whole family was usually imminent. Seeing as Mihkel wasn't eighteen yet, or old enough to work in the mines, if both his parents died, he would have to rely on the kindness of others for shelter or be put in an orphanage. He wouldn't have the option of staying in the house; they were usually burned down. A feeble attempt to stop the spread of Stigma.

● ● ●

"I'm sorry," I said, not knowing what to say. What does one person say to someone who is going to lose their entire family?

"My mother doesn't know yet, so don't tell anyone." Mihkel took a couple steps toward me. Unable to stop myself, I went up to him and wrapped my arms around his neck. He didn't hesitate hugging me back. I had ended what we had a few years back and I never wanted to look back, but I found myself, right now, wanting to go back to those days. Feeling relieved, Mihkel had never left those days to begin with.

"Of course," I whisper.

"Think you'll be able to learn how to hunt in a day or two?"

"Definitely."

"We'll meet up in our usual spot in a couple days then."

Our conversation was interrupted by Craig coming into the house. I took a step back and tried to act nonchalant. "Mihkel, you need to start on your chores."

"I'll see you later then." I walked out of the house.

I had gotten maybe five steps from the door when I heard it open again. "Elena," I turned to see Craig coming up to me. "Don't tell anyone what my son told you."

"I won't."

"You and I both know that his mother and I will die from this." Craig put his hand on my shoulder and squeezed it lightly. "Don't do anything stupid to get false hope in my son's head."

Chapter 12

I wanted to go see Sindri, but I had already spent too much time at Mihkel's. It would be bad if Enrik beat me home with quite a bit of time between us. My mother would start to ask where I was and it would get back to my father. Or worse, his boss. Right now, with what I had just learned, I wasn't in the mood to maneuver around the political games of Elias Nolan's mind.

As I was just about to pass the boundary line to where my family lived, I stopped when I saw a man in a CROSS uniform. He looked at me with his dark auburn eyes. As soon as his eyes met with mine, I knew exactly who he was. "Elena Hawthorne, is that you?" the man asked, walking over to me and placing his hand on top of my head. "You've grown quite a bit."

I couldn't help but smile. Drake Fisher, a member of CROSS from the Royal Province and the only man I liked from the militaristic city.

"What are you doing here?" I asked, taking his hand off my head.

"I'm part of CROSS, I have business here," Drake said. "I'm actually going to see your father."

Drake and my father were old friends, as my father was with Sayers. The only difference is I actually like Drake. That, and he was married to a distant family member of mine before she died during childbirth. "He's probably still at the Justice Building."

"Not to bring up the obvious question, but what the hell happened to your face?"

"It's been a long couple days," I said. "I'm sure my dad can fill you in."

"How is your father doing these days?"

"Working a lot. We barely see him anymore, not that he wants anything to do with me at the moment."

Drake raised his eyebrows at me. "I think I will ignore that comment, but I'll try to get him to come home tonight."

"Only try?"

"Things are bad all over." The look on his face just made me very curious as to why my father's hours have doubled in the past month. "Why don't you get yourself home? I'll see you later tonight. With that, Drake walked away.

++++

I made it home to see Selig was in the kitchen making pine tea. He did a double take of me. "What in the Gods?"

"It's a long story and I don't feel like telling it."

"Mom's been going out of her mind."

"I'm aware of this." I sat down at the table and sighed. My head was pounding. That Drake Fisher was in Ragnar City meant something bad was happening. Drake was the highest ranking officer of CROSS outside of Ragnar City and the liaison for the other provinces. "Do you think I do all of this on purpose? I don't. Our family has been damned from the beginning. If there is something I can do to help, I'm not going to stop."

"Elena, you think if I could, I wouldn't be doing what you do? I hate it as much as you do that dad has been fucked and things will never get better." Selig rubbed the back of his neck and sat down next to me. "Have you eaten at all?"

"No," I said, realizing I haven't eaten anything since the piece of stale bread Frost had given me. "I'm starving."

"This was dropped off this morning." Selig placed his hand on a package wrapped in brown paper. "It's food, very high quality."

I raised my hand to look in the package but hesitated. Selig motioned for me to open it and I did. My heart skipped a beat. "Is this beef?"

"Yes. Cheese, butter, bread, oil, hydration tablets, and medicine," said Selig.

"What is this medicine for?" I held up a small, round, silver container.

"All those cuts and bruises you keep getting."

I gave my brother a playful shove. We saw Damien the same amount of times every month. Only, we saw him for different reasons. I saw him after I was disciplined for breaking rules, Selig saw him when he got hurt. "You could use some of this just as much as me."

• • •

"This is for Stigma," Selig picked up a black cylinder and put it on the table. "Enough for two months. Dad is up high in the city, but not even Elias Nolan could get this much medicine for Ally."

Elias Nolan, also known as the General, the son of the Regent in charge of the Blackwater Province. Everything that happened in the Province went through Regent Nolan. I had only met the man once and I never wanted to meet him again.

"It was Drake."

"Drake? As in Drake Fisher? Our Uncle? He's here?" Selig asked.

"Yes. He'll be here later tonight." I picked up the medicine to see that it was divided into two separate months. Taking half of it, I slipped it into my pocket.

"What are you doing?" Selig asked, grabbing my wrist. "That medicine is for Ally, no one else."

"You know we always give some to Craig's wife."

"We're not going to give her a month's worth. Two months of this will give Ally two months of no pain. Why deny her that?"

"Craig has Stigma."

Selig stopped, "Are you serious? What about Mihkel?"

"He doesn't have it, but both his parents are going to die. The least we could do is give them a little longer with each other." I pulled my wrist away from my brother.

"When did everything go to hell?"

"Things have always been bad, it's just been catching up with everyone. I'm taking this to his family."

"Whatever you two are talking about, I suggest you postpone it."

We both turned to see Father and Drake coming into the kitchen. "I see you found the package I left for the family," Drake said. "That medicine is meant for your sister."

"We usually try and spare some medicine for Craig Tiitus' wife," Dad said.

"Craig Tiitus, he's a good man. There was a reason I picked him to run the mines." Drake held out his hand and Selig shook it. "You two look older for some reason."

"We've been stuck with the bad life in Ragnar City," said Selig.

"That's enough," Dad snapped. "Where's your mother?"

"She took Ally to visit the doc."

Our father didn't say anything to that. "Ration the food Drake brought and make sure Enrik is tied up out the back."

Selig went outside and left me to the food. I wiped my hands off and started to ration, attempting to ignore the conversation between my father and uncle.

I finished rationing out the food for three weeks and had just started on making dinner when my mother and Ally came home. My mother smiled when she saw Drake stand up. "Drake, what are you doing here?"

"I can't come to visit family?" Drake asked, hugging my mother.

"You're going to have to come up with a better lie than that." I hadn't seen my mother hug someone like she was hugging Drake in a long time.

"Business in the city." Drake took something out of his pocket and put it in my mother's hand. It was a silver necklace. "I can't keep this anymore. Cristina would have wanted you to have this to give to one of your daughters."

"Thank you…" my mother said, slipping the necklace on over her head.

"I had that made for her," my father said. "As a wedding present." I noticed the look on Drake's face wasn't a normal one. His eyes flicked to mine and back to my mother.

I decided to take this moment to take Ally back to bed and give her a dose of medicine. My father, mother, Drake, Damien, Cristina, and Claire, my father's surrogate sister, were very close. Every time that Drake was in the city, they would reminisce. They were part of happier times once. It was brief, but they were happy.

"Did Uncle Damien give you a shot of anything?" I asked, helping Ally back in the bed.

"He gave me some medicine."

I pulled the covers up to her chin and started rubbing her back slightly. "Uncle Drake brought us a two month supply of medicine."

"Are you going to give any to Mrs. Tiitus?"

"Of course I am," I said. "Are you okay with that?" After all, it was her medicine. I didn't want to take any from her without hearing her say it was okay.

Ally nodded and put her bandaged hand in mine. "Are you okay?"

"I'm fine, don't worry about me. Just try to get some sleep. I'll bring in some dinner for you later."

Chapter 13

After dinner, I was gathering up the dishes when Drake stopped me. "Let's take a walk. I want to talk to you and Selig about a few things."

We looked at our father who motioned that it was okay for us to go. "Be back before dark," he said.

"I'll make sure they get home," said Drake. "They won't get in trouble if they're with me."

"I want them home before dark," he repeated. "They start their real lives tomorrow."

"Carter, they haven't see Drake in a couple of years. You know they'll be fine with him," our mother said.

"Fine." Our father picked up a bowl of stew for Ally and went into the bedroom.

Drake looked at our mother who just shrugged. If anyone was going to be able to find out what was going on in my father's head, it was going to be Drake.

++++

Selig met Drake and me out front after retrieving Enrik. "Has he ever stopped growing?" Drake asked, scratching Enrik behind his ears.

Drake didn't say anything as we started walking. Ten minutes from the house, Selig stopped. "What did you want to talk to us about, Drake?"

"How are you two doing with everything?"

Selig raised his eyebrows. "What do you mean?"

"I mean, how are you handling all the bad that is happening to your family?"

"We're all about survival, even if it is a lost cause," I said.

"You really believe that?" Drake looked at the two of us. "You really think living and surviving is a lost cause?"

Selig sighed. "Sometimes. Do you know why dad turned down being the head of GUARD? Why would he give up an easier life for his family?"

Drake rubbed the back of his neck, pondering an answer. "I think that's a question for your father to answer."

"That's bullshit," Selig snapped. "Ally is dying because we can't get her the medicine she needs. It will be amazing if she lives through the winter. I want to know why our father is being such a coward."

Drake punched Selig, sending him to the ground. He then took off his gloves and grabbed Selig by his shirt. "Don't make assumptions about your father being a coward. You have no idea what he has gone through to make sure you two actually have a life. Yes, times are hard, but that doesn't mean you can go around saying your father isn't doing everything he can for the family."

I put my hand on Drake's shoulder. He turned to look at me, letting go of Selig. Slowly, he stood up straight and pulled Selig to his feet, despite his protests. I noticed a tattoo or a brand on the inside of his left wrist. Before I could get a better look at it, Drake pulled his gloves back on. "You two don't know the sacrifices your father has made for you."

"That still doesn't justify that our sister is going to die," Selig said. "She's twelve and she is going to die scared, in pain, and alone."

I knew what he meant by Ally being alone. We would be there with her, but that didn't mean any of us knew what she was going through. It just meant we were going to witness her death rather than experience it with her.

That got Drake thinking. His wife died from Stigma, as well as his daughter. Even though he was heavily exposed to both of them while they were alive, he didn't contract the disease. "It wasn't that your father turned down the job of being in charge of GUARD. It was because of something else."

It suddenly hit me. I had seen that tattoo on his wrist before. Our father had one in the exact same spot, I had just never gotten a clear look at it. "Does it have anything to do with that tattoo on the inside of your wrist?"

Drake touched his wrist as if it were out of habit. "You're perceptive."

"What does the tattoo even mean?" I asked quickly before Drake could change the subject.

• • •

Drake opened his mouth to answer but Selig interrupted him. "Don't give us the answer that it's something for our father to explain. We all know he won't."

"It's not so much a tattoo, more of a brand. Or a mark, if you will. It signifies something from around from twenty years ago."

Selig and I both looked at each other. Twenty years ago, Niklaus Kahler was crowned the new King. I remembered learning about it in school. It was a big deal because he wasn't of the bloodline. The flame of a worldwide rebellion started to ignite, but it was snuffed out before catching fire. The rebellion only lasted six months, proving Kahler was truly the man for the job. He, himself, ended the rebellion and talk of him killing the previous king died almost immediately.

"Twenty years ago..." I started to say. "Did you and dad have something to do with the rebellion?"

Drake scanned the area before answering. He knelt down and started to pet Enrik on his head, their eyes on the same level. "We were accused. There were around...twenty accused. But, they couldn't find evidence that pleased the new King so we were branded. Kahler didn't want us dead since we were still serving him under the crown. He wasn't about to lose nine of his best soldiers." He slowly took his glove off his hand and pulled his sleeve up.

For the first time, Selig and I got a real look at what our father, Drake, Nolan, and Sayers hid from the world so very carefully. It was a dissolving black feather with a thin wire wrapped around it. "What's it supposed to mean?" Selig asked.

"It symbolized how we were once great and now we're dissolving into nothing," Drake answered automatically. "Your father wanted to take the job with GUARD, but he wasn't allowed due to the mark he carries. It's why a lot of us are in CROSS, we don't have any other skills. But being soldiers, it's all we know."

Chapter 14

That next morning I was dressed and ready to go by the time my father had gotten up. This time, since I knew what the mark on his wrist was, I could see it clear as day. My acting like I was still asleep didn't work. I felt a rough hand on my shoulder and slowly opened my eyes. "I know you're awake, Elena. I want to talk to you," he said. "I'm going to start making tea. When it's done, you better be ready to talk. No exceptions."

"Yes, sir," I said quietly.

I waited until my father left the room and closed the door. Gently, I got out of bed and put my half of the covers over Ally. "Any idea what he wants to talk about?" Selig asked, lazily raising his head and rubbing the sleep out of his eyes.

"Probably something about how I disappoint him more than I don't?"

"Who haven't you disappointed recently?" He sat up and sighed. "What are you going to tell him about what Uncle Drake told us?"

"I don't know yet, I'll think before I answer him."

"That's not something you're very good at."

I picked up my ragged pillow and threw it at him. "And you're better at being an annoying twin brother than not."

Walking into the kitchen, I saw my father pouring the pine tea into cups. There was a peeled orange on the table. "Sit down," my father said, motioning to a chair. "Selig, you sit down as well. You're a part of this conversation."

Selig and I studied each other for a brief moment before we sat down. Whatever our father wanted to speak to us about was important. The rarest fruits in the Blackwater Province were reserved for the most crucial conversations.

"I need you two to step up," he said, suddenly. "I don't mean do more for the family, both of you do more than your share. I meant, step up with your attitude about this place. You both start working soon, that means you will be put into the system. Once that happens, I won't be able to help you. Selig, concentrate on doing your best as an apprentice with whichever merchant takes you on. If you do well enough, you could take over, creating a better life for you and for your family. Elena…I

• • •

need you to start trusting me. When I say I will get whatever this family needs, I need you to not go out and break the rules. What goodwill I have with city officials needs to be used for the family. Not just you."

Our father tore the orange into thirds. As we each took a piece, I could see juice already dripping from my fingers. Sticking the whole piece in my mouth, I savored the sweet and tangy taste.

"I'm not going to work for a merchant," Selig announced. "I'm going to go work in the mines. Craig Tiitus gave me the job a couple days ago."

"Tell me what I did to get such defiant children," our father muttered, standing up. "Elena, is there anything you want to tell me before I go to work?"

I shook my head. "So be it then."

Selig and I waited for the door to close before we did anything. "You really want to go work in the mines?"

"Don't really have a choice, do I? Have you ever heard of a merchant taking on an apprentice from the north?"

My brother had a point. The merchant businesses were mostly kept in the family. I had only heard of one time an outsider was hired. That was the apprentice at the masonry shop. "You do what you have to do then," I said, holding out my hand.

"Same," said Selig, running his hand across mine.

As I was pulling on my boots, Enrik came over to me. I scratched him behind his ears and he licked my hand. "What do you think? Think the family can make it without everything Selig and I do?"

Enrik nudged my face with his nose. "I didn't think so, either."

++++

Selig and I left at the same time, walking in the same direction. Not saying much to each other, we stopped at the road where it split in two directions. Selig would go north to the mines and I would go south to the Justice Building. "Some birthday this is going to be…" Selig grumbled.

• • •

"I'll see if I can trade for a sweet roll or something." Sweet rolls were regular rolls with a light dusting of sugar and cinnamon. The baker was usually a man who didn't like to haggle, but he would make an exception for a special occasion for some of his favorite customers. That, and he liked the loons that Mihkel or Sindri would find on a hunt once in a while.

"I probably won't be in the mood for anything. Not after my first day of working in the mines." Not knowing what to say to each other, Selig went further north and I went south.

Only miners and merchants were up at this hour, along with the various CROSS and GUARD members. I thought about stopping off at the Lore but decided against it. The Lore was where all the illegal trading, buying, and selling took place. My father swore if he caught Selig or me there, it would be the death of us. So far, we had both been lucky he hadn't seen us. Yet.

"Look who is up on her feet completely…"

I stopped walking to see General Nolan coming over to me. "General Nolan…surprised to see you up at this hour. Not a long line of girls last night?"

"Still have that mouth." Nolan removed his sunglasses. "Word on the street is that your Uncle, CROSS First Class Captain Drake 'Lionheart' Fisher, is in our *beloved city*." The way he said beloved city made me realize he hated Ragnar City just as much as the next person.

"He's in the city on business," I said with raised eyebrows. "You're in charge of CROSS, how did you not know he was coming?"

"I was being sarcastic, Elena." Nolan sighed and slipped his sunglasses back on. "You know if you actually get the hang of being part of the medical staff, you will have to become part of CROSS."

"I think I'd rather work in the mines."

"With your talents, CROSS would suit you better. Though, you're not the only one."

"I'm sure CROSS would be the perfect job if I want to serve a man that I loathe."

Nolan started to walk toward the Justice Building. "You know, Elena, surviving means doing things you don't want to do aside from just breaking the rules."

• • •

As much as I hated to admit it, he had a point.

I saw a few CROSS members as I walked toward the medical wing. Ballory and Nazar were talking with my uncle. "Look who is up and around after the beating she received from Captain Sayers," Ballory said with a smirk on his face.

"Medicine is a wonderful thing," I said. "Especially when it's administered."

"Watch what you say around here, Elena," Drake said, putting his arm around my shoulders and pulling me close. "Some might call that treason."

"Never thought you had a death wish, but you may have changed my mind," said Nazar.

"I'm going to be late," I said, pulling myself out of Drake's hold.

"That's right…" Ballory said. "This is the newest member of CROSS in the making."

"No," I snapped.

"Too late," Drake said. "If your brother hadn't went into an apprenticeship, he would have ended up being recruited into CROSS. You two have some natural talents. Plus, you know working for Nolan and your father is better than the life Selig is going to have being a miner."

"Thinking you can't recruit a miner to work demolitions for CROSS?"

Our conversation was interrupted by Nolan and Sayers coming over. "There's a situation," Nolan said. "Nazar, Fisher, go to the mines. Creid is already there with Captain Hawthorne. Sayers, I suggest alerting Bogdan to the situation. I'm hoping to contain this before it gets too out of hand and he feels the need to exert his power, along with his lust for blood and death. Ballory, take her somewhere out of reach of all this shit."

"What's going on?" I asked.

"I don't know, but let's go," Ballory said, giving me a shove toward the offices.

Chapter 15

Ballory kept his hand tightly on my shoulder until we passed my father's office. "If you put any more pressure on my collarbone, you will snap it in half," I said, trying to loosen his grip.

He didn't get a chance to answer. The ground shook violently sending us to the floor. "This is why I hate being in the mining province…" Ballory muttered, blinking some blood out of his eye. "They have to dig all over the underground of the city looking for coal and other minerals."

"Your head is bleeding."

"I'll be fine," said Ballory as he slowly stood up, pulling me to my feet. "Come on."

As Ballory was leading me toward the exit of the Justice Building, I could feel more tremors under my feet. I walked as quickly as I could with Ballory pulling me along.

It wasn't until there was another massive tremor that I lost my balance, taking Ballory to the floor with me. I felt the wind get knocked out of me when his shoulder hit me in the abdomen. "Either the whole mine is collapsing or there is another rebellion."

I didn't have the energy to make a comment about a rebellion, which Ballory seemed to be grateful for. I felt his weight being lifted off me and then someone's hands on my shoulders pulling me to my feet once more. "I suggest going to the southernmost part of the city, the furthest away from the mines." It was Sayers.

"So, it is the mines?" I asked.

"An explosion was miscalculated, causing part of the mine to collapse. The problem is, GUARD will see it as a threat and report back to the Capitol," Sayers said, examining the cut on Ballory's head. "It's not that deep, but a bleeder. Let's go."

The tremors were getting weaker and weaker as we made our way to the south side of the Justice Building. "So much for you and Selig having a choice in working for CROSS or not," Sayers said. "After today, we're going to need more recruits."

"You actually told Bogdan, Captain?" Ballory asked.

"The lesser of two evils."

"How many dead?" I asked my heart in my throat.

"Your brother is fine, he wasn't down in the mines when the explosion happened." Sayers turned to look at me, revealing a cut on the left side of his jaw stretching to the middle of his neck.

"Captain, from the force of the tremors, it has to be more than a mine explosion," said Ballory.

"I am praying to the Gods Bogdan doesn't pay too much attention to this disaster. Craig Tiitus has been fighting for better work conditions since he took the damn job. I wouldn't be surprised if he did this himself."

"Craig would never hurt innocent people," I said. "He, like everyone else, hates Ashton, but he would never hurt someone who didn't deserve it."

"Why do you think the explosion happened this early in the morning?" Ballory asked.

I stopped walking. "You knew about this?"

"Let's go, Elena…the last thing anyone needs is GUARD taking up a permanent residence in this dying city. It will be the death of us all."

Outside the Justice Building, it was almost total chaos. Various CROSS members were attempting to sort through the madness, getting citizens to safety. The problem was, they were having to do their job with the random tremors that interrupted their progress from time to time. Or the citizens were too weak from not having enough to eat, or had gotten hurt the falling debris. Most of the CROSS soldiers were too green to have any idea what they were supposed to be doing. Making this a worthless effort. Almost. Ballory gripped my arm hard, his nails digging into my skin. Another shock happened, sending me off my feet. Ballory wrapped his arms around me, trying to break my fall. Both of us landed on the rock and stone, I felt a sharp edge split a small area on my arm. I felt the heat from my blood trail down my arm. I managed to get a look at Ballory, he had another cut on his head. This one was deep and he was going to need medical attention for it.

I felt Sayers pull me to my feet. Once I gathered my bearings, I helped him get Ballory to his feet. "Only Fenrir could do this much damage…" Ballory said, allow Sayers to look at his head again.

• • •

"Religion has nothing to do with this," Sayers snapped. "Elena, we have to get to the mines. I need you to do one of the things you do best and survive right now. The quicker we get this thing under control, the better for everyone."

"Okay, but can Ballory do anything with that head wound?"

"He'll be okay. Don't worry about your brother or father, they'll be alright," Sayers said.

++++

I maneuvered my way through the city, having to fight my way through the crowds. Not knowing where I was going, I just kept walking. I didn't stop until I heard my name. Turning, I felt a sense of relief when I saw Mihkel pushing his way toward me. "What are you doing in the southern part of the city?"

"I was just in the Justice Building when everything started going to hell," I said.

We stood there, looking at each other, when someone shoved their way past us. Mihkel's eyes started to move, ending up following the blood trail and stopping at my arm. "Come on, Sindri and Kara are at their house."

Mihkel took my hand and started to push his way through the Ragnar citizens. It surprised me that he took hold of my hand. But, it surprised me more when I didn't protest. I was feeling safe when he was around me, and the more he was near, the more I wanted him to be. Right now, though, I just wanted to get indoors and find solace with familiar faces.

When we were almost to Sindri's house, I pulled my hand out of his grip. He stopped and turned around, a confused look on his face. "Elena, what's going on? I think it would be best to get inside somewhere."

"Mihkel, they think your dad did this on purpose," I said. "Did he?"

Mihkel gave me a look. One I had never seen before on him. It was hard, cold, and sent a shiver down my spine. "What makes you think he had anything to do with this?"

• • •

"Your father is an outspoken man and everyone knows it. Sayers is going to relay his thoughts to my father and General Nolan or go directly to GUARD with it. You know he will."

"CROSS is there for the people...such an ironic statement," Mihkel said, rubbing the back of his neck.

We didn't say anything else until we got to the Anton house. Going inside, I saw that Kara was fast asleep with her head in her brother's lap. Sindri had a relieved look on his face when he saw Mihkel and I were pretty much unscathed. "I guess it's a good thing we didn't go hunting today," said Sindri as Mihkel and I sat down.

"I still want to go," I said.

"We will, if CROSS can get a handle on this," Mihkel said. "Without the bloodshed."

"Blood will only be spilled if GUARD gets involved."

We all stopped talking when Sindri and Kara's father, Robert, came from the downstairs shop. "Glad to see you four are okay and smart enough to stay inside." He walked over and easily lifted Kara into his arms. "Stay inside until this blows over."

Robert Anton had a similar build to Mihkel's father. He was strong from the work it required to run his shop. He had short, grey hair with several scars on his hands and arms. All from his job. Unlike Craig and my father, he was a kind man and never struck his children. While he got angry from Sindri's actions, he just gave him more chores to do, never struck him.

"Us, staying inside until it blows over? That could be days," I said.

"Your father is in CROSS and his father is in charge of the mines. It's too dangerous to go outside."

He didn't wait for a response, instead he carried his daughter out of the room.

After an hour, I was getting restless. We hadn't heard anything and I couldn't sit around any longer. "I'm going," I said, standing up.

"Going where?" Sindri asked.

"To the mines," said Mihkel, standing up as well.

"Okay...are you two going to tell me when you started to be so close?" This question wasn't out of jealously. There had

● ● ●

94

been nothing romantic between Sindri and I. We had been friends for as long as I could remember, and we had an understanding. If something happened in my life, I told him. As he did with me.

"We're not," I said quickly. "We just have a couple things in common."

Around a minute later, the three of us were walking through the streets. It felt like I was in a completely different city. I had never seen the streets of Ragnar City so bare before. Not that it was a vibrant place to live, but there was always someone outside, homeless or not.

"Why do I get the feeling that if we get caught it will be worse than when we got at the reservoir?" Sindri asked.

"Probably because whatever is going on has something to do with GUARD?" Mihkel asked.

"Whatever is happening has to do with everything," I said simply.

Chapter 16

The first person that recognized us was Solomon. As he came running over, Mihkel and Sindri pulled me out of the way of five GUARD soldiers running toward us. Luckily they stormed past, not stopping for anyone or anything.

"What the hell are you three doing here?" Solomon snapped. "What is it going to take for you to do what you're told?"

"Creid!" We all turned to see General Nolan coming up to us. Blood was running down his left temple and he was trying to hide the fact that he was favoring his left arm. "As much as I hate to admit it, these three can take care of themselves. The only reason I enjoy being in charge of CROSS is because I don't have to deal with shit like this. I haven't bled for the damn job in fifteen years. Get back with the others and let them worry about themselves."

Solomon didn't say a word as he turned and walked back toward the entrance of the mines. General Nolan turned back and glared at us. "Don't make me regret not having you dragged into the Justice Building and restrained." He wiped the drying blood off his face and slipped his sunglasses on. "If you three survive this day, I don't care how much you protest, I'm recruiting you into CROSS." He walked out of earshot before any of us could protest.

Our break from reality was interrupted by some miners coming toward us. They were all covered in black dust, only a couple of them bleeding. "Mihkel, what are you doing out here? It's way too dangerous, even for you." It was Rockson Galloway, Craig Tiitus' right-hand man.

"What's going on?" Mihkel asked.

"One of the main tunnels collapsed in on itself causing a ripple effect. Your father is trying to stop the collapsing by bracing the tunnel with debris from another explosion. There is only one problem: the only place it can be done properly."

Mihkel, Sindri, and I looked at each other. "That will cause GUARD to put Ragnar City under martial law," said Mihkel.

● ● ●

The most stable area in the city was around the Justice Building and the only way to stop the mine from completely collapsing in on itself was to use an explosion around the building to block off the unstable area. "Any damage to the Justice Building will be an automatic execution for those who played a part in it," said Galloway.

As the ground became unsteady under our feet again, I put my hand on Sindri's shoulder to steady myself. "What about a controlled explosion in one area?" Mihkel asked. "Where it's detonated from a safe distance and the building is saved from any more destruction?"

"It's possible," Galloway said with a look of pondering in his eyes. "I only know of one person that could rig the explosive material in that way."

++++

"Absolutely not," my father said. "I will not allow any of my men to kill themselves for a lost cause."

"Captain…" Ballory said.

My father raised his hand up. "I don't want to hear another word out of you, Lieutenant."

"Carter, you know he's the only one that can do it," Drake said. It was rare for Drake to call my father by his first name when they were in uniform. "Then I can ignite it."

"It's either that or GUARD comes in and takes over," said Sayers.

My father sighed and rubbed the back of his neck. "Where's General Nolan?"

"He's helping out Regent Nolan in making sure martial law isn't called too early, if at all."

"The last thing anyone needs is Captain Bogdan in the city on a permanent basis," muttered my father. "Do it. Have Craig Tiitus act as your guide through the mines and get out of there as soon as possible. You have thirty minutes, tops, to get this done."

With that, my father started to shove the three of us north. "Right now, I don't care if this is the only time you actually do what I say. Stay out of the area. I mean it, Elena."

• • •

"Where's Selig?" I asked.

"He's fine. He was evacuated with the other miners. Go home and make sure your mother and sister are okay. When everything is all clear, I'll send your uncle by with Selig." He then kissed the top of my head, something he hasn't done since I was young.

++++

At home, I saw a relieved look on my mother's face. She pulled me into her arms and did the same with Sindri and Mihkel. "Thank the Gods you're all okay. Have you heard anything about your brother?" she asked, squeezing my arms.

"He's with the evacuated miners," I said. "They're going to stop the tunnel collapse by bracing it with debris from a controlled explosion."

"That doesn't sound like an idea of your father's," my mother said.

"It was Mihkel's," said Sindri.

"Ally needs some medicine applied to her sores, would you go do that?"

I stayed silent as I picked up the metal cylinder and went into the bedroom. Ally was awake, playing with a rag doll that had once been a hand me down to me. "Hey, sunshine," I said, sitting down on the bed. "How are you feeling?"

"My neck hurts," she said, touching the back of her neck.

"Let me see…" I gently lifted her hair up and my heart skipped a beat. There was a gaping sore the size of my hand on the back of my sister's neck and shoulders. It wasn't there yesterday, so it had to be a new one. But, it looked like it had gone untreated for months. Not knowing what else to do, I picked up a rag we used to clean the Stigma spots and started to wipe the pus and dried blood away. When I cleaned it up the best I could, I picked up the cylinder of medicine. "This will sting."

I felt Ally's back and neck muscles tense up as I applied the medicine on the fresh sore. My heart sank as I realized the rate of the disease was spreading. My sister didn't have much longer, even with the medicine Drake sent our way and Damien

● ● ●

98

doing all that he could. My twelve year old sister was going to die.

"What's wrong?" Ally asked.

I, only then, realized that I was crying. Quickly, I wiped my eyes dry and smiled at her. "Just something in my eye," I said, sighing slightly. "I have an idea for your birthday."

"I'm not allowed outside unless Uncle Damien says it's okay."

"What if I can convince him, mom, and dad to let you out in the backyard for a little while with Selig, Enrik, and myself? We can play together like we used to."

Ally opened her mouth to respond when she started coughing violently. I put my hand up toward her mouth, stopping when I saw red flecks on her gown. Slowly, I turned my hand over to see it was covered in blood. With Ally coughing our mother came into the room and I stood up. "What happened?" she demanded. "Elena, where are you going?"

I picked up the black jacket that Selig didn't wear anymore and pulled it on, my jacket wasn't wearable now. "I'm going to do something I should have done a long time ago." I ran out of the room like I was on fire.

"Elena?" Mihkel asked, standing up. "Everything okay?"

"You're coming with me," I said, grabbing his wrist and pulling him out of the house.

"Elena, did you not hear what your father just told us?" Mihkel pulled his wrist out of my grip. "What's going on?"

I couldn't keep it to myself anymore. "General Nolan and my dad...they are the ones who caused Stigma to spread throughout the city."

Mihkel just stared at me. "Wait, wait, wait..." he said a rapid pace, holding up his hands. "Did you just say that two men who are supposed to be there for the people are the ones that started the downfall of the city?"

"Yes..." I said, feeling the tears starting. For the first time in my life, I didn't care. "There's something else..."

"I'm suddenly afraid to ask."

"It's Ally...the Stigma has spread, a sore the size of my hand appeared on her neck and shoulders..." I looked at Mihkel to see that tears were streaming down his face as well.

* * *

"That means my mother is going to die soon." Blaise Tiitus had contracted Stigma not a week after my sister had.

"The open sore looks like it hasn't been treated for months. The disease has sped up and I don't know what else to do."

"Elena, you're not thinking—"

"We have t—"

Mihkel halted the conversation by kissing me. His lips tasted salty, from the mixing of our tears. His hands encircled my face, and I welcomed his familiar touch again.

Our kiss was interrupted by a massive ground tremor and the sound of an explosion. Suddenly, I was off my feet and lying on the ground with Mihkel covering me.

When the tremors stopped, Mihkel slowly lifted up his head. He looked down at me and sighed, "Are you okay?"

"Yeah…" I said.

Mihkel stood up with the grace that came naturally to him and pulled me to my feet. He ran a hand through his hair, shaking the dust loose. I redid my hair into a simple ponytail. "I need to know that you know exactly what you're getting us into. CROSS? What is your plan with joining CROSS?"

"We join up, which is what General Nolan, Sayers, and my father want, and maybe we will be able to see what research they have on the cure for Stigma."

Mihkel ran a hand through his hair again. "So, this is why you chose me to drag along with you instead of Sindri?"

"He hasn't lost anyone to Stigma. We will."

"Lead the way."

++++

Even though it was cold, I had to strip my jacket off and cover my mouth and nose due to all the mineral dust in the air. I felt Mihkel take hold of my hand and lead me through the turmoil.

Unable to see, I walked into Mihkel when he stopped abruptly. Hey, you two!" someone yelled. "Get inside! The dust is too thick to be out in!"

Mihkel started to walk again, causing me to almost trip from the sudden movement. We got inside as quickly as we could, the doors slamming behind us. The person that had yelled at us was Drake.

Drake started to strip out of his uniform. "I suggest you two shed your clothes that has dust on them, it's toxic."

I dropped my jacket to the ground and started to work on my boots when I stopped. "We need to speak to General Nolan, Captain Sayers, or Captain Hawthorne." If I was going to be part of CROSS, I would have to get used to calling my father by his title.

Drake stopped and raised his eyebrows at me. "Captain Hawthorne? Well, well, well…" He pulled his gloves off and dropped them on top of his military coat. "So, you two want to join CROSS?"

"Yes," said Mihkel.

"I'll see if I can find the General, he's been wanting you two for a while," Drake said, turning his head and looking around. "Lieutenant Ballory, take these two to get some clean clothes."

Ballory stayed a couple steps in front of us as we followed him down the hall, his hands behind his back, holding his CROSS-issued sunglasses in them. "Why do I get the feeling I'm going to be seeing the two of you a lot more than usual now?"

"Did everyone know it was only a matter of time before we joined CROSS?" Mihkel asked.

"Those with talents for CROSS always end up coming here, even if they don't want to."

"You sound like you're speaking for experience," I said.

Ballory stopped walking and looked at us. "Everyone in CROSS has had an experience like that in one way or another. I just pray to the Gods that you two have a firm grasp on your humanity. If you don't, you will lose it quicker than most do."

"Lose our humanity?" Mihkel asked.

"You join up with CROSS, life does get better for you. At a cost. You take the generosity from Ashtan and the price is steep. I've been standing in my grave for ten years, waiting for them to decide I'm no longer of use to them."

"Why do I suddenly feel like we're going to sign our death warrant?" asked Mihkel, looking at me.

● ● ●

"It's not too late for you to turn back," Ballory said, putting his hands on our shoulders. "I know why you both are doing this, and it's admirable. Forgive me for saying this, but it's a lost cause. There is no cure for Stigma, there never will be."

"Have you ever lost someone to this disease? Watching them dying in pain day by day and not being able to do a damn thing about it? You would do anything you could to at least stop the suffering," I retorted.

"If you want to stop your parents' or sister's suffering, then I suggest taking a syringe and filling it with a medicine that makes them stop breathing," Ballory said. "Doc Aryen has performed his share of mercy killings like everyone else has. Just as you two will soon enough."

I started to put my hand into a fist to punch him, but Mihkel beat me to it. "You better hope my talents aren't needed as much as everyone with the uniform on thinks they are, or I will rise above you and perform a mercy killing of my own."

"Mihkel, stop! You want to get executed?" I hissed in his ear.

"That's enough!" someone yelled.

The three of us didn't have time to look up before everyone was being pulled apart. "For someone who claims they will be loyal to the royal family…you're making it harder on yourself to be trusted," Nolan said, coming over to us.

"All a misunderstanding," said Ballory, wiping blood off of his lower lip. "I just wanted to see how hard he could punch."

"Test his strength another way," Drake said, not letting go of Mihkel. My father had his arm around me.

"Sign them both up now," said my father. "Let them prove the hard way they can be useful."

"The hard way?" I asked with raised eyebrows.

"Haven't done that in a while," Nolan said. "This should be interesting. Schedule it for next week and we'll have some fun."

"I suggest you two go home and prepare for your life to change, for the worse," my father said.

I walked with Mihkel back to his house. "I'm sorry for getting you into this," I said.

"Don't," Mihkel said, with a smirk on his face. "If I didn't want to do this, then I wouldn't have gone with you."

"Will you teach me how to hunt tomorrow morning at daybreak?"

"I wouldn't have it any other way. Tomorrow morning, daybreak."

Chapter 17

Luckily no one else was awake when I got up. Ally would ask where I was going, mother would give me a lecture on how I'm not bulletproof, and Selig would try to stop me. Which, there was a strong chance he would. I was fast, but if Selig got a hold of me, I wouldn't be able to get away. He was strong and carried the same determination that I did.

As I was pulling on my boots, Enrik came over to me. I scratched him behind his ears and he licked my hand. "Want to learn how to hunt?" I asked him softly. It was a stupid question seeing as Enrik was already a master hunter. I remembered seeing Mihkel and Sindri hunt for the first time. Sindri had skill, but it was from a lot of practice. Mihkel was like Enrik, a born hunter. I wonder what Enrik would be like if he was in the care of Mihkel? They pretty much rivaled each other in their abilities. Enrik had the better eyesight and sense of smell, but Mihkel had the human mind on his side. They would be an unstoppable team.

Mihkel was already waiting for Sindri and me by the time I had gotten to the woods with Enrik. "You're here early," I said.

"I couldn't sleep," said Mihkel, not able to look me in the eye. Of course I knew why he had a lot on his mind. It was then I remembered that I had snuck some of the medicine Drake had given us. It seemed like it happened so long ago, though it had only been a day or two.

"Medicine, take it."

"I can't take that from Ally."

"Where do you think your mother has been getting her medicine?" I asked. "It's okay, here is a month. Ally has a month. Your family needs it more than mine does right now." I hated saying that. I loved my sister and would do anything for her, but Mihkel was in a different situation. He was going to lose both of his parents in a short period of time. He was going to be on his own. Normally that wouldn't be a problem, but he was the same age as Sindri. I had just turned eighteen. At eighteen we could work anywhere, you could risk your life for meager wages every day in the mines or, in our case, serving the royal family. Sindri was a few days older than Mihkel but, since his father ran the masonry shop, he was set for life.

It was then Mihkel had turned his head to the side and I felt my chest tighten. I saw a long line of stitches. "What happened to your head?"

"Like your family, mine needs water. I went back to the reservoir after we separated. Or, I tried to. I didn't even make it to the meeting point. I stepped on a snare or something like that. Some blade came out of nowhere and split my scalp. Before I passed out...I-I...saw something, a flash of...something."

A flash of something, I had a feeling it was similar to what I've been seeing at random moments. "Who stitched your head up?"

"I have no idea. When I came to, my head was cleaned and the wound was stitched closed." I lightly ran my fingers over the stitching. It wasn't smooth and clean like Damien's.

We stopped talking when we heard a branch snap. We both looked up seeing Sindri walking over to us. "Ready to hunt?" he asked, a cold tone in his voice. Mihkel and I glanced at each other. Sindri had to know.

"Yes," I said, taking a bow from Sindri.

"How about we make sure you can actually shoot an arrow first," said Sindri. The three of us knew he saw the line of stitches on Mihkel's head, but he didn't say anything. Just as he didn't say anything about the two of us becoming closer and closer.

"I think that would be my area of expertise," Mihkel said, taking the bow from me and tossing it to Sindri. He started to take my jacket off when I shoved him against a tree.

"Easy there, fireball," said Mihkel. "You can't shoot with that jacket on."

"I've seen you do it a thousand times."

"That's the catch. I'm good at it and I've had practice, you're just learning." Mihkel slipped out of his own jacket and laid it on the ground. "Come on."

I shrugged out of my jacket and laid it down next to Mihkel's. Sindri followed suit. It was a cold morning, making the hair on my arms stand on end from goose bumps. Mihkel tossed me a shooting glove and I slipped it on my left hand. He did the same. Sindri had his on his right hand.

I slipped my index, middle, and ring fingers into the holes for my fingertips. I was surprised to see it was a perfect fit to my hand. "It fits perfectly."

"I made it a couple nights ago," Mihkel said. "Something tells me you'll be one hell of a shot."

Sindri handed me the bow and an arrow. As I readied the bow, I felt someone's hand on my shoulder. "Level out your shoulders and keep your arm straight." It was Mihkel. "Legs apart, like mine."

I mimicked what Mihkel was doing. "Aim for that crevasse in that tree." He pointed with two fingers and then put his hand over mine, showing me where to aim my fingers.

I aimed the arrow at the tree. "Take a breath and let it out slowly," said Sindri.

Taking in a breath, I let it out, feeling the release of the arrow. It hit the mark dead center. The two of them clapped slowly. "That's amazing," Sindri said. "There is only one other person I know who did that on their first try." He walked up to me.

"Who?"

"Me," Mihkel said simply, as if it weren't a big deal.

We spent the next hour practicing until my arm was growing sore from the repetitive motions and the shooting glove was digging into my skin. As we were getting ready to go back into the city, we heard the sound of engines. "Airship…" Sindri whispered suddenly. "Go." In an instant, we grabbed out stuff.

We started to run down the hill, navigating through the trees. Enrik had gone off on his own earlier to hunt, but as we were running down the hill, he showed up again. "Is it CROSS or GUARD?" Sindri asked as we stopped to gather our bearings for a second.

"By the engine sounds, GUARD," said Mihkel. "Keep going."

A few minutes had passed with us running at full speed. The engine sounds weren't getting softer, they were getting louder. "We've been spotted!" I yelled.

● ● ●

"It's GUARD technology, heat seeking," Sindri shot out between breaths.

Just as I was getting another burst of speed, I was pulled to the ground by the back of my jacket. It was Mihkel. "What are you doing?" I hissed, starting to get up.

"We're back at the top of the reservoir tower," said Mihkel. "We can lose the tracker inside the tower."

I looked down the tower, remembering what Mihkel told me about his head. "I don't think so, what about what happened to your head?"

"If we're going, we need to go now," said Sindri.

I tightened the straps on my bag and took a deep breath. "Let's go."

We jumped down into the top level of the tower, just a few feet away from the cliff we were on. "Take whichever way is easiest for you, it doesn't matter," Sindri said, as the engines were getting louder. The airship was getting close enough that it was getting hard to stay on my feet.

Mihkel had to yell at us to be heard. "Go!"

I went with the trees again, as did Mihkel. Sindri went with the ruined buildings path. We moved as fast as we could without killing ourselves.

As I was bracing myself to go to the next tree, I felt a sudden sharp pain against my neck. Clutching my neck, my fingers came away with blood. Looking around, I saw one of the black metal claws splinter the branch I was going for like it was a toothpick. "Was that on purpose or did they miss?" I asked. I looked at Mihkel when he didn't respond to see part of the claw latching in his arm. Without thinking, I took out my knife and started to cut around the metal. I pulled it out and saw Mihkel had bitten his lower lip hard enough that he had to spit out blood.

Just then, another claw shot past us, causing my foot to slip on the moss covered branch. I felt my balance go. Mihkel grabbed my wrist, letting me hang from the branch, nothing but air and branches below my feet. I didn't have my gloves on, so there wasn't a prayer for me to drop and catch a branch without breaking bones.

Mihkel started to pull me up when I suddenly had a flash of something. It wasn't the white room, though. It was something

• • •

different, as if I was seeing the bottom of the water. "Stop," I said, getting a sick feeling in my stomach. He had grabbed me with his injured arm and his blood was trailing down to my hand.

"What? It'd be better to pull you up," said Mihkel. He was showing signs of pain now.

"Let go."

"No way, are you insane?"

"Trust me on this," I said. The image was getting clearer; I could see the water and the bits of dirt and bark falling from the bottom of our feet and splashing into the water. It was…surreal.

Mihkel hesitated. As he was staring at me, the branch started breaking. "Mihkel, drop me. If the branch breaks, both of us could die."

"So, only you are allowed to die?" he snapped, trying to tighten his grip on my hand. The mixture of blood and sweat was making it rather difficult.

I opened my mouth to say something when I noticed my hand was slipping out of Mihkel's. "Mihkel, what are you doing? Pull her up!" Sindri called out.

Taking advantage of Mihkel distraction, I pulled my hand out from his. "No!" he yelled.

I started to fall, managing to turn myself around so I could see if I was going to slam into anything. Whatever I was seeing in my head was even clearer. I was maneuvering through the branches and I was almost at the bottom. Suddenly, the flash changed. Not because I made it into the water, because I was in an intense amount of pain.

Something wet hit me in the face. It wasn't water, it was blood. My blood. It had to be. I was able to move my arms, but there was still an immense amount of pain. The pain was too much. I blacked out.

Chapter 18

Michael

The church was dimly lit due to the lack of electricity that was allowed in Ragnar City. I sat down on one of the middle pews, disrupting the layer of dust that had long since settled. Leaning forward, I intertwined my fingers, resting my wrists on the back of the pew. The rank of Chief was still tattooed on the wrist of my flesh arm. Slowly, I reached into my pocket and took out the necklace of prayer beads and Cosmos symbol of the once glorious Valefor shaped in the form of water and feathers. Wrapping it around my Shinar hand, I sighed. Gripping it tighter, I could see the wire as the beads were being pulled apart.

"Never thought you would be one who would look to one of the Gods for guidance."

I turned to see one of the only friends I had left alive in this world. Drake Fisher adjusted his uniform sleeves and just looked at me. When he saw what I was holding, his expression went from blank to stern. "I've turned this god's forsaken world upside down looking for that. I wasn't going to be able to forgive myself if I never found it." He walked over to me and leaned against the pew. "Why...did you take it?"

"You weren't the only one in love with her." I stood up. "In case you have forgotten, she was-"

"Even though Ragnar City is slowly dying, that doesn't mean you two can fight or take the Lord's name in vain."

Both of us stopped to see a priest walking over to us. "The Lord?" Drake asked. "Aren't there two gods?" he asked, his voice thick with sarcasm. Like me, he found that praying to a man that writing depicted as a giant bird or a giant wolf, was something pointless in this life.

The Priest smacked Drake and then me. Both of us took it by surprise, making it hurt more than it normally would. "I may have faith in both of the gods, but that doesn't mean you two can disrespect me."

"How can you? The world is dying and you think the God of Cosmos or the God of Chaos can do anything? Livia is dead!" I rubbed my mouth and looked at the priest. "And…so am I."

I walked out of the church and had to shield my eyes. I had lost track of time again. It had been pitch black when I had gone into the church. Now, I would have to stay here all day to avoid everything and everyone. "I know both of you are still hurting. I am, too."

Turning my head, I saw Father Kane standing beside me. "Just because you raised me after my parents died doesn't mean you know me."

"I know you better than you think, both of you. Did I try and push either of you into the clergy?"

I couldn't help but smile, even though it came with a sigh. "No, you didn't."

"How long has it been since you've been to see their graves?"

"Their?"

"You did have a child with her."

"It wasn't a baby, it died before it was born."

Father Kane looked at me in disbelief. "You should be ashamed of yourself. Your son was not an 'it'. He was part of you, a part of her."

"Are you done with this lecture? If you don't mind, I'm going to go home and drown myself." I started to walk down the steps, suddenly feeling a sharp sting in my neck. Slowly, I reached up and pulled out what looked like a dart. I looked up at Father Kane, the world becoming blurry and shaky.

"I'm sorry, Michael, but this is the only way," he said, his voice fading.

"Everything went dark.

++++

I woke up to a regrettably familiar ceiling. My head was pounding and my whole body felt heavy. I remembered this feeling from years ago, being hit with the dart multiple times; the only calming agent strong enough when it came to a few of us. "You look better than the last time I saw you. Maybe about the same."

Attempting to sit up, I felt a strong wave of nausea come over me. I bent over and emptied the contents of my stomach into a waste basket, which wasn't much. "What the hell did you put in that dart?"

"The same thing used those many years ago," the man said. I could smell smoke from his cigarette. I could also smell the scent of the aftershave he wore when he was wearing the uniform. It helped to cover up the smell of coal and oil embedded into everyone's skin.

When my vision became clear, I slowly managed to sit up and get a clear view of my visitor. My captor. "Carter Hawthorne…I thought I told you if I never saw you again, it would be too soon?"

"Still as drunk as ever though I made it clear that I own you," said Carter, pushing the waste basket away with his foot. He put his cigarette out and looked at me with tired eyes. "Your skills are needed again."

"I don't do that anymore," I said. "That was the deal. I don't do that anymore and you let me stay dead."

"Clearly…" said Carter, standing up. "You've forgotten the conversation we had."

Carter suddenly grabbed me by my throat and threw me to the ground. He took out his gun and put it to my forehead so I wouldn't use my Shinar limb on him. "I know what your true wish is, don't tempt me."

"What would you know about it?"

"I know a lot more than you think." He forced me to look at him. "You'll create a Shinar limb and stay on as the girl's mechanic."

"Girl?"

"…my daughter."

"Ally?"

"Elena."

"Since when is Elena your daughter?"

"Since your wife gave birth to a stillborn." Carter holstered his gun. "Get to work."

With that, Carter left. Leaving me to figure out what the hell I was to myself.

Chapter 19

Keeping my sunglasses on, I walked into the Justice Building. I had considered putting on my old CROSS uniform, but decided against it. I wasn't trying to get myself noticed and reinstated. I was trying to return to my lifestyle of everyone thinking I was dead. Though, I had a feeling that this wasn't going to happen. "You know, you just standing there doesn't mean it's going to all go away?"

I turned and smiled when I saw Amon Ballory standing there. "Amon Ballory, I didn't think I'd see you in Ragnar City. I thought you would have gone back to Aion. Even Solanum."

The two of us shook hands, Ballory pulling me into a brief hug. "You know the only way to get out of CROSS is to die," Amon said. "You were the closest one to that idea."

"Until Carter Hawthorne reminds you that he owns you."

"You'll have to get fitted for a uniform before you see your client."

"Uniform?"

"Oh, you've been reactivated into CROSS. There is no debating that." Amon patted me on the shoulder.

"Only the Gods could have planned this..." I muttered.

"That would be the second in command, Captain Carter Hawthorne," Amon said. "Come on. You'll need a shower as well. You smell like burnt food and bad spirits."

"That's the whole point in trying to kill myself with drink."

++++

After Amon shoved me into the showers, I stood there under the hot water. It had been many years since I had hot water, but it wasn't welcomed. Turning the water off, I wrapped a white towel around my waist, leaving the water beads clinging to my chest.

I went into the locker area to see a brand new CROSS uniform laid out for me. There was a note attached to it. *'Don't fight fate. You know as well as I do, we both belong in this life.'* It was signed by Amon. There was also a pair of thin black

● ● ●

gloves for me to wear. The sole purpose was to hide my Shinar arm.

Getting dressed, I was pulling on my boots when my last moment of pure solitude was interrupted. "Look who cleans up nicely." It was Amon. He leaned against the wall with his arms crossed. "You had to know you were going to come back to CROSS someday, whether you wanted to or not."

"I should have taken up the offer that old man gave us way back when," I said.

"Then Livia would have had an even shorter life than she did. You may blame yourself for what happened to her. But, you were the one who saved her. Giving her the extra nine months, she was happy."

"And what would you know about it?"

"I know that she gave up her life in the end to make sure your son had a chance at living.'"

"A lot of good that did…"

"If you ladies are done reminiscing about the old days, I believe Chief Engineer Crane, here, should get to know his client's file," Captain Sayers said, holding a file out to me. "Get to work, Chief."

++++

It had taken me over two hours and three cups of coffee, without the shot of spirits in it, to get through the first half of this girl's life. Now that I was officially back in CROSS, drinking was not allowed under the command of Elias Nolan, Carter Hawthorne, and Dragan Sayers.

Leaning back in my chair, I sighed and closed my eyes. Removing my gloves, I put the cold metal of my Shinar hand on my face, breathing in the fumes of metal, oil, and blood that had so long ago been permanently set in.

"How's it coming?" Amon asked, bringing me back to reality with another cup of coffee.

"If this girl was anyone else, she would have had her tongue cut out a long time ago," I said, sighing again.

"Hate to tell you this piece of news, but she and someone else who has gotten away with a few things are going to be joining CROSS."

"That is one of the worst lies I've ever heard."

"Then, you will really be shocked when I tell you it is true. Elena Hawthorne and Mihkel Tiitus were going to be tested and starting training next week. But, now, with Elena as badly hurt as she is…it'll be at least two seasons."

"It will be more than two seasons, it's her leg. She'll have to learn how to do some simple things all over again."

"I hope you two get along then," said Amon, squeezing my shoulder slightly. "Finish reading the file, you're going to meet her tomorrow."

"Elena, being who she is, do I attach her limbs the normal way or my way?"

"I would start with your way, depending on where you are and who is in the room with you. I always found attaching the nerves one-by-one is not something I would want to go through. I would use your alchemy."

"That won't get me executed?"

"You're employed by the Royal Province of Arcadia, as long as you use your ability for their causes, it's fine."

"Who says saving a civilian is something in their best interest?"

Amon just squeezed my shoulder slightly again. "Wait till you see what she can do."

Chapter 20

Elena

I shot awake to an unfamiliar ceiling from the same intense pain I felt before I blacked out. Sitting up, my heart skipped a beat when I saw my reflection in the adjacent mirror. I had quite a few cuts and scrapes on me.

I pulled the blanket off to see that I wasn't in anything but a pair of light blue shorts. My torso was bandaged, but it seemed to just keep my chest covered. I didn't think I was hurt other than the scrapes.

As I was trying to get out of bed, I fell, unable to use my legs. I slowly sat up, realizing something was wrong. I looked down, finding my right leg was gone. Flashes suddenly came into my mind again. Falling to the water, I had tripped a snare. It had to be similar to the one Mihkel had hit. Only the one I had hit was more dangerous. I had lost a limb.

I couldn't get my breathing to slow down. I must have been hooked up to machines. Two pairs of white shoes came running into the room. They picked me up and put me back on the bed. I didn't start to struggle until I saw they were strapping me onto the bed. I felt a sharp stick and the world went hazy.

++++

I woke up to the same white ceiling. My mind was calmer. I reassessed my body, hoping it was all a dream, maybe even a flash. It was real. I saw something. I saw the way down through the trees and could maneuver through them in my mind.

Raising my head, I saw I was strapped on the bed. I looked around, the room was stark white. It wasn't the same room from the memory flashes or visions, whatever they were. As I started to lay my head back down, I felt the sheet bunch up under the small of my back. The lump was now the one thing my mind was focused on—and how to get rid of it. "Have you calmed down?" a man asked, bringing me back to reality. Blinking a couple of times, I saw it was my father.

"Where am I?"

He came over and leaned over me. "You're in the hospital that is mainly used for CROSS members. I am going to take the straps off, but you have to stay calm or they will come back and drug you again. Understand?"

I nodded slightly in understanding and he removed the straps. "What happened?"

"What do you remember?"

"We were being tracked and we went back down the reservoir tower to get away. I slipped and Mihkel caught my arm."

My father held up his hand, "He caught your arm while you were falling?"

"Yes," I said simply. I watched him think for a moment. "What else?"

I still didn't want to tell him about the memory flashes, or that I could see the water in my mind before I could see it with my eyes. My father was part of CROSS and, after what happened with Frost, I didn't want to relay any information to a current member of CROSS. Not when I would be put into GUARD's custody and then brought to the Royal Province. It wouldn't matter that I was about to be sworn into CROSS. "That's it. I passed out pretty quickly."

He sighed and sat down on the bed, careful not to touch what was left of my right leg. "You're lying to me. I can always tell when you or Selig are lying to me."

"I'm not lying," I protested. What my father said was true, it was almost impossible to lie to him and get away with it. But, right now, I wasn't in a trusting mood with anyone.

My father sighed again and kissed me lightly on the forehead. "If this doesn't keep you from breaking anymore rules, then I don't know what will aside from death."

Not knowing what to say to that, I just kept silent. It was very hard to read my father when he was in a certain mindset. I knew he wasn't outright threatening me but, beyond that, I had no idea. A couple days ago, I would have thought he was just saying this to scare me. But, now…with Frost in CROSS or GUARD custody, I wasn't so sure. With something this severe, I didn't think he was against using Sindri, Mihkel, or me as an example to prove once and for all that breaking the rules had

● ● ●

very severe consequences. "Try and get some rest. Sindri and Mihkel are doing fine."

Our conversation was interrupted by the door opening. My father stood up and brushed some of my hair off my forehead.

My father walked out of the room without saying anything to the person walking in. "I just have one question for you," the man said. "How high is your threshold for pain?"

I turned my head and looked at a man wearing a CROSS uniform with black gloves on. I suspected he had his rank tattooed on the inside of his wrist, but I couldn't see it. Right now, I didn't care. "What?"

"Maybe I should introduce myself first," he said. "My name is Chief Engineer Michael Crane and I am going to be your mechanic."

"Mechanic?"

"As a mechanic, I will be the one who will attach your Shinar limbs and do the upkeep on them," said Michael, pulling up a chair and sitting down.

"Shinar limbs are for military personnel only." I wouldn't be allowed to get them. Not without having some experience in CROSS.

Shinar limbs were metallic arm and leg replacements used in cases of limb amputation. These were military grade instruments used only for CROSS or GUARD personnel. Sometimes, they could be used as an upgrade, removing their flesh limbs voluntarily. The ones who did that were usually from GUARD. And, if you saw one of them, someone was going to die.

"Captain Hawthorne…your father, pulled some favors. Besides, you don't want to start out your new career sitting behind a desk and not being able to do anything. Your life is too valuable to not go through with the procedure." He gave me a small smile. It wasn't like the one Sindri or Mihkel would give me when they wanted to get a rise out of me. It was genuine.

"Why did you ask me about my pain threshold?" I had a feeling I already knew the answer and I wasn't going to like it.

"It is a very painful procedure. Only the strong willed can go through with it, let alone survive it."

* * *

"How do you know that?" I asked, finally managing to open my eyes completely, getting used to the bright light in the room. I just looked at him.

"I've done a lot of the procedures. Even lost a few clients in the process. It can go from fine to a disaster in five seconds."

"That's all?"

"That's a little optimistic. It's more around one to two seconds."

"Then why perform the procedure?"

"I'd be out of a job otherwise and the Royal City of Ashtan wouldn't find me useful anymore." Michael brushed some of my hair out of my face. "I will only do the procedure if you say yes to it. It's a lot of pain and it can take anywhere from one month to a full year to recover."

I tried to sit up and felt a hand on my back. As Michael helped me sit up, he picked up a robe and hung it around my shoulders. I was freezing with just the bandages around my torso. He put two fingers under my chin and forced me to look at him. "A word of advice—decided quickly. The goodwill of the head of CROSS doesn't last long."

Staring at him, I saw his dark brown hair and equally dark brown eyes, with a tattoo on his neck. His five o'clock shadow was like my father's, permanent. "What else do you know about me?" I asked, fighting to look away.

"If you decide to go through with the procedure, then we'll talk." He stood up with his back turned and I saw more of the tattoo on his neck. Something in the back of my head told me it covered most of his body. Though, I still couldn't tell what it was.

"What do you know about a man named Crispin Frost?"

Michael turned and looked at me. "Where did you hear that name? Actually, the better question is, how do you know of him?"

"I met him," I said as if it wasn't a big deal. "He's in custody of CROSS or GUARD now." But, it was a big deal to me. I knew exactly what was going to happen to him. If he hadn't stuck his neck out for me then he would still be in hiding or presumed dead.

"Frost is a friend of mine," Michael said. It seemed that that was all he was going to say, so I didn't press on it. "I suggest you think on the decision of getting the Shinar limbs and try to get some rest. I'll check on you in a day." With that, he left, leaving me to my thoughts.

Chapter 21

I must have fallen asleep again. When I opened my eyes there was a tray of food and some clothes laid out for me. There was also a note attached to my clothes. Picking it up, I saw it was from Michael. '*Elena, make the smart decision.*' I made a mental note of the fact that Michael didn't say make the 'right' decision.

As I was picking up the shirt, a nurse came in. She gave me a smile and helped me put the clothes on. They were simple hospital wear, but they were better than my current outfit of bandages and blue shorts. "Do you know if I could see my friends?" I asked.

"The two young men that were brought in with you?" she asked.

"Yes."

"I'll have to check with your doctor first," she said. "But, I don't see why you wouldn't be able to see them for a few minutes."

The nurse helped me get dressed before she left the room, leaving me alone again. A minute later, I heard the door open. I opened my mouth to say something when I saw it wasn't Sindri or Mihkel, it was my father's boss.

General Elias Nolan was a ruthless man just like his father. But, even with what he was willing to do, he still wasn't in the same league as the members of GUARD. They still looked down on him as they did any member of CROSS and he would never be appointed to GUARD. He was in the normal CROSS uniform, but his sash had changed to a white and blue holster that held his weapon of choice during times of distress for the city. He also had a white scarf on that was tucked under the black vest he was wearing.

His brown-and-grey hair was combed back with some sort of oil and he was wearing his sunglasses. It didn't matter the time of day or where he was, there were very few people who knew the color of his eyes.

"You caused a lot of trouble in a very short period of time," he said, closing the door behind him and locking it. "If I even let one thing slip to someone in the Royal City, it would be an automatic death sentence. No one steals from the King."

I didn't say anything. I didn't know what to say. Even as a little girl, this man had scared me. The only time he came over to the house, my father had to tie Enrik up out in the back so he wouldn't try to bite General Nolan. This was one man you did not want to irritate. But, there was something that he liked. He liked young girls around fifteen to eighteen in age who were in dire need of food or water. I remembered one particularly bad winter when there was a line of teenage girls outside his house. My father swore he would take a whip to me himself if he ever caught me trying to get supplies that way. I didn't blame him. I still remembered like it was yesterday when Sindri's younger sister ended up in his bed trying to obtain medicine for a nasty chemical burn their father had gotten in their shop. My father had to arrest Sindri to keep him from trying to kill the General. There was also the one secret my mother was keeping from her husband. All needed Stigma medicine and we had nothing to trade for it. So, she spent the night with him. She made Selig and I swear that we would never tell our father. For one, it would break his heart and two, it would break up the family. Like Sindri, my father would go after his boss. He would have probably succeeded in killing him, though he would have died in the process. My father and the General would spar once in a while and it was truly a frightening sight. Even though they weren't supposed to hurt each other, they always did. And, they always ended up on medical leave. Luckily, they haven't permanently disabled each other.

"What are you going to do?"

"I hear you're quite handy when it comes to getting down to the reservoir," he said, sitting down in the same chair Michael had sat in earlier.

"What does that have to do with anything?"

"When you are healed from the Shinar procedure, we'll talk. You and Tiitus will be on special assignment." General Nolan stood and leaned over me. He put two fingers under my chin as Michael did, but he applied pressure, forcing me to look at him. He kissed me lightly on the lips. I could smell the oil in his hair and I wanted to vomit. When he broke the kiss, he looked at me. "You remind me of your mother…" He kissed me again. Only, this time, he forced his tongue into my mouth. As I tried to push him away, he grabbed my wrist and forced me to lie flat on my back. He put his weight on my leg, making it impossible for me to fight him off.

A flash of panic shot through my mind when I felt his hand slid under the hem of my pants and underwear. He broke the kiss and put his free hand over my mouth. "I suggest you calm down…"

Breathing heavily through my nose, I felt the heat creep over my entire body when he touched me. I froze when I heard a zipper being undone.

++++

He straightened up after he was done and patted my cheek. "See you around, Elena. I'd hate to see the daughter of a good CROSS Captain—fail."

I waited until he left the room and closed the door before forcing myself out of bed, ignoring the clothes he had carefully taken off me. I dragged myself over to the sink, ignoring the trail of blood from my stump. Pulling myself up with my arms, I vomited bile into the sink. The taste was strong, but it didn't mask the taste of the General's tongue and breath on my lips and in my mouth. Or the smell of oil lingering around me.

"Elena?" I looked up to see Willow standing there with a basket in her hands. "What happened?" She set the basket down and ran over to me, grabbing the blanket that had fallen on the floor and wrapping it around me.

I grabbed her wrist and looked at her. Willow and I weren't that close, but I was glad she had found happiness with Selig. "I need to talk to Michael Crane…"

We were interrupted by the door opening again. "What in the Gods…what happened?" The nurse asked, rushing into the room with Sindri and Mihkel behind her. "You three out," she snapped.

I collapsed on the floor and started to cry. I hated crying but I couldn't stop the tears. "Elena…" I felt someone's hands on my back. It was Mihkel. "Hey, look at me. Look at me."

• • •

I managed to calm my crying for a moment. "Get my dad to tell Michael Crane I want the procedure."

"You three need to leave," the nurse repeated, ushering Mihkel, Sindri, and Willow out. Not thirty seconds later, Captain Sayers came rushing in.

Without saying a word, he wrapped the blanket tightly around me, scooped me up like my father did when I was young, and carried me out of the room.

Chapter 22

I awoke in a different room. The rooms were identical, but this room lacked the pungent smell of blood.

I had been put in new hospital pajamas and there was a food tray next to my bed. My stump had been rewrapped and I felt rather heavy. I must have been drugged quite a bit. Yet, I was hungry. Something I hadn't felt since waking from the accident.

As I was reaching for the food tray, the door opened. I reached for the knife, pulling it into my grasp. I looked up to see Michael standing there. He walked in and closed the door, locking it behind him. "It's good to see that you're hungry. That means whatever the General gave you is out of your system."

"Gave me?" I didn't want to relive what he had done to me so soon.

"Do you remember much?"

I shook my head even though I remembered just about everything. A decision I regretted as soon as I did it. "How long have I been out?"

A day or two, you freaked out after my boss came to see you. Sayers picked you up and carried you back to surgery. Several eyebrows were raised when it was seen that you were in nothing but a blanket." He pushed the tray closer to me and sat down on the side of the bed.

"What did Nolan do to me?" I asked, putting my fingertips to my lips. I didn't want to have everyone know that I couldn't take care of myself. The General struck me as the type of man who didn't kiss a teenage girl for no reason. There had to be something he wanted to happen from it.

Michael held up a small glass bottle. It held some sort of liquid with a dark blue tint to it. "This," said Michael, setting the bottle down on the table, "is a poison created by the Royal Capitol called Nightbane."

"Nightbane?" I had never heard of it and I knew about most of the plants in Ragnar City. My mother made sure of that.

"Yes." Michael sighed and rubbed the back of his neck. "If it comes in contact with a solid matter, it causes the victim to vomit and go insane until they die."

● ● ●

"How am I alive then?"

"The amount applied in your case was enough to kill you, but I'm willing to bet it was altered by the General so you wouldn't die. Or, maybe, the surgeon got the poison out in time. You sure you don't remember anything else?"

"Why would he do what he did?" I asked. The General may be a man you didn't want to be on the bad side of, but he would never endanger the life of family members to someone in CROSS. The job was too important to him to have his subordinates lose focus, causing negative attention to be directed toward him. I was still trying to figure out how my father wasn't losing focus with Ally slowly dying. I was having a hard time focusing on the things I do in day to day life. But, I wasn't my father. As much as I wanted to be sometimes, I never would be.

Michael looked at me with a simple look. "He's a prick. I got the message from your friends. Mind if I ask why you want the limbs?"

It was what the General had done to me and what he said afterwards. Something about failing and I didn't want to be helpless around him ever again. "I felt helpless around Nolan."

"That tends to happen to his female…victims." Standing up, he took out a small cylinder that was metallic in color. "I need a couple things from you before I can start."

"What?"

"I need some information and measurements. Age?"

"Eighteen." My birthday was on the seventy-eighth day of the fall season. A few days before the day of the explosions.

"Height?"

"5'7."

"Weight?"

"115."

As he wrote the number down a smirk appeared on his face. "I hope you don't mind, your weight will go up at least eight pounds."

I shook my head.

"All right then, let's get your measurements and I will get started on your leg."

Michael helped me stand up on my good leg and held up the metallic colored cylinder. He turned it on, a red laser

• • •

125

appearing. "What is that?" I asked, having to hold myself steady with the bed rail.

"It gets your exact measurements," said Michael, running it up, down, and around my leg. I was surprised I didn't feel a thing.

He then measured my arm as I sat back down. He also measured the stumps and slipped the cylinder back into his pocket. "All right, it will take me about two weeks."

"That's all?"

"Well, with the usual workload I have, it would have taken about two months. Normally. Since I was in…retirement, I haven't had any work for quite a while. But, if I were to take the normal amount of time, I would get even more unwanted attention. So, I will be getting them done as quickly as I can. It will take you about two weeks to recover enough so I can attach them, anyhow. Eat something and try to get some rest."

I opened my mouth to ask him a question, but I decided against it. I wanted to ask him more about Frost, but it was probably safer for me not to. After all, we were in a government building where everything was probably monitored.

"Could I see my friends?"

"I don't see why not. I prefer my clients to be upbeat rather than depressed." He reached out to touch my shoulder, but hesitated. "I'm here to talk or listen if you need someone."

I pulled the food tray over to me, looking over the contents. I had been given a meal of meat and vegetable soup with two rolls and a glass of water. The soup was amazing. I had never tasted anything like it before. The meat was actually beef, something I had only one other time in my life. The vegetables were fresh, not dried, and there was actual pasta in the soup as well. I ate the solid food, leaving the dark broth to soak up with the rolls. As I took a bite of bread, I recognized it immediately. The young baker and his wife must have sent them over.

As I finished eating, the door opened and my heart skipped a beat. I relaxed when I saw it was Sindri, Mihkel, and Selig.

At first, Selig just stood there looking at me. When I held up my arms motioning that I wanted a hug, he came over to me. Gingerly, he gave me a hug with both arms. We rarely showed affection for each other, but this was one of the times it was called for. We both were very open with our love for Ally, but not with each other. I looked at Sindri and Mihkel.

Sindri had a bandage that looked like it was for a burn on his left elbow. Other than that, he looked fine. Mihkel was a different story. He was already in a CROSS uniform and, the scary part, he looked like he was a part of CROSS all along. He had a tired look in his eyes and multiple cuts on his face and hands. They both looked relieved that I was okay.

There was another knock on the door. It was Michael again. He tossed me a little black box that Selig caught it for me. "Happy birthday, Elena," he said before leaving the room.

Sindri, Mihkel, and Selig just looked at me with raised eyebrows. "That mechanic has taken a quick liking to you," said Sindri.

I sighed. "Shut up."

"Ally is doing okay with everything, but mom is worried about you," Selig said.

"I'm sure dad has already talked with her, you'll never guess who came by the house and asked if I wanted a job?"

"The General?" I asked, feeling my stomach turn into a tight knot.

Selig raised both his eyebrows. "How'd you know?"

"He paid me a visit as well."

"Apparently you two weren't the only ones, Mihkel is now a part of CROSS," Sindri said with a glare.

Mihkel uncomfortably adjusted the cuffs on his jacket and gave me the briefest of glances. "Leave these two alone to talk," said Selig, pulling Sindri out of the room.

As the door closed, I looked at Mihkel. "You're already sworn in? How is that possible?"

"I was going to ask you the same question," said Mihkel, sitting down. "The General came to my house and dragged me to the reservoir tower."

"What did he have you do?"

"He wanted to see how I could disable the sensors and the process of getting down to the water."

"I am suddenly terrified of the General."

"You and me both."

• • •

127

"How did you and Sindri get hurt?"

"Sindri took a bullet and I tried to play hero."

Attempting to shift, the oversized hospital shift fell off my shoulder, causing me to blush. I had no idea why I was feeling this way around Mihkel. We never got along before that fateful day on top of the reservoir tower. Pulling the shirt up, I sighed and rubbed the back of my neck.

"Want to open what Chief Engineer Crane got you as a birthday present?"

I had completely forgotten about what Michael had dropped off. Opening the box, I stopped when I saw it was a pair of earrings. "They're beautiful…" I said.

Mihkel looked at the earrings, "They're black onyx…I thought anything that had black onyx in it was taken by Arcadia."

"Could you help me get them in?" I asked.

I had my ears pierced three times in each ear. On my right ear, I had two in my earlobe and one in the cartilage; the left ear, I three in my earlobe. Mihkel took out the top studs and put the black onyx ones in. "There's a note," he said.

Picking up the folded piece of paper, I read it aloud. *"Elena, these belonged to someone very special to me once. You remind me of her: strong, determined, and full of life. Also, a stubborn streak that doesn't weaken for anyone. I have no use for them, so I thought you would enjoy them."*

"Something tells me Michael is either very blunt or has no emotion," Mihkel said.

"Could you do something for me?" I asked. "Could you tell Captain Fisher I would like to see him?"

"Is it weird to call your uncle by his title?"

"A little bit."

● ● ●

Chapter 23

The birds had fallen silent by the time Drake had come by my room. I was feeling drowsy from whatever the pills the nurse had forced me to take a little while ago. "Hey, you look pretty good for what happened to you," said Drake, moving to kiss me on my forehead, causing me to flinch. He looked at me with a curious look and then started to sit down on the edge of the bed before deciding to take the chair. "The newest member of CROSS informed me that you want to see me? I'm not going to lie, it's strange to see Craig Tiitus' son in a CROSS uniform."

"I need to talk to you about something," I said, blinking a few times.

"Okay..." he said with raised eyebrows. "What's the big emergency?"

I took in a much needed breath, trying to figure out how to ask him about what was happening to me. "Something is happening to me and I don't know what it is."

Drake just looked at me and, without saying anything, he got up and closed the door. "What do you mean something is happening to you?"

"I have these...flashes or visions. I don't really know how to describe them." I was having to fight the pills that I had taken while choosing my words carefully in a government controlled building. "They're like memories, but they come at random times."

"How random?"

I thought about it for a couple seconds before realization dawned. "Whenever I'm tree jumping."

Drake smiled slightly, catching me off guard. "You taught your father how to do that, didn't you?"

"Yes..."

Drake sighed and rotated his neck. "What are you seeing?"

"A white room. I'm hooked up to a machine and I'm...terrified. I can see things in my head before I see them with my eyes."

He stood up and walked over to the sink. Sighing, he turned and looked at me. "Does your father know?"

129

"No."

"Why would you talk to me about this and not him?"

"I'm not sure how much I trust him."

"A few days ago, I would have said that is a stupid concept to have in your head."

"What would you say now?"

"I'm not sure, I have a feeling you know more about your father than he wants you to know."

"So, you know what I know?"

"Elena, I was married to his sister for a short time. We fought alongside each other. I know just about everything about your father."

"You're okay that he helped cause the deaths of one-third of the population in Ragnar City?"

Drake sighed and fingered his wedding ring. "Yes. I do know and I suggest you stop talking about it."

I knew I wasn't going to get anything else out of my uncle, so I changed the subject. "Did you hear what happened a week ago?"

"Yes. Your father told me," Drake filled up a glass with water and brought it over to me. "Crispin Frost is a dangerous man."

"What happened to him to make him like that?"

Drake held up his hand. "That is something you don't want on your mind."

"And, what is happening to me I want on my mind?"

"You've got a point there, but I'm not sure what is happening to you. If you trust me enough to look into it, I'll let you know what I find out."

"As long as you don't tell my father."

He gave me a soft smile that he used to give my brother and me when we were younger. "You are going to have to get over not trusting him sooner or later." He started to kiss me on my forehead but stopped himself. He put a small unwrapped package in my hand. "Happy birthday."

"Thank you…" I said, opening the box. It was a new pair of gloves for tree jumping.

"I saw the pair you have. You need a new pair. Besides, once you get your Shinar limbs, the ones you have won't hold up to your newfound strength."

"I thought you would be one for me not doing what I do anymore?"

"I am. But, I know you. You're a whole lot like your father and, for some reason, you carry some of my characteristics. So, I figured I might as well help you out by making sure you have decent equipment. That, and you'll be…showing off what you can do to the General when you're able to."

I physically cringed and felt sick at the mention of the General. Drake noticed the change in my demeanor. "Elena? Is there something you need to tell me?"

I started to shake my head when Drake forced me to look at him. "I can't."

"Elena, I can protect you…you know I can."

Not saying anything, I showed him the mark on my neck the General had given me. Drake didn't say anything as he stared at the mark. He simply adjusted my shirt and sighed. "Try the gloves on."

He helped me pull one of the gloves on and I found it fit rather well. "How is it that everyone knows my size?"

"Relax," he said. "I got the measurements from Michael."

Looking at him again, I didn't speak for a moment. "How well do you know Michael Crane?"

"I've known him for a long time. He's a good man with a dark past like everyone else in CROSS. You'll get to know him as he is now, your mechanic. Those with Shinar limbs can't go through life without a good mechanic." He pulled the gloves off my hand and looked at me. "You won't be able to use these for a while. This procedure you're going through—is going to be more pain than you could ever imagine."

"How do you know? You don't have Shinar limbs."

"Michael will be attaching all of your nerves to the limb. I know it's going to hurt because I've seen it done multiple times. Now, get some rest."

Chapter 24

The next two weeks went by rather quickly. I had to begin working with a physical therapist. Her name was Sartana and I found out real quick that her physical therapy was different than what I expected. Instead of strength and conditioning, it was a lot of balancing and stretching to work my muscles.

"Why am I not working on strengthening my arms and leg?" I asked, taking a sip of water from a bottle she had given me.

Sartana just looked at me as she took the water back. She took a drink and set the bottle down. Without saying anything, she pulled up her pant legs to show that she had Shinar legs. "Being able to walk normally is more important at this time than anything else. Balance is key."

I didn't ask how she had lost her legs; she was quiet most of the time, talking only when she had to give me new directions. I noticed that she had a similar looking brand as Michael did on his neck.

Her dirty blonde hair was to her shoulders and she usually kept it back in a ponytail. She had silver, square framed glasses and was very slim, but she didn't look weak.

Today was our final session before the Shinar limbs were going to be attached. "You have a knack for this," said Sartana, applying some type of gel to my stump.

The gel had a cool feeling to it. "What does this do?"

"It's going to help when the metal is attached to your skin and bone. You sure you want to do this?"

"Yes," I said without hesitation. What the General did was still strong in my mind and I wanted to prove to him that he wasn't going to get rid of me that easily. I wasn't going to be his, either. "Who put your Shinar limbs on?"

"A man who shouldn't have that much power," said Sartana. "You're lucky your father cares about you, Michael is the best."

I wanted to tell her my father isn't who he used to be, but I was interrupted by the door opening. It was Michael. "Speak of the devil," Sartana said. She easily lifted me up and put me in the wheelchair. I wanted to protest, but she just gave me a stern look.

"Alright, let's go," said Michael, coming up behind me.

As Michael was pushing me down the hall, I turned my head to look at him. "Where are we going?"

"Back to your room."

"Is anyone else going to be in there?"

"The nurse and Doc Aryen."

"Why did you decide to become a mechanic?"

"It more or less wasn't much of a choice with my talents. That, and what good is a mechanic when they don't have a Shinar limb of their own?"

"You have one of your own?"

"I do. Sweetheart, you have a lot to learn. Just because you're going to have a new leg doesn't mean you know anything about Shinar. It takes a while for people to learn how to pick out people who have these limbs; unless they chose to go through the procedure just because they can."

"Was yours attached because you lost a limb?"

"Not exactly," said Michael. The tone in his voice said he wasn't going to say anything else on the subject.

We had gotten to the hall where my room was when Michael stopped pushing me. Drake and Solomon were talking to each other with hushed voices. It was Solomon that noticed we were there first. He started to walk toward us when Drake grabbed his arm. Drake said something to him. "Let go of me," Solomon said.

"Is a Lieutenant giving an order to a Captain?" asked Drake. "If she doesn't want to talk to you, then you leave her alone."

"Ordering me to stay away from my own girl?" Solomon snapped. That did it.

I could feel the stares from Drake and Michael on me. "I'm going to assume that was supposed to be a secret. Judging from that look Captain Fisher is giving you," Michael whispered, so only I could hear him.

"It doesn't help that he's related to my family, either."

"You're dismissed, Lieutenant," said Drake.

* * *

Solomon gave me a brief look before straightening his uniform and walking out of sight. "I'm going to give you two a moment alone…Captain," Michael said and then left before I could say anything. Just because I was about to go through a painful procedure didn't mean I was going to get off easy from this.

"Creid?" asked Drake when he came up to me. "Are you trying to give your father an ulcer? Or me, for that matter? Elena, it's not allowed. Not for you."

"Is it any of your business?" I snapped glaring up at him. Selig was in deeper with Willow than I was with Solomon, but I wasn't about to sell my brother down the river.

It wasn't against the rules to be involved with a member of CROSS. But, depending on who it was, it was frowned upon. Or at least, my father heavily frowned upon it. He would rather have his children marry a miner or merchant. Not someone from CROSS, or heaven forbid someone from GUARD. I remembered asking my mother once why father was so against us getting involved with someone from CROSS. My mother simply replied that they didn't want this life for their children. I wanted to ask why she married my father if she was so unhappy.

Drake took in a breath and let it out slowly, as if he was trying to fight the urge to smack me. "I won't keep this from him."

"Why isn't this allowed?"

"I'm sure you'll find out soon enough. Be careful, Elena, I'm not the only one looking out for your best interests."

++++

Back in the room, Michael lifted me up in one smooth motion and placed me gently on the bed. He shed off his jacket and lay it across the chair. It was the first time I saw his Shinar arm. "It's a work of art, isn't it?" I asked.

"Yes, it is," Damien said filling up a syringe.

"I'm going to attach your leg first," he said, sitting down on a backless chair and pulling the cart over that was covered with a white sheet. "Getting nervous yet?"

"Not even a little," I lied.

• • •
134

"Liar." He pulled the sheet back with a smirk on his face.

I propped myself up on my elbow to get a better look. I just stared at what was my new leg. "Now I'm nervous."

Michael pulled on gloves and started to undo the cloth that was wrapped around my leg stump. I was already starting to figure out why Sartana had put whatever that gel was on my stump. It was a numbing solution. "Okay, the first thing I have to do is attach the metal connector to your body, so the Shinar limb will actually attach. Then, I will have to attach all of your nerves, which is the most painful part."

"How painful?" I asked.

"I suggest to the clients that they are strapped to the bed so they won't struggle," Damien said, injecting my stump with whatever the medicine was. "To fight infection."

"I'm fine."

"Don't believe yourself." Michael stood up and rotated his Shinar arm. "You start to struggle and I will strap you to this bed. Understand?"

"Yes," I said, not looking forward to feeling helpless again.

"I can't knock you out for this," said Aryen. "I'm only here to make sure nothing gets out of control."

"Does anyone regret doing this?" I looked at Michael.

"Yes," said Michael plainly. "Word on the street is that you're already a member of CROSS, so there is no going back."

"Never thought I had a choice to begin with."

"That's the problem with destiny," Damien said.

Chapter 25

Michael

Staggering into the restroom, I managed to make it to the sink before I vomited everything in my stomach. It had been years since I performed a procedure. Somehow, I had forgotten the screams that came with the job. Turning the water on, I splashed the iced water on my face. I felt the need to vomit again when I saw that I had some of Elena's blood on my neck.

"Easy there, Michael..." Someone had put their hand on my back. "It's just a little bit of blood."

"An eighteen year old's blood who went through something I wouldn't wish on anyone." I spat a mix of bile and spit into the sink. "What aren't you telling me?"

"I don't know what you mean," Drake said, tossing me a towel.

"Don't you fucking like to me!" I shoved him against the wall, pushing my Shinar arm against his neck. "We both know with her and Tiitus' skills, they would have never gotten caught. The General was alerted to what they were doing at the reservoir tower. The question is, who was it?"

"Tell me something..." Drake inquired, something changing behind his eyes. "Why do you care all of a sudden?"

"She is going to be scarred the rest of her life, they will be trapped under the Arcadian rule. They would be better going to where those suffer for believing in one God."

Drake's dark eyes suddenly diminished into their familiar red flame I hadn't seen in years. A thin flame started to circle around his hand and the end wasn't an inch from my face. "Step back or I will burn off your other arm," he said through gritted teeth.

The heat went from noticeable to unbearable on my Shinar limb. Clutching where my skin met metal, I took a couple steps back, having a hard time keeping steady on my feet. "Who gave them up?"

"It was for their own protection," Drake said, not extinguishing the flame.

• • •

"You admit it?"

"It wasn't me. Think of someone else, someone who has a lot more to lose than I."

"They're children…" I said backing up to the far wall and sinking to the ground. "What in the Gods names have I done?"

"Something that will change the course of this world…" Drake said, finally extinguishing the flame.

++++

I barely noticed that I passed my friend Amon by in the hall with what rage I had inside me. "Michael, what's going on?" Amon asked, catching up with me.

"I don't care what they do to me, I am going to put an end to this once and for all."

"Michael, you're going to have to tell me what is going on." Amon grabbed my shoulder, jerking his hand back almost immediately. "It feels like it's on fire…"

"Thank Captain Fisher," I said through gritted teeth. "Where's Captain Hawthorne?"

"He went home," said Amon, a very confused look on his face. "His youngest took a turn for the worse."

"My apologies for her, but there are much bigger things that are happening."

Amon just looked at me. "When did you find out?"

"You knew?"

"Of course I knew. You would have known if you didn't go off to try and drink yourself to death. There are problems that are going to bring total destruction to this pitiful excuse of a world. Not even the trees would survive what is coming."

"You speak of something that is supernatural and doesn't exist."

"What makes you say it doesn't exist? Cedomir is still alive. Anything is possible." Amon sighed heavily. "There is only one man who can create that much heat to Shinar metal. Are you saying that he isn't completely human? Are you? It isn't the traditional definition, but we are all dealing with something dark."

Part II: The Darkness Awakens Within

"Your life will only be spared once on this journey. Make it count."

—Michael Crane

Chapter 26

As an attempt to rescue the world from the destruction of the human population, an idea was formed. Work with the genetic engineering of trees. Save the world by allowing the trees to survive in the most arid conditions.

The greatest minds from five of the six provinces were gathered in the city of Ashtan to see if the impossible would be done. It took only nine months. What was thought to be a pipe dream had been accomplished, but at a terrible cost.

Instead of just having enough trees to keep the planet alive, they overtook it, evolving themselves for protection. Growing at an incredibly fast rate, a newly planted tree looks like it's been around for a hundred years.

The problems didn't stop there. With the trees overtaking everything, multiple regulations had to be put in. There wasn't anyone left alive that knew what it was like to breathe in clean oxygen. People were getting sick, their bodies unable to process the abundance of oxygen that was being put into the air. Filters were put in everywhere to help those left alive to adapt to the rapidly changing world around them.

Water instantly became the most precious item around. With the trees in their state, they were taking up all the water. The minds that solved the original problem had to scramble to fix the new problems the solution had brought out. The various ideas were tried, proving to be too expensive or not working fast enough. Then, the unexpected happened. The trees were dormant. Water reservoirs were created and guarded. If caught stealing water, the punishment was death.

• • •

Chapter 27

Elena

It took only a full month for me to recover from the procedure. No one was more surprised than Michael. He simply couldn't believe that I was able to get up and walk around like nothing happened in only a month. Damien had been coming to check on me and kept me on a steady supply of pain medication. But, now that I seemed to be recovering in record time, he was starting to wean me off the drugs.

The first day I was completely off the pain medication, I felt very hungry. The nurse that had been taking care of me brought in what I ate the last time I remembered eating solid foods, beef and vegetable soup with pasta and the rolls from the Ragnar City bakery. I inhaled the food so fast that I threw up everything in my stomach. This got me a scolding from the nurse. Then all I got to eat was broth, vitamins, and water.

As I was finishing the broth, my father came into the room. He motioned to the new earrings I was wearing. "Black onyx. Those are quite rare and somewhat illegal. Who gave them to you?"

"Michael. They used to belong to his wife."

My father sat down on the bed and looked at me. "Drake told me something interesting."

"What's that?" I asked, a curious look on my face even though I knew exactly what he was talking about.

"Don't play innocent with me," my father snapped. "What the hell were you thinking? Getting involved with a member of CROSS? My Lieutenant? MY personal assistant!"

"If it makes you feel any better, I don't think it was going anywhere," I said. I was feeling lousy and wasn't in the mood to be lectured by my father.

My father stood up and had the look on his face when he was about to discipline Selig or myself. But, he stopped himself. He merely put a finger in my face and looked at me. "If this isn't broken off by the time you're released from here, I will make both of your lives miserable."

● ● ●

"My life is already pretty miserable," I said. "What could you possibly do to make it worse?"

"You would be surprised," he said, pulling his gloves on as he was getting ready to leave. "I am your father, you will listen to me. Your brother will listen to me; you will also listen to me as your commanding officer."

Our conversation ended with a knock on the door. It opened and Michael, along with Drake, came into the room. "Are we interrupting anything?" Drake asked.

"No," said my father. "Crane, make sure she's fit to leave the hospital. Then have Doc Aryen clear her."

"Yes, sir," said Michael.

"Carter," said Drake. "Where are you going?"

The three of us stopped and looked at Drake. My father and Drake were close friends but, even in front of family members, my father was always Hawthorne or Captain to Drake. Drake was always Fisher to my father. If they used their first names in front of people, it was usually something quite serious. Whatever was on my father's mind was on Drake's as well. And it was big. As long as I've known Drake, I have never heard him question my father in front of people. For all I knew, he never questioned him or his motives.

My father didn't answer. He just left the room. Michael and Drake looked at each other before Michael spoke. "I'm going to go check on something before I make sure you can function with your Shinar limbs."

Drake waited for Michael to close the door before he spoke. "I found out a few things, feel up for taking a walk?"

"Yes."

I didn't take long for me to get dressed. My Shinar leg moved just like the limbs I was born with. The only difference was the dull ache where the metal was attached to the skin. Then I remembered Michael saying something about this as he was doing the procedure. When the barometric pressure changed, my thigh would ache.

I had gotten dressed in black cargo pants, a white tank top, and the jacket I always wore. I ran my fingers through my hair and pulled it back into a messy knot. As I was pulling on my boots, the door opened. Michael came back into the room. "I

● ● ●

guess I don't need to make sure your limbs are working. You seem to be getting along just fine." He leaned against the wall and crossed his arms. "Any pain?"

"A dull ache."

"That's normal, I wouldn't worry about it. You'll get used to it over time. I don't even notice it that much anymore." Michael adjusted the glove on his metal hand. "Despite the tension between you and your father, he is glad you're okay. He just has problems showing any emotion other than angst or disappointment."

"I'm aware of that," I said simply, surprised that I wasn't used to it yet. My father had been this way for as long as I could remember. Witnessing the kinder side of him had become strange to me. "How unusual is it for someone to recover within a month?"

"It's highly unusual," said Michael. "I only know of one other person who recovered that quickly."

"Who?"

"No one you know," Michael answered too quickly. "Doc Aryen wanted to run a few tests. The results weren't completely clear, but he thinks it's the Nightbane that was in your system. It may have something to do with your speedy recovery."

"I thought it was a poison."

"It is. However, there have been some experiments done to see if a low dose can help instead of hinder. Doc Aryen will be able to tell you more, it's not my area." Michael handed me a pair of thin black gloves. "You might as well get used to wearing these."

I wriggled my fingers into the glove and was surprised at how well I could move my fingers. "Every CROSS member wears these?"

"Officers do. Try wriggling your toes," said Michael.

I did. It came as easily as wriggling my fingers. "Wow...you truly are an artist. I think you truly found your calling."

"That can be a good thing or a bad thing."

Our conversation stopped abruptly by Drake coming back into the room. "Come on, let's go before we lose the light."

• • •

"I'll check on you later," Michael said, squeezing my shoulder. "Don't overwork yourself."

++++

Drake and I walked out of the hospital and I had to shield my eyes from the remaining sunlight of the day. I had been inside for almost sixty days, not once seeing the light of the sun. Put these on," said Drake, handing me a pair of sunglasses.

Slipping on the sunglasses, my vision was instantly better. "Are you going to tell me what you know or do I have to guess?"

"Easy there, turbo," said Drake. "Let's make sure you can actually walk before we start talking."

"Didn't you just see me walk out of the hospital?"

"I did, but I want to see you walk again. Just to make sure." He motioned for me to start walking.

I walked about thirty steps when I felt a hand on my shoulder. "You've proven enough, to me anyway," said Drake, slipping on his own sunglasses.

As we walked around the property, Drake continued to make forced small talk. I had had enough. "Tell me what you found out."

He stopped walking. "When I tell you this, I need you to understand that I am going against everything your father wants for you."

"Wait a minute. My dad is involved in all of this?" I honestly had no idea why I was surprised. My father had been living what seemed to be three lives at once recently.

"Let me finish," he said, holding up his hand. "If he finds out that you know, there will be consequences. Do you understand?"

"Yes."

He took my arm and led me into the garden area. The only place I knew where plant life was planted on purpose. "I need to know something first. Have you ever heard of a program called PULSE?"

I opened my mouth to say no, but something from one of the memory flashes popped into my head. There was a closed file on the table beside me. PULSE and a name I couldn't remember was written on the tab. "Yes. Well, kind of. I saw it on a file."

"That's what I thought," Drake sighed and motioned for me to sit down on the bench. "I don't really know how to explain this, so bear with me. You're awakening."

"Awakening?"

"The flashes you're seeing means something has dissolved in your brain. Nothing that will kill you, but it was a safeguard set in place to make you unaware of…certain events." He thought for a moment, trying to find the right words. "This happened to you when you were two."

"When I was two? But, I was my age now when I saw the flashes…or visions, whatever they are."

"I can't explain that, but it happened when you were two years old. So, from what I understand those flashes are…are memories."

"Memories of no one…" I stood up and turned my back to him. I needed to think without him watching my face. "You knew about this this whole time? You knew about it. You didn't have to check into anything, did you?"

"Elena, it's more complicated than that. Something I can't…explain to you now. You don't have enough information."

"Why did my parents let this happen to me? Did it happen to Selig, too?"

"It didn't happen to Selig." Drake sighed heavily, loosening his jacket collar. Just as he did that, the temperature dropped rapidly. All of the sudden, I could see my breath. "This is something I really wish you weren't hearing from me."

"Just tell me."

Drake held out his hand. "Give me your hand. It's better to show than tell you something like this."

I was back in the past, Drake standing beside me. Looking at myself, I was back in the clothing I was in when Frost took me back. I also had all of my flesh limbs back. "What is this?" I asked. "Frost showed me how Stigma was spread."

Drake looked at me with raised eyebrows. "So you've been through this before? That makes my job a lot easier.

Elena…you and I are bound. There are at least fifteen of us that are bound like this."

"Bound?"

We were interrupted by a young man dressed in Arcadian style clothing rushing past us holding a little girl in his arms. I then realized we were in Ragnar City.

The man from Arcadia, mostly likely Ashtan, made sure that the downpour of rain was kept off the girl's head as best he could, not caring that he was getting soaked in the process. Drake and I followed him, sloshing through the mud, already chilled to the bone from the rain.

He openly stopped, when the girl started to cry. "Shh…" he whispered, trying to comfort her. "We're almost there."

"Who is that? And where is he taking that little girl?" I asked looking at Drake.

Drake didn't answer me, he just motioned for me to keep walking. I recognized this part of the city, it was my borough. We were not ten feet away from my house.

The stranger started to pound on the door, when he didn't get an answer he pounded again. "Captain!" he said in an urgent whisper. "Captain! Open the door…"

The door opened, and I saw a man who resembled my father, but didn't have the look of battle fatigue as a permanent part of him. "Micah…you're late. Get inside before you both catch your death." My father ushered the man inside and closed the door.

"Come on…the most—interesting part is coming up," Drake said, walking toward the house. He touched the door, causing it to fly open, and we took the opportunity to get inside.

My father closed the door, and I saw my mother take the little girl from Micah's arms. She wrapped her in a blanket, and went to sit by the stove. "Were you followed?" My father asked, not taking his eyes off of Micah. I saw he had a gun in his hand with the safety off, his finger on the trigger.

"I made sure that I wasn't," said Micah picking up the mug of tea in front of him.

"The boy?" My mother asked, holding the girl in her lap.

"Already dropped off."

• • •

"Which family?" My father asked, not taking his hand off the gun.

"A miner's family—they are unable to have a child. Those who needed to be bribed were."

"Bribed? Who authorized that? Bribing means they are still alive, if this is to work...then those who would go again this...should have their throats slit," said my father, finally taking his hand off his gun.

"Carter, there hasn't been enough bloodshed for you?" My mother asked.

My father and Micah ignored her. "I gave her a new name," Micah said. "Elena."

My heart skipped a beat, Drake was showing when I became a Hawthorne. "She's two?" My mother asked.

"Yes..." Micah said.

"Then she will be Selig's twin sister."

I felt the air escape my chest just as Drake let go of my hand. "It can't be..."

"Carter and Elise...they aren't your biological parents."

I stood there, dumbfounded. I couldn't speak, couldn't think. "B-But I look like my father."

"It was one of the reasons the Hawthorne's were chosen as your new family. You have physical characteristics that Carter has."

"Do Selig and Ally know? Or is it just my parents?"

"Only Carter and Elise."

"Did they lose a daughter?"

"No."

"Then why did they take me in?"

"To protect you."

"From what?"

"Not from what, from whom," said Drake simply. "There is one other person in the city that is in the same situation as you."

"Who?"

"One of your friends."

"It's Mihkel, isn't it?"

"Yes. Craig and Blaise Tiitus aren't his biological parents. Elena, you've seen his ability when it comes to archery, it's almost unnatural. I need you to—"

"Captain Fisher," a familiar voice called out.

Both of us turned to see Captain Sayers, Michael, and my father standing there. "Carter, Dragan," Drake said, standing up slowly. "What's going on?"

"Hand over your service weapon to Captain Sayers," my father said.

"Dad?" I stood up.

"Elena, come with me." Michael held out his hand, ushering me to come toward him.

"I'm not going anywhere," I snapped. "What the hell is going on?"

"Elena, go with Crane. Now!" my father countered.

Michael didn't give me another chance to protest. He forced me to walk away from whatever was happening.

It wasn't until we were out of sight that Michael let go of my arm. "What's going on?"

"Captain Fisher is being arrested," said Michael, like it wasn't a big deal.

"What? Why?"

"Because he did something he shouldn't have."

Chapter 28

Part of me was expecting to be dragged out of my hospital room in the middle of the night with a black bag over my head. As the night went on, it didn't happen. Unfortunately, that didn't mean it wasn't going to happen.

Unable to sleep due to nerves, the events that happened earlier in the day kept replaying in my head. I was worried, scared, or whatever term was most appropriate for what was going to happen to my uncle. I was so dumbfounded with his arrest that I had completely forgotten about Frost, but not quite. He was still in the back of my mind. Barely, but he was there.

I pulled on my clothes and was tying up my boots when the door to my room opened without warning. Right now, I had never wished to have my hunting knife on me more. Holding my breath, I waited to see who was coming in.

"Take it easy, Elena," said a familiar voice. "It's just me."

Sighing, I relaxed instantly. It was just Michael. He closed the door behind him before turning a light on. "Can't sleep?"

"I could ask you the same thing," I said. "What are you doing here?"

"Came to check up on my client," Michael answered, leaning against the wall as he did yesterday. "Come on."

"Where are we going?"

"I don't know about you, but I tend to get sick of hospital food rather quickly." He gave me an innocent look. "Come on, if you're with me, then they can't do anything to you."

"Are you sure about that? They just arrested my…uncle."

"Coming or not?" he asked, a serious look on his face.

I responded by zipping up my jacket partway and pulling on the gloves Michael had given me.

++++

I kept up with Michael easily enough, staying quiet until I figured out where we were going. I took in my surroundings and determined we were going to the Bakery. By the time we had gotten there, I could smell the freshly baked rolls coming out of the oven. It wasn't even dawn yet.

Michael opened the door and went in, holding it open with his fingertips. I walked in, letting the door close behind us.

Like most of the merchant shops in Ragnar City, the bakery was small. Or, at least, the area where the customers came into was small. I'm willing to bet the back was quite large in order to accommodate the large ovens. "Michael," a woman said. "It's been awhile, I didn't think we were ever going to see you again."

The baker's wife gave us both a smile and came out from behind the counter. Though she was moving around without much trouble, she had to be at least six months pregnant. Her long, light colored hair was pulled back into tight bun and she was wearing a maternity dress. "Elena," she kept the smile on her face. "I'm glad to see that you're doing better."

"Thank you for the rolls you sent over, they were very good."

"I was hoping you would like it." She first patted Michael on his cheek and then me. "My husband just took out your favorite rolls."

With raised eyebrows, I looked at her, not sure which one of us she was talking to. At the moment, I hoped it was me. I was starving and bakery rolls would hit the spot right now.

She went into the back, letting the door swing behind her. Not even a minute later, she returned holding a tray. It was now apparent she was talking to both of us. She had three sweet rolls on the tray along with three cheese rolls. Setting the tray down, she put them in a paper sack and sealed it off. Michael took out a few coins and held them out to her. "It's our pleasure," she said, pushing Michael's hand away.

"If you don't take it, then I'm starting a tip jar for you," said Michael.

"Just take the money," said the baker, coming into view. "He'll find some way to make us take it."

Michael and the baker shook hands. They spoke softly to each other for a minute before he went back into the kitchen area, patting me on the back before he did so. "Let's go," Michael said.

● ● ●

Twenty minutes into our walk, he suddenly stopped. "Where are we?" I asked.

"My place," he said. "Come on, the rolls are getting cold."

++++

Michael's home was the same size as mine, but it was almost barren. As it seemed, he only kept things that he absolutely needed around. "Sit down," he said, taking a couple of cups from the sink and filling them with water from a metal basin. "Sorry about the state of this place. I haven't been able to really do anything with it. Or wanted to, for that matter."

"How long has it been since your wife died?"

"Going on...a long time. Stigma."

"Do you have immunity to it?"

Michael, who was in the middle of taking the bread out of the bag, stopped. "I'm going to assume there is something else on your mind for bringing this up?"

"I think Mihkel is the same way."

"There are more people who are like you and me than you realize."

"How many more?"

"I'm not sure of the exact number, but they're around. Their identities are usually kept secret. Doc Aryen is a good man."

We ate in silence for a few minutes. I savored every bite of the sweet bread. Michael seemed to be enjoying himself watching me eat. I slowed down on the third roll and looked at him, feeling my ears go red. "I only get part of one once a year."

"I figured as much. Usually, I have one every other month," Michael said. "I figured, what the hell? Times are bad enough to treat you and myself to something."

We finished eating and I drank the water he had given me in two gulps. He offered to refill my glass, but I declined. Water was scarce and I didn't want to take more of his than I had to. "What do you know about PULSE?" I asked out of nowhere.

Michael set his glass down, making it a point to looking everywhere but me. "I really wish Drake didn't tell you anything."

• • •

150

"What do you know?"

"I know what Hawthorne knows, what Drake knows. You have no idea how deep this goes and you don't want to know. Not now."

"Tell me."

"If I tell you what Drake didn't get a chance to tell you, then there is no going back." He had the same serious expression on his face had earlier. "You should really be hearing this from Hawthorne."

"Carter Hawthorne isn't my dad," I said even though I didn't truly believe it. I still thought of him as my father and Elise as my mother. Selig and Ally were my brother and sister.

"Drake revealed more information than I originally thought," he said, rubbing the back of his neck. "What do you know?"

I told him what I knew; about Mihkel being like me, the memory flashes, and that I was awakening. Michael had a blank look on his face as I retold the information. For a little bit, I thought he wasn't listening. But, he would look at me once in a while to show he was. "Do you know what a person with certain abilities is called?"

"No. I didn't even know there was a name."

"Contractor."

"Contractor?"

"Yes. The term came from an experiment that was done," said Michael. "When someone uses their ability, it comes at a cost."

"What cost?"

Michael let out a sigh and rubbed his eyes. "Say a Contractor has the ability to create and manipulate fire. Whenever they use their power, they get burned in the process. A cost. Equivalent exchange, whatever you want to call it."

"Do you know of someone who can use fire?"

"Nothing gets past you, does it?"

I shook my head. "Is Frost one of them?"

Michael just nodded. "Drake?" I asked, and he nodded again. "My dad? You? Mihkel?" He gave the briefest of nods.

Chapter 29

I was silent on the way back to the hospital. Michael didn't try to force conversation on me, for which I was grateful. I had too much on my mind to think about it. I did want to ask him who my biological father was, but I couldn't get my mind to form the question.

He left me alone in my hospital. It wasn't until after he left that I realized how much I didn't want to be alone right now. Just as the revelation made itself clear, I heard a click.

Mihkel closed the door behind him and looked at me, staying against the door. "Hey…" he said humbly.

"Hi."

"I'm sorry about your uncle."

"You heard?"

"I'm part of CROSS, just like you. I'm actually surprised they didn't have me come and arrest him."

"True…"

"Your father really arrested his own brother in law?"

"Yes. Him and Sayers."

Mihkel walked over to me and sat down on the bed. I couldn't get over how well the uniform fit him. It seemed like he was born to be part of CROSS. I shuttered at the thought. Before I knew it, he pulled me into his arms. "You're shaking."

"You look too good in the uniform."

"It scares me too. They put me up in the barracks for right now, to keep me away from my parents." He put his forehead to mine. "I heard Captain Sayers talking to Lieutenant Ballory. As soon as you're well enough, you will be put into the uniform."

I gave him a chaste kiss, the briefest one I ever gave him. The familiar feeling was still there between us. He returned the kiss, putting his hands on my shoulders. We kissed again, and this time, the memory of us happy together, was back in full force. The next thing I knew, his arm was wrapped around my waist, and my arms around his neck. The pressure of his lips on mine, making hair on the back of my neck stand on end.

I broke the moment. "We can't do this. Not right now." Mihkel sighed and kissed me on the forehead before pulling away.

"Captain Fisher being arrested, he's not going to survive this is he?" He tugged at his collar a couple of times. He wasn't the only one with heat rushing up his neck.

It wasn't a secret that General Nolan and Drake rubbed each other the wrong way on various occasions. Lately, it's been whenever Drake has been in Ragnar City or if the General has gone to Ashtan. Usually, my father would stop any fighting before it began but something told me that wasn't going to happen anymore. Mihkel had a point, Drake was going to die.

We were interrupted by the door opening again. Damien walked in, slipping his glasses on. "Elena, let's see if we can't get you out of here today," he said, stopping when he saw Mihkel. "Lieutenant Tiitus, would you mind waiting outside?"

Mihkel gave me the briefest of looks, and left without another word. "How are you feeling?" Damien asked.

"Fine, just some minor pain."

"How are you doing with what happened? You've been through more than most people in this city in just under two months. Elena, you can talk to me."

"I could talk to Drake and then my father arrested him."

Damien took his glasses off. "Not even your father can save someone from a treason accusation."

"Treason?"

"I shouldn't even be telling you this."

"How do you even know the charge?"

"My profession isn't just being a doctor."

"What about Crispin Frost?"

Damien, who was writing something on my chart, stopped. "He's been charged with treason as well. I'm not going to ask how you know about his problems." He continued to write. "I don't see why you can't go home today."

Mihkel was walking with Damien and me out of the hospital wing when we saw Craig come running up the steps. "Something is wrong with my wife," he said, almost out of breath. Craig was a strong man and I had never seen him out of breath before. He must have been sprinting the entire way here.

"What is it?" Damien asked.

"I don't know, I gave her some medicine and she starting seizing."

"I need to get something from my office. I will be there as soon as I can," Damien said.

++++

At the house, Craig and Mihkel had rushed in with me right behind them. I grabbed the medicine on the counter and followed them upstairs.

I stopped when I saw the state Blaise was in. She was writhing in pain, curled up on the floor in a ball. "Mom?" Mihkel asked.

"Blaise, can you hear me?" Craig asked, cradling her in his arms. "Blaise?" My heart skipped a beat when I saw her face. She was bleeding from her eyes, nose, and mouth.

A couple minutes later, Damien came into the bedroom. "Lie her down flat and keep her head still," he said, going to his knees. "How long has she been like this?"

"Thirty minutes, slightly less," said Craig.

"Okay, Elena, give me the medicine. Mihkel, go get some water," Damien said, opening up his messenger bag that doubled as his medical bag.

I gave him the medicine jar without hesitation. "Mihkel, now!" Damien yelled.

I pushed Mihkel toward the kitchen, which got him moving. He dunked a cup into their water and hesitated for a couple of seconds. "She's dying, isn't she?"

"I-I don't know," I said.

We were brought back to reality by Craig yelling, "Mihkel!"

The two of us ran back into the bedroom to see that Mihkel's mother was now bleeding from her ears, eyes, nose, and mouth. Damien was filling up a syringe with some sort of medicine. "Hold her down," he ordered, pushing the air out of the syringe.

Damien jabbed the needle into her chest and injected the liquid into her heart. "Is that going to save her?" Craig asked.

"No, but it will hopefully stop the bleeding."

"Hopefully? You just injected her with something and you don't know what it will do?"

"I have never seen a reaction like this before," snapped Damien. "Either keep her still or wait outside."

He picked up the medicine jar and looked at it. "This is what you gave her?"

"Yes," Craig said. "Selig dropped off the new batch a few days ago."

Damien opened up the jar and scooped some onto his finger. He sniffed it and then smeared it onto the inside of his wrist. "This is the problem."

"What?"

He held up his wrist and showed the discoloration from the medicine on his skin. "Someone tampered with it," Damien said. "Where did you get that amount of medicine?"

"Drake supplies some people with it," I said.

"I want to talk to him," Craig said, through clenched teeth.

"He didn't do this," I said. "Drake would never do anything to hurt anyone from Ragnar City."

"My wife almost died just now, I'm going to talk to him."

"He's been arrested, Craig," Damien said, lifting Blaise up gently and lying her down on the bed. "You won't be able to get near him."

"What was he arrested for?" Craig asked.

The three of them looked at me, causing me to hesitate before I answered. "Suspicion of treason."

The conversation stopped when we heard glass breaking. "No—" Craig said. "No..."

He moved over to his wife as she went limp. I put my hand over my mouth and looked at Damien. He walked over and hesitated, his hand hovering over Craig's back.

Mihkel suddenly left the house at a run. I started to go after him when Damien grabbed my wrist. "I am going to tell your father about this so Captain Fisher will be interrogated."

I didn't say anything, just pulled my wrist free and went after Mihkel.

++++

"Mihkel!" I called out. "Stop!"

Mihkel didn't stop running until we got to the square. Turning to look at me, I had never seen him so vulnerable. "My mother is dead…" He started to breathe rapidly. "Only the Gods…I can't—I can't…"

I put my hands on his face, forcing him to look at me. "Look at me, slow your breathing down. Breathe with me…" It was then, the tears came.

At a loss for words, I pulled him into a hug. "I'm sorry," I whispered. I felt the urge to tell him what I found out, but decided against it. The square was too public of a place and I didn't want to put more of a burden on him at this moment.

He started crying on my shoulder and I just kept my arms around him. I felt his body tense up slightly before he broke the hug. He put his forehead to mine and then kissed me. This kiss was different from what seemed like an eternity ago. I could taste his tears, and I knew he just wanted to feel something. "Sorry…" he said, putting his fingers to his lips.

I didn't say anything until I felt the heat leave my face and neck. "Don't be," I whispered, putting my hand to his cheek. "Your father is going to need you."

"He is going to want to be alone for a while," Mihkel said. "My mother was his whole world."

It was depressing to hear Mihkel talk like that. His parents truly loved and cared for him, but Craig and Blaise were like Carter and Elise. They would be devastated if they lost each other.

"I can't be here right now. I have to get out of here."

"There isn't really any place to run away to." It was stupid, but it was also true. There wasn't any place to run to in this world. Xing was the only province that had the least amount of GUARD personnel on its lands, but there were still quite a few. You couldn't hide anywhere, not for long, especially if you had a target on your back.

Mihkel suddenly held out his hand to me. "Come with me."

"Where?"

• • •

"It's a surprise." The familiar warmth was coming back to his eyes.

"I hate surprises."

"I know, but I need you…" He hesitated slightly, his cheeks blushing with color. "I need you to come with me. Trust me on this."

I just stood there looking at his hand still held out to me. I looked at him again and he met my eyes. The blush had already gone from his face, the warm look he usually had when it was just him, Sindri, and myself back in place.

Chapter 30

We went back to where he first showed me how to shoot a bow. "Isn't this a little dangerous?" I asked seriously. The last time we had come here, we had to run for our lives from an airship and I ended up losing a leg.

"It's easier to get away with just two people if we need to. Besides, who else knows you've been released?"

I didn't know, probably my family. Which would probably be about it. But, I needed a distraction. We both did. Mihkel because his mother had just died and I was thrust into keeping a nightmare on my shoulders, which I wanted to share with Mihkel so the burden wasn't all mine. I was selfish even in this world. Mihkel tossed me my shooting glove. I slipped it on.

It being around two months since I last shot an arrow, I was very rusty. Mihkel didn't make an effort to hide the fact he was laughing at me. Which, right now, didn't bother me. I actually welcomed it. We were distracting each other and that was the plan right now.

Mihkel hit every shot where he wanted it. Me, it took a while. First, I had to get used to my new leg, which was harder than I thought. All this extra activity was making the dull ache become a noticeable pain. I was going to have to learn from Sartana or Michael on how to use the leg to its full extent. Mihkel would be the ideal teacher, but he didn't have Shinar limbs. And, I hope he nor Sindri ever have to go through that pain. I couldn't imagine anyone doing this voluntarily.

Taking a break after about an hour, Mihkel sat down and opened up the bag he had carried with him up here. He took out a roll and tore it in half, tossing me the slightly bigger half. "Are you going to tell me what's wrong?" he asked, tearing a piece of bread and popping it in his mouth.

"What makes you think anything is wrong?" I asked, knowing he would see right through it.

"You are one bad liar once someone has seen how vulnerable you can be." He had a point. There were certain people in Ragnar City that could read me like an open book. Selig, Sindri, and Drake were the only three before two months ago. Now, the list had been growing too quickly for my taste. It

* * *

was now Selig, Sindri, Drake, Mihkel, Michael, and Frost. It would usually take months for me to open up to someone that I had just met, but, for whatever reason, Michael and Frost were different. Probably because we were in the same nightmare, even though they had experienced more than I have in this lifetime.

"This is something you shouldn't have to be weighed down with just after—" I let my voice trail off.

"I'll take whatever I can to distract me." The look on Mihkel's face showed he was serious.

I had no idea how to start telling him about what was happening to us, or what was happening to me. I had no way of knowing if he had started to go through the awakening process or not. Michael or Drake didn't tell me how to know if it was happening to someone else. I actually wasn't sure if I wanted to know. Something told me the more I knew about this, the more dangerous life was going to get.

Looking at the boy who I used to find irritating, I found this company more comforting than Sindri's at the moment. So, I decided to tell him everything, even the things Michael suggested I didn't.

He only raised his eyebrows when I told him my birth name and looked relieved when I said I was going to continue to go by Elena Hawthorne. He didn't say anything while I was talking; just listened, eating his half of the bread slowly.

He ran a hand through his hair and sighed deeply. "What happens now?"

"I'm not sure, we work for CROSS."

"So, you decided to share the bad news with me and make me terrified as well?"

I shrugged. He was right. I didn't want to handle this trouble on my own. I wanted to go to Sindri since he was the one person I could truly talk to about anything, but I couldn't now. Not with this. Michael would have said something if Sindri was like us, but they didn't bring him up, except to say don't say anything to him.

We walked back to the city and I still hadn't decided if I wanted to go home or not. I didn't get a chance to make a decision. When we walked back to Mihkel's house, we both stopped. My father was standing there with a furious look on his

* * *

face. He was talking to my mother and Craig as well. When Craig saw us, his facial expression changed from upset to hatred. All three of them stopped talking and glared at us. "Where were you?" my father asked, coming up to me. Before I could react to anything, he slapped me, sending me to the floor. He held up his hand to Mihkel. "Don't even think about it, Lieutenant. I am your boss, and can order your execution in a heartbeat."

"I suggest you get out of my house, you're not welcome here anymore," Craig said to his son.

Mihkel gave me a look before he walked out of the house. He was getting far more punishment than I was going to receive.

Chapter 31

"You think you can just keep breaking rules and not have to face the consequences?" my father hissed in my ear. He kept his hand on my collar, forcing me to walk. "What is it going to take for you to let go of this death wish you have?"

"Carter, stop," my mother said. "Let her go."

My father just glared at her, his expression almost instantly changing from the anger he had looking at me to slight confusion. "What did you say to me?"

"Let her go before you make it so we lose both our daughters," my mother said.

I had never truly thought of my mother as a strong willed woman. But, at this moment, she had changed my opinion of her completely. Very few people stood up to my father. I did my best to avoid it at all costs, as did Selig. If we stood up to him, it just meant we were going to be disciplined.

My father released me. I adjusted my jacket and rotated my neck slightly. When I touched the back of my neck, my fingers came away smeared with blood. My father cut me; that was a first.

The three of us were quiet on the walk back. My mother had never spoken of Ally dying before. That was usually because Selig, my father, and I were just in permanent denial about the whole thing. I stayed a couple steps behind them and wasn't surprised when my father's fingers grazed my mother's hand and she walked a little closer to him. It seemed to be no matter what happened, they were always going to love each other.

When we reached the house, my father stopped me from going in. "I can't protect you if you keep walking that fine line when it comes to the rules. You know what I had to do to get you that Shinar leg? They're allowed to military personnel only." He put his hands on my face. "I had to get in so deep with the General, I will never get out from under his fist."

"Why? I'm not even your daughter. You took me in for whatever reason. That, and I was just recruited by CROSS," I said, pulling myself away from him. I didn't care that I had hatred showing on my face. Right now, I was angry at him. I was angry at anyone that kept his from me for eighteen years.

● ● ●

He let me move away. The look on his face showed that I had really hurt him when I saw that. He walked into the house without another word, leaving the door slightly ajar.

++++

The first one to greet me was Enrik. He sniffed my metal leg and started to growl. I knelt down and took my gloves off. Once he sniffed my hands, he went from snarling to being overjoyed to see me.

Standing up, I scratched him behind his ears and looked at my brother. He was leaning against the door frame with his arms crossed. At this moment, he never looked so much like Carter Hawthorne. He was almost a mirror image of him aside from the weariness my father carried with him at all times. Selig was like Mihkel and could tell when something was wrong, but he wasn't going to push the subject. At least not in front of the parents. It was then I saw he had something on his mind as well. "Are you going to tell her the news?" our father asked, sitting down on the table.

"Tell me what?" I asked.

Our mother covered her mouth and walked into the bedroom, slamming the door behind her. Now I was very curious. "What's going on?"

"I start on the demolitions team for CROSS the same time you start."

I about choked on the breath of air in my throat. Working in the mines was one of the most dangerous occupations in this world, but I would rather work in the mines than work for CROSS as a demolitions expert. They were the most expendable. I was surprised Ballory had lasted as long as he has in the area.

Our staring contest was interrupted when the door to the bedroom was opened. We looked with raised eyebrows to see Ally standing there. It was rare that she had enough energy to get out of bed and walk around. Our father took the opportunity to leave the three of us to talk.

"I missed you," I said, hugging my sister.

"Me, too…" she said hesitantly.

"Just go ahead and ask," Selig said.

"C-Can I see it?"

I sat down and pulled my pant leg up, letting her look at my Shinar leg. She came over and brushed her fingertips across the cold metal. "Can you feel that?" she asked.

"Not exactly, my nerves are attached to the limb so I can move them around. But I can't feel anything."

"There's blood on your hand. "

Looking at my hand, I saw that Ally was right. Instinctively, I checked where our father had cut the back of my neck and found that it was still bleeding. "Since you're able to act like your normal self again, mind helping me bring some wood in?" Selig asked. That was code for he wanted to talk to me without Ally hearing.

"Sure," I said.

We left Ally in the company of Enrik as we went out back. Selig didn't say anything until we both heard the door click shut. "What's going on?" Selig asked.

"Mihkel's mother just died," I said.

Selig rubbed his mouth and sighed. "How? I dropped off that medicine. A new batch."

"The medicine was tampered with," I said. "Has Ally had any?"

"Yeah, she's been getting a normal dosage since Uncle Drake gave it to us. She just had some not ten minutes ago."

We looked at each other then ran back into the house. "Ally!" Selig called out, both of us stopping when we saw Ally was just sitting there looking at us.

"What?"

"Are you feeling okay?" I asked, kneeling down beside her. I looked at her eyes to see they looked normal; there wasn't any blood.

"Yes," she said with a confused look.

The bedroom door opened and our parents came out. "What's wrong?" our mother asked.

"You have been giving Ally the medicine, haven't you?" I asked.

"Yes."

"That is how Craig's wife died, why is Ally okay?"

• • •

163

"That's something that I will be talking to your uncle about," our father said simply. "I suggest you two get some rest. You're going to need it," he said, motioning to Selig and me. After all, we were now part of Cross, whether we wanted to be or not.

++++

I must have fallen asleep quicker than I thought. The next thing I knew, it was morning and my father was currently pulling on his CROSS uniform. I slowly sat up to see Ally was fast asleep next to me and Enrik was lying down next to Selig. He looked at me and motioned with his hand to follow him out of the room. I got dressed quickly. Just as I was pulling on my socks, I noticed that Selig had woken up.

My father had started heating up water for the pine tea we drank every morning and sat down at the table. "Sit down, we need to talk."

"Are you going to hit me again?" I asked. It wasn't that I was afraid of him; that was how he disciplined us. That is how most parents in Ragnar City, possibly, the entire world, disciplined their children. Or at least one of the parents did.

"Depends, are you going to say I'm not your father?" Looking in his eyes, I saw he was still hurt by the comment I made yesterday.

I opened my mouth to say something when Selig walked into the kitchen. He had a blank look on his face, but I could tell he was nervous, probably scared. Both of us had seen what happened to someone who is permanently tied to CROSS.

Glancing at Selig and our father, I wondered how much our parents sacrificed to have Selig and then take me in. Years later, they had Ally. Most families in Ragnar City only had two children. Three or more became too many mouths to feed. It wasn't that Arcadia put a limit on how many children families could have, it was a basic thing for survival. The less mouths to feed, the more food that could go around. Although there was an exception to the rule, mining families typically had five or more children, so food was very scarce.

"What do you want to talk about?" I asked.

• • •

Our father hesitated now that Selig was in the room. I wanted to say he was going to find out sooner or later, but I kept my mouth shut. "You need to be aware that you'll have to go through training, both of you."

"Training?" Selig asked looking at me.

"For her new leg and you for being in demolitions, there's a certain way things are done." Our father got up and went to put the pine needles in the water, along with a few mint leaves. "If you haven't figured it out already, that new leg of yours isn't the same. They're close, but no piece of metal could replace flesh and bone."

He must have known I was having trouble with shooting an arrow yesterday. "I just have to get used to it," I said. I gingerly touched my face where he had slapped me yesterday. I was honestly surprised I didn't have a fractured cheek bone. It was tender, but the swelling had stopped. That was one thing I liked about the weather getting colder; the air would act as a cold compact.

"Which is where your training comes in." His eyes flicked from Selig to me, the look in them showing that he had more to tell me, but now wasn't the time.

The smell of the pine needles and mint leaves filled up the kitchen, announcing that the tea was ready. Selig poured three cups and set them on the table just as the front door opened. It was Sayers. "We need to go, now."

"What's going on?" our father asked, standing up.

Sayers hesitated when he saw Selig and me. Our father motioned for Sayers to keep talking. "There's a riot starting over the abnormal shortage of water. General Nolan would like to dissolve it before GUARD comes in."

Our father muttered something under his breath. He went into the bedroom and came out armed. He looked at the two of us. "You two get to the Justice Building, something tells me we're going to need everyone."

"Clear eyes today," Sayers said.

Chapter 32

I was pulling on my jacket when there was a knock on the door. My mother had gotten up slightly after my father and brother left. I opened the door to see Sindri and Mihkel standing there. "You heard?" Mihkel asked, already in his CROSS uniform.

"Yes, a riot."

"Kara went into the main part of the city earlier to get our order in." Sindri gave me a worried look.

There was only one other reason why their father would allow Kara to go into the square and that would be to get bread. "She hasn't come back yet?"

"They shut down the square, I was hoping, you two, being in CROSS, could look for her or let me through."

"We can try," said Mihkel. "But, Elena and I don't really carry any weight the moment. I'm a Lieutenant, but that's just because of the knowledge I carry."

"It's better to sweet talk someone," I said. "Which one, though? Drake is currently in custody."

"Lieutenant Ballory or Captain Sayers?" Sindri asked.

"No, at least not directly…" I said, thinking for a second. "Michael."

++++

Mihkel and I went directly to the square, bringing Enrik along with us. I did a double take at his neck. He had a large burn stretching the side of his neck, blood running into his uniform. "What happened?"

"Just because I wear a CROSS uniform doesn't mean anything," said Mihkel.

"GUARD? GUARD is already here?"

"A few of them are."

We made it to the town square without any issues. When we got there, we saw firsthand just how out of control everything was.

Sayers had said a riot was starting. It was already pure chaos. "Come on," Mihkel said, taking my hand and pushing a path through a group of people. "Mr. Anton?" he asked when we got to the barricade formed by CROSS members.

Robert Anton turned and looked at us, cradling his left shoulder. "What happened?" I asked.

"The shop was overrun, have you seen my children?"

"Sindri is looking for Kara on the other side of the square," said Mihkel.

"Hey!" a voice yelled. "Let these two through, they're CROSS."

We turned to see Solomon coming up to us. "Lieutenant Creid, these two are to be let in. Lieutenant Tiitus and Lieutenant Hawthorne. Let them in."

Two CROSS soldiers looked at each other and then moved aside. Solomon pulled the two of us through. "Thank you," I said.

"Don't thank me, you're probably going to get yourselves killed. After all, you're not armed and aren't allowed until you're sworn in and qualified."

"Have you seen my dad or brother around?" I asked.

"He's probably up at the Justice Building trying to get some sort of order before they stop the riot," said Solomon. "You two should get out of here, things are going to get very violent."

"We're looking for Sindri's sister," Mihkel said. "Unlike CROSS members, the people of Ragnar City actually care about their families."

"I suggest you watch your tone, you are wearing the uniform."

"And we're the same rank."

I got between them. "Mihkel, go over there. I'll be there in a minute." I waited for Mihkel to walk away with Enrik. "What's wrong with you?"

"What's wrong with me? What's wrong with you? That thin line your friend has been balancing on? It's shrinking like the one you're doing your act on."

"Are you threatening me?"

"I'm warning you," he said and walked away. The look on his face was telling me our relationship was over. Before he found out about me and Mihkel, which I was grateful for. He wasn't about to throw his career away for me. Luckily, I was already over it. And, it looked like he was as well.

Mihkel looked at me as I ran up to him. "Everything okay in paradise?"

I ran a hand through my hair and pulled it back into a messy knot. We haven't ever been in paradise, I thought. "Let's just find Kara, Sindri, and my brother. Then we can get out of here."

"Selig was supposed to learn how to blow stuff up today, right?"

"Yeah…or at least start. I think he's shadowing Lieutenant Ballory for a couple weeks."

"If they were going to be in the mines, they won't be. It was my father who started this riot, the shortage of water was only the breaking point."

"Only the Gods can help him now…" I was never a big believer in religion, but right now we were going to need all the help we could get to get out of this mess alive.

"I saw Sindri for a second—somewhere over there." Mihkel scanned the crowd. Someone suddenly knocked me to the ground. Mihkel pulled me to my feet before stopping abruptly. I looked up to see my father standing there. He had a deep gash on his temple and he was cradling his right side. "What in the name of Valefor and Fenrir are you two doing here? Should I start telling you to try and get yourselves killed so you stay out of the danger?"

"Kara's out in the mess somewhere and we are part of CROSS," I said, forcing myself to be steady on my feet.

"Not until you are carrying a weapon, get out of here before it gets completely out of control. I'll find her." My father ignored the blood running down his face.

"It's already out of control, we're not leaving her!" Mihkel yelled.

My father made a fist and just glared at us. "You'll find her and get out of here. Once GUARD gets here with full numbers, bullets will fly. They don't care who they hit."

"Captain!" a CROSS soldier yelled.

My father took out my knife that I had always carried and put it in my hand. "Don't make me regret giving this back to you. Get Sindri's sister and get back to the house. And for the Gods' sake, don't let Enrik bite anyone." He started heading back into the crowd when I grabbed his wrist.

"What about Selig?"

"He's with Amon Ballory. Don't worry, Ballory is one of the best shots I know. They're rigging something for General Nolan."

"Let's go," said Mihkel, taking my hand again.

We made it to the masonry shop and got pushed in from the mob growing in size. I had never seen the shop so empty. Everything that used to be in front of us had been taken. I stopped when I saw blood on the floor; it must have been Robert's. "The roof," I said. "We can use the height to our advantage."

++++

We left Enrik in the shop to ensure he didn't attack anyone. Going out the back, we climbed up the ladders which lead to the chimney. I got up there and immediately started to scan the square. "See her yet?" Mihkel asked right behind me.

I didn't answer right away, "I see her!" I pointed in the direction of the Justice Building even though Mihkel couldn't see me.

Kara was standing on the steps, looking terrified. My heart skipped a beat when I saw a man notice her by herself. "Go!" I said.

"What's happening?"

"Go!"

We flew down the ladders and forced our way through the growing crowds. "She's on the steps of the Justice Building!"

I let Mihkel lead, for he had an easier time getting through the mob. "Kara!" he yelled when we made our way to the building. He ran up the steps and charged the man that was trying to take the supplies she had away from her.

Running up the steps behind him, I went to Kara and looked at her. "Are you okay?"

● ● ●

169

"They wouldn't let any of us leave," she said softly. I treated Kara like a sister. She was the same age as Ally and I had known her since she was born. "I'm sorry."

"It's not your fault, are you hurt at all?" I put my hands on her face and forced her to look me in the eyes. "Kara?"

Kara suddenly collapsed in my arms. I had to go to my knees to make sure I didn't drop her. I desperately tried to get her to respond. "Mihkel!"

Mihkel ran over with a cut over his eyes and a few cuts across his knuckles. "What happened?"

"She just collapsed.

"Give her to me, we've got to get her out of here." Mihkel lifted Kara up in his arms. He stopped when he saw blood on her shirt. Gently, he set her down and lifted up her shirt. There was a three inch cut on her abdomen.

Mihkel stripped his jacket off and then tore the sleeve off his shirt and started to wrap it around her abdomen when we heard a familiar sound. "GUARD is here," I said.

Slowly, we looked up to the sky to see the airships approaching. There were three of them which meant around fifty GUARD members with guns. No one was going to be safe once their feet touched the ground. "You know I didn't give you that new leg just so you could get sought out and killed."

Turning, I saw Michael standing there. He had lost his jacket and his shirt was torn, leaving his Shinar arm in full view. Luckily, since he was back in the military, it didn't matter. "What happened?"

"She got hurt somehow. I have no idea how, though."

Michael looked at the wound for a second. "I don't think it's that deep, you need to get out of here."

"What about you?"

"Officially, I'm part of CROSS again. It's penalty of death if I abandon my post. Go to the left for two blocks. There will be an opening for you to get around the chaos and GUARD." He started to stand up when I grabbed his arm.

"Sindri is out in the crowd somewhere," I said.

"I know where he is," said Michael.

"Is he...?" I couldn't finish the question.

* * *

"He's a little banged up, but he's okay for now," Michael said, forcing us to our feet. "You might run into something that will find her blood...appetizing. What do you have to protect yourselves with?"

I showed him my hunting knife. Michael hesitated for a second before taking out a small sidearm that was hidden under his pant leg. "You see anyone, you throw the gun away. I don't care if it's lost forever. Do not let anyone see you with this. It wouldn't just be me in front of a firing squad."

"Okay..."

"Five shots only. If nothing, when we make it out of this alive...you can give me back my gun. All right?"

"Watch your back," said Mihkel, trying to wipe blood out of his eye.

"You two do the same. Get out of here."

I slipped the gun into the small of my back, adjusting to make sure my jacket covered it. In the struggle, my hair had come loose from the hair tie. I hastily wrapped around it, pulling it into a knot before continuing our mission.

++++

We made it to the spot that Michael directed us to. I spotted the opening and stopped. "You get her to Damien, I'm going back."

"Wait, what?" He just stared at me. "Are you crazy? GUARD was landing when we left."

"My father is still out there and so is my brother. He has a high chance of getting killed because he'll be setting explosives. Michael is also still out there and so is Sindri."

"No. Most are part of CROSS. They're safer than we are the moment."

"Selig hasn't gone through training; he's going to be expendable."

"I would trust your father in keeping him safe. After all, Selig is actually related to him by blood." He stopped when he said that. "I'm—" I cut him off by kissing him.

I didn't say anything as I left Mihkel and started to run back. I knew he wouldn't follow me because of Kara. But, if we made it through all of this, he would be furious. So would my father, accusing me again of having a death wish, and possibly granting me the death I've been avoiding for some time.

Making it back to the square, I saw GUARD as they were just landing. I was wrong about the number of them. There weren't fifty, there were more like one-hundred and fifty. The one in charge, I had never seen before. From just glancing at him, I knew he wasn't someone to mess with. You didn't want to mess with any GUARD members.

I watched as the General walked up to them with my father beside him. Both of them had fresh wounds on their faces. They spoke for a couple minutes. Or, rather, argued. General Nolan was a man you didn't want on your bad side, but he did care in his own way about the people in Ragnar City. He, like everyone else, knew once GUARD took charge, things would go from bad to worse.

Suddenly, I was grabbed by someone and was forced into the square. My father did a double take of me and had to fight not to do anything. But, from the look in his eyes…he was disappointed in me. So was Michael, who was being rounded up with the other CROSS members. They had given me an out and I had been stupid enough to come back.

"I was going to be surprised if I didn't see you back here," a voice said.

Sindri was standing beside me. Like me, there was also a GUARD member forcing him to move. Sindri had torn a sleeve off from his shirt and had it wrapped around his arm. It was bloody. "Why are you here?" I asked.

The man in charge called himself Bogdan and was like General Nolan, keeping his sunglasses on the entire time. He took out his sidearm and motioned for one of the GUARD members to bring over a miner; probably one of the ones who started the riot. If they caught Craig, they were going to save him for last.

Bogdan didn't say anything, he just raised his weapon and fired one round, hitting the miner right between his eyes. Two other GUARD members brought up a woman I didn't recognize and forced her to her knees. She was crying, pleading with Bogdan to let her live. He shot her in the same manner, looking annoyed when some of her blood splattered on his uniform. It was then a third person was brought up. My heart skipped a beat when I saw it was Willow. "No…" I said. I felt time stop when I saw Selig running over to her, Ballory behind him.

"Stop!" Selig yelled, looking like any other person wearing a CROSS uniform. "You can't touch her!"

"Give me one reason why I can't, boy," Bogdan said.

"You can't harm the spouse of a CROSS, or GUARD member, especially if they're pregnant," Selig said taking out a folded piece of paper. "We were married a month ago." They really did it. I couldn't believe it.

A GUARD member snatched the paper from Selig and handed it to Bogdan. "So it seems to be true. I don't need to get any more blood on my uniform at this moment."

I could feel our father's eyes burning holes into Selig. Getting married at eighteen was rare. It was considered a stupid thing to do. Most people waited until they were in their twenties after a few years of saving what money they could.

Suddenly, Sindri and I were forced to the ground and searched. I knew they were going to find the gun. I should have hidden it or given it to Mihkel when I had the chance. The fact that I was in possession of a firearm would be thirty lashes at least, probably more because of the riot and the fact that I was Carter Hawthorne's daughter. There was always tension between GUARD and CROSS, even though they were both employed by the Royal Province Arcadia.

I stayed still throughout the search. Just as I feared, whoever was searching found the gun. They pulled me to my feet so fast that I lost my balance and fell, landing hard on my hands and knees. A sharp shot through my thigh, where my Shinar leg was attached. "Get up, you stupid bitch," a GUARD soldier snarled, dragging me to my feet by my hair.

He started pulling me toward the middle of the square while I was trying to gain my footing. I ended up being dragged. "Found this on her, sir," the GUARD soldier said.

Bogdan took the gun and looked at it. "CROSS issue, who gave this to you?" he asked. Without waiting for me to answer, he put the gun in the soldier's hand and pulled me to my feet. "Tell me who gave you the gun!"

"It was me."

Bogdan and I turned to see Solomon standing there. "I gave it to her to protect herself," he said with his hands up.

Bogdan released me, sending me into the arms of Sayers. Sayers held me to his chest as if he already knew what was going to happen. "Don't do anything and you might get out of this alive," he breathed into my ear.

"What's going to happen to him?" I wanted to look up to see the look on his face, but he kept his grip tight so I couldn't move.

"Just watch," Sayers said softly.

Solomon was forced to his knees and Bogdan took out a long, thin sword from a sheath. He turned the blade in his hand, the sharp edge pointing toward the sky. In a flash, blood was pouring from Solomon's throat. I couldn't look away as he gave me the briefest of looks. The look wasn't goodbye, it was more of keep fighting.

Chapter 33

My legs sagged and Sayers had to hold onto me tighter. He was saying something to me, but I couldn't comprehend any of it. I just stared at the life draining from Solomon's body. Watching as it spilled from his throat and splashed onto the ground. The two GUARD soldiers holding him up, let go; allowing him to drop to the ground in his own blood. "Elena," I heard Sayers say, but I didn't respond. "Elena!"

"They just kill him..." I barely whispered.

"Something tells me that wasn't his gun that you had on you," he said slowly, releasing his grip from me. "Who gave it to you? It wasn't me, it wasn't your father. The General would rather shoot you than give you a gun."

"I found it," I lied. I didn't want to give Michael up. If Solomon was just executed for saying he gave me the gun, I didn't even want to think about what they would do to him for actually being the one that gave me the gun.

"You're a bad liar," he hissed. He pulled a bloodied Sindri to his feet. "You two need to get out of here before something else happens."

"What about my family?" I asked.

"Carter will be fine, he's CROSS, and they won't take out the second in command on a whim. Selig put a target on his back for marrying the only daughter of Renner Nolan. He's on his own right now, but I will find him when I get a moment."

"What about Mihkel's father?" Sindri had a look on his face that was more determined than mine.

Sayers shoved the two of us against the Justice Building and kept an arm across Sindri's neck. "Craig is the one who started this riot. Do you know what he did? Do you want to know what he did to a CROSS soldier to start this up?"

Both of us were silent. "He shoved one of my men to the ground and beat them with a piece of mining equipment. He beat them to death. He has dug his own grave and now he's going to die in it. Get out of here." He took a step back.

Neither of us moved. "Go!" he yelled.

I pulled Sindri's arm and that got him to move. We started walking and I realized I had go back for Enrik. "Come on," I said. "We need to stop by your father's shop. I have to get Enrik."

"Where's my sister?"

"Mihkel's got her. She'll be okay."

I gave Sindri the short version of what happened. "I would be surprised if Enrik was still in there," Sindri said.

"If he's not there, then he'll be at home," I said. "Or, out hunting somewhere." I wasn't too worried about Enrik. He could take of himself better than anyone else I knew.

Sindri led us to the masonry shop. He kept a strong grip on my wrist, making me want to yank away from him. But, I didn't blame him. His father was hurt, his sister was hurt, and thing were only going to get worse. But, there was something I couldn't get out of my head. It was what Sayers had said about Mihkel's father going to die today. I wasn't sure how Mihkel would react. Even with everything I had learned about Mihkel and myself, all I knew was I regretted saying I wasn't my father's daughter. If we all survived this day, I was going to apologize to my father.

When we got to the masonry shop, I saw that the door had been broken. Quickly, I stuck my head in to see that Enrik wasn't anywhere in sight. "He's not here."

Sindri looked at me, "I have an idea where he might be."

"Where?"

"You're not going to like it." With the look on his face, I already knew where he was thinking of. And, no, I didn't like it.

"You're serious? You want to go back to the square?" I had surprised both of us by saying this. Normally I was all for jumping into dangerous situations, but right now, I just wanted to make sure my family was safe and at home.

"What about Selig? I bet Enrik went looking for him."

Sindri had a point. Whenever Selig, Enrik, and I were out in the city square, we would usually split up. If Enrik started out with me, he would end up with Selig or the other way around. "Let's go," I said. I started to walk back the way we came when I felt his fingers close around mine.

"Tell me something first, who gave you that gun?"

"Michael," I delicately said. The few people that were around us weren't paying attention to us. But, I didn't want to get into more trouble than I already was. I had a feeling I wasn't going to get away with anything this time.

++++

We were careful about how we got back to the square. We ended up on the far side of the Justice Building. It was Sindri that spotted him before I did. "Hey, I see your brother over there." He pointed across the square. Selig was with Willow and Ballory. It looked like Ballory was yelling at him for making a scene.

I blocked the sun from my eyes to get a better look. It was Selig and, like everyone else, he had blood on him. I must have moved like I was going toward him because Sindri grasped my arm. "I wouldn't go straight through the square," he said hesitantly as he blinked some blood out of his eyes.

"Let me see." Gingerly, I touched around the cut on his forehead to see how deep it was. He winced. "Sorry."

"It's fine."

"The bleeding isn't going to stop." I looked at Sindri. "You should stay here."

"You think you can get to your brother on your own? No way. Hell, I would prefer that Mihkel was with us on this. Things tend to go better when there are three of us breaking rules. Not just two."

Sindri had a point. Usually when it was the three of us, things went a little more smoothly.

As we were about to go the long way, Amon Ballory got our attention from across the square. He simply motioned to us to get out of here with a jerk of his head. I had a feeling I didn't want to fight him on this.

We made it to Damien's private residence without any problems. GUARD and CROSS were busy rounding up people and were on a power trip.

I knocked on the door a few times. "It's Elena," I said. "Come on, Damien, open the door."

I was surprised when it was Mihkel that opened the door. He had blood on his shirt and also on his hands. "He's just finishing up with Kara, come on in." Mihkel helped Sindri in and closed the door.

This was only the third time I had actually been in Damien's house. It was small like everyone else's, but it was clean without any coal or mineral dust, which usually was impossible in this part of the city.

We went into the bedroom to see Damien was just bandaging up Kara's abdomen. "I see that you two have seen some excitement out there today," he said.

"How come you're not out there?" Sindri asked.

"I may be part of CROSS, but they only call me in when one of our gets hurt. I'm only a doctor."

"Our own?" I asked.

"You know that CROSS is like GUARD, and they watch out for those in the uniform even before their families," Damien said, as he started to wash his hands.

Mihkel helped Sindri to bed so I could rest. I was still recovering from the Shinar procedure and seeing Solomon executed was both physically and mentally draining.

"From the look of you two, I'm going to assume that GUARD is already there?"

"Yes."

Damien sighed and handed a pill bottle to Sindri. "This will kill any infection she might get and will keep the pain level down. One in the morning and one at night."

Sindri slipped the bottle into his pocket. "Thank you."

"It's my job."

"I don't have any money to pay you."

"Next time you catch a turkey, clean it, and bring it by. That will take care of your bill, for all three of you. I suggest you get your sister home while you can."

Sindri lifted up his sister and I walked to the door with them. "Be careful," I said.

"I take it, you're staying here?"

"Yes, he just lost his mother and his father is going to die." I rubbed the back of my neck.

"I'll see you when this is all over." Sindri sighed heavily. "If he needs to smash anything, tell him to come by the shop."

I walked back into the bedroom to see Damien was stitching up Mihkel's head. Not looking away from what he was doing, he spoke. "Did I hear you right?"

• • •

"What do you mean?"

"That my father is going to die," Mihkel said.

"If it's true that he started the riot, then, yes, he will," said Damien. "Somehow, I don't think telling you how sorry I am is going to cut it."

"No, it's not," Mihkel snapped.

I opened my mouth to tell him to calm down, but I decided against it. I kept my mouth shut until Damien was done with Mihkel's stitching. "Elena, I'd like to have a word with you," Damien said.

"Sure."

Damien led the way out of his bedroom and into the kitchen area. "How's Ally doing?"

"She's going to die."

Damien rubbed his mouth while he thought about something. Was her medication tampered with?"

"If it was, then she's showing different side effects."

"Who does Craig think tampered with the medicine you gave his wife?"

"Drake."

"That doesn't make any sense. Did he know that you would split the amount of medicine he gets for Ally?"

I shook my head. With how quickly Stigma has spread in such a short period of time, telling people we had extra medicine, even though we didn't, would have turned out very badly.

Damien took something from his pocket and put it in my hand. It was a small silver cylinder, like one he had used a couple months ago. I opened it and saw a single tablet in the cylinder. "This isn't?" I started to ask.

"Yes, it's a black capsule."

Black capsules were given to CROSS and GUARD members during times of war in case they were captured. Or if they were a big enough embarrassment. But they hadn't been used in over thirty years. "I thought they were all destroyed."

"I like to keep a small stock of certain medicines that were used in an earlier time," said Damien. "Sometimes they come in handy."

● ● ●

"Wouldn't you get in trouble if certain people found out?"

Damien simply shrugged; there wasn't much that the citizens of Ragnar City could get away with. I was willing to be that Damien would get at least forty lashes, possibly dying from the shock and blood loss. "Who do you think is luckier in life, those who die quickly or those who die slowly?"

I didn't know how to answer that. Judging from the look on Damien's face, he didn't know how to answer it, either. There have been a couple of times I wished Ally would just die in her sleep to escape the constant pain she was in, but then there were other times that I had no idea what I would do if she died. She was one of the few good things in my life and I didn't want to lose her.

"I don't know."

"If you get a chance, give that to Craig or someone who can get it to him. I have a feeling the citizens are going to need a martyr before all of this is over."

I must have had a frown on my face when we went back into the bedroom. Mihkel raised his eyebrows when he looked at me. I slipped the capsule in my pocket and met his eyes. "Has the pain medicine started working yet?" I asked.

"It started working almost as soon as he injected it near the cuts."

"The beauty of Arcadian technology," Damien muttered.

Suddenly there was banging on the door. "Damien Aryen! Open the door!"

"CROSS or GUARD?" Mihkel asked.

"GUARD," said Damien. "Someone from CROSS wouldn't be acting like they wanted to break down the door. Also, CROSS would have used my title."

Mihkel and I looked at each other for a second before there was more banging on the door. "Damien Aryen, open the door!"

"Go out the back," said Damien, taking a small black box and putting it in my hand. "Take this and go."

"What is this?"

"Give it to your father," he said, picking up a syringe. "Mihkel, this will get you through the rest of the day. Its adrenaline." He injected it into Mihkel's inner forearm and tossed the syringe in the trash.

It was then we heard the door being broken down. "Go," Damien said pushing us toward the back. "They must have seen you come in."

"Does this have anything to do with what's happening to us?" Mihkel asked.

Damien didn't even act like he didn't know what we were talking about. "I'm betting your tracker was activated on its own or someone activated it for you. Now go!"

He shoved us out the back and shut the door behind us. As soon as the door was shut, we heard gunfire. I started to reach for the door when Mihkel put his hands on my face. "We have to go before they find us."

"If one of our trackers has been activated, what's the point?" I asked.

Chapter 34

Mihkel kept dragging me away until I forced him to stop. "We can't just leave him…" I said. "We can't just leave everyone."

"What can we do?" he asked. "You want to go up against GUARD with a hunting knife? I don't think Aryen would have wanted you to go on a pointless suicide mission."

I started to take out the capsule Damien had given me when Mihkel pulled me into a hug. Feeling my eyes start to water, I fought to blink so they didn't slide down my face. There was no way I was going to start crying now. "Let's get back-"

Our conversation was cut off by the sound of the clock tower. We look at each other and ran back to the square.

We were about twenty feet from the square when we stopped running. Something else was happening and it wasn't anything good. I could tell by the somber looks on the people's faces, but it was Mihkel who saw what was going on before me.

Slowly, I turned my head and my heart skipped a beat at what I saw. Craig was being dragged to the middle of the square by GUARD members. Bogdan was unraveling a whip that had a long, metal spike at the end of it. That only meant one thing; this was a death sentence being carried out without a trial. Ashtan must have given Bogdan orders to cease any activity dealing with the riot. To kill any sort of hope the citizens of this city might have in living freely, not having to worry about starving or dying because they couldn't get the medicine they needed. Rebellion was always on the minds of the citizens, but there were few people who would actually try to do anything about it. It was too great a risk to try and overthrow Ashtan. I couldn't bear to think about losing my family and being alone, or losing Sindri. Now, there were two more people to add to the list, Michael and Mihkel. I didn't want to lose them either. Mihkel had started to move through the crowd of people to get to his father. Not knowing what else to do, I followed him. Pushing our way through the crowd, we stopped when we made it to the front. Mihkel stood there as if frozen to the ground. It was just now that he seen the spike at the end of the whip. "Dad…" he whispered. I took hold of his hand and squeezed. He squeezed mine back, still lost in the sight about to unveil in front of us.

My father was the one tying Craig up by his wrists to the wooden post. We were too far away to hear anything, but we could see that Craig was saying something to him. My father took the necklace Craig always wore off his neck and slipped it into his pocket. He put his hands on Craig's face and put his forehead to his, saying something to him. He then did something that I had only seen him do for my mother. He put his left hand up, with his thumb on his palm and his index finger touching his lips. Craig took in a breath and closed his eyes.

"They can't do this," Mihkel pleaded with no one.

Having no idea what to say to him, I just kept hold of his hand, letting him know I was there beside him.

Bogdan brought his arm out and flung it forward, sending the nail directly into Craig's back. Craig's shrill scream seeped into my skin, causing the hair to rise on the back of my neck.

Mihkel must have made a move, for someone put their hand on his shoulder. "Don't make this any worse for your father than it already is." It was Michael.

"He's going to die, how worse can it get?"

"This is a relatively quick way to die. You have no idea how much Captain Bogdan loves this part of his job."

"We can't just stand here and do nothing." Mihkel looked at Michael.

"You will if you know what's best for you," said Michael. "Captain Hawthorne ran out of favors to help out Elena. He can't and won't do the same for you."

"I don't care."

"You will," I said remembering the fear running through my mind when I first realized I was missing a leg. I jumped when I felt a wet tongue on my fingers, it was Enrik. I felt myself smile as Enrik kept licking my fingers.

"Both of you listen to me, your life will only be spared once. Don't waste it," Michael said, with a sense of urgency.

"That's what happens when you have a brother in CROSS."

I raised my eyebrows to see my brother standing next to me with Willow. I let go of Mihkel's hand and hugged my brother, then Willow. They hugged me back and then Selig slipped the leash around Enrik's neck.

"The four of you, get out of here," our father said, coming up to us.

"I'm not going anywhere," snapped Mihkel.

"Do the last thing your father wishes of you," my father said taking out the necklace he took from Craig and putting it in Mihkel's hand. "Get out here before you four do something stupid."

"No."

"Your father doesn't want you to see him die."

It was then Bogdan's arm raised the whip again.

Suddenly, Mihkel was moving in front of his father. He knew he wouldn't be able to stop the pain, he was making the choice to endure it for Craig. As he got in front of his father, the spike on the whip met his collarbone.

The sound made me feel sick to my stomach. Everyone in the square knew the exact moment Mihkel's collarbone was broken, possible even shattered.

"Oh, shit…" muttered Michael.

Part III: The Snow-Covered Path

"When you play this game, you win or die. There is no middle
ground."
-Dragan Sayers

Chapter 35

The Fallen: Entry I
Winter 38th, 2466

I remember the first execution I witnessed like it was yesterday. It wasn't just because my father was the one that carried out the sentence; it was because it was the first time I witnessed actual death. That, and Dragan Sayers was beside my brother and I, telling us that if we looked away, our father would know and would consider it a sign of weakness. The look on Sayers' face was more sickening than the actual act of my father killing a man who was trying to get water for his family.

Chapter 36

Michael

Captain Sayers moved toward one of the newest members of CROSS before I could, sending Elena into my arms. As I was wrapping my Shinar limb around her, I felt her leg shaking. Captain Hawthorne was the one who pulled the spike out of Mihkel's collarbone, not caring if he was causing more damage or not. The two Captains pulled him to his feet and started to take him inside the Justice Building when Elena started to pull free from me. "I don't think so," I said.

"What?"

"We need to go."

"Where?"

"Anywhere but here."

"I have to see if he's okay."

I sighed and tightened my grip around Elena. She could struggled against me with all her might, but she wasn't used to her new leg. I had the upper hand. "You'll probably get the chance, whether you want to or not," I said to her in her ear. I started to pull her in the direction I was going. "We're going to Doc Aryen's place."

Elena stopped walking. "We can't."

"What do you mean we can't?" I asked, looking at her.

"He's dead..." she said. I heard her voice crack slightly.

"What? How?"

"GUARD."

I pulled Elena over to the side of the Justice Building and pushed her against the wall. "What do you mean he's dead? He's one of the most important people to CROSS and GUARD."

"I mean he's dead. GUARD broke down the door and he shoved Mihkel and me out the back way. Right after he closed the door, we heard gunfire."

"So, you didn't see him?"

"What does it matter?" She pushed me away. "GUARD shows up with guns, people die."

● ● ●

Our conversation stopped by Amon coming over to us. "Michael...Captain Hawthorne wants you and her in the Justice Building."

"In a minute," I said.

"He said now," Ballory said, wiping blood off his forehead.

"Okay..." I sighed and rubbed my mouth. "We'll be right there."

Ballory's eyes flicked to Elena before he walked away. I sighed again and rotated my Shinar limb. "I'm sorry I pushed you."

Elena just looked at me with blank face. "I'm fine. I just want to make sure Mihkel is okay."

"He will be physically. Mentally, I have no idea."

++++

I escorted Elena to the Justice Building, Amon waiting for us on the steps. "Your father wants you to wait in his office until he's done with the Tiitus kid," he said.

Elena opened her moth to speak but I beat her to it. "I'll take her there and wait with her."

"You're needed elsewhere, I'll wait with her," Amon said. "Captain Sayers wants to see you."

I raised my eyebrows, but nodded. "Okay, Lieutenant." I put my hand on his shoulder and walked into the Justice Building, leaving Elena with one of the few people I trusted.

Captain Sayers was waiting right inside for me. He hadn't changed out of his bloody uniform and didn't seem to care that his normally clean image was gone. "Engineer," he said. "Walk with me."

From the look on Sayers' face, I knew I didn't have a choice. "Captain, what's this all about?"

Chapter 37

Elena

"Elena," said Ballory. It was one of the few times he had ever used my first name. "This way."

"I know where my father's office is."

He smiled slightly and motioned for me to walk. Ballory walked beside me, his arm almost touching mine.

Ballory opens the door to my father's office and I walk in, Ballory following behind me. He closed the door and motioned for me to sit down. I did and looked at him. "Do you know how long it's going to be?" I asked.

Ballory leaned against the desk and crossed his arms. "You father wanted me to let you know you're leaving the city tonight."

"Wait…what?" I asked, dumbfounded.

"You, the Tiitus kid, Michael, and some other are leaving Ragnar City tonight."

"Why? What's going on?"

"I don't have time to explain everything to you. That, and your father wants to explain what's going on to you and Tiitus himself." Ballory just looked at me.

"What are they doing to Mihkel?"

"Making sure his tracker has been destroyed."

"What about mine?"

"Give me your knife," he held out his hand.

"What knife?"

"Cough it up," he stated, flexing his fingers. "Come on."

I took my knife out of my boot and placed it in his hand. "What are you going to do?"

Ballory didn't answer as he flicked opened the blade. "Hold still."

"What the hell are you doing?" I started to stand up.

Ballory pushed me back down in the seat. "Hold still, this will only sting for a bit."

I hesitated but then slipped out of my jacket. "I'm not going to get an infection from this, am I?"

"No. Relax, and stop stalling. You're going to make me nervous."

"Make you nervous? I'm the one getting stuck with a knife."

Ballory rotated the knife in his hand a couple of times and pulled the collar of my shirt down and over to expose my collarbone. "Take a deep breath."

++++

He gave me a shot after placing a bandage over the incision. "That wasn't so bad, was it?" he asked, a smirk on his face.

"Asks the man who used the knife instead of having the knife used on him," I retorted.

Ballory pointed to his collarbone. "It was done to me, except I didn't get the shot or the bandage afterwards."

"Aren't I lucky…" I slowly stood up and pulled my jacket on. "Can I see my father now?"

"I don't see why not, they should be done with Tiitus."

"He already had his collarbone opened up," I said.

"It was probably in a couple of pieces, at the very least. It would take a little white to get it out and get him cleaned him up."

We went down the hall and Ballory stopped me. "I heard about what happened to the Doc, are you holding up okay?"

"I wasn't shot, he was," I said coldly.

"I know he meant a lot to your family," he said. "He meant a lot to me, too. He meant a lot to many people."

"My sister is going to die a lot sooner than she would have if he was still alive."

Ballory held up his hand. "He knew what we were getting into when all of this started. Everyone knew what would happen eventually. Only those who were willing to see this through to the end, are here. Craig, was one of those people. Doc Aryen, was one of those people. Sacrifices had to be made and they were willing."

I didn't say anything else until we reached the medical wing. Ballory sat down on a bench in the hallway and I went inside.

• • •

The first person I saw was Sayers. He was leaning against the wall with his arms crossed and his eyes closed. When he opened his eyes, he looked tired, but relieved to see me. "Took you long enough, Lieutenant," he muttered.

"Where's my father? Where's Mihkel?"

"Through that curtain." Sayers pointed with two fingers.

I ran over to the curtain and pulled it back. I stopped when I saw Mihkel sitting up on a bed with his shirt off and his shoulder heavily bandaged. Next to him was a tray covered in bloody tools. My father was wiping blood off his hands. He looked at me and gave me a smile I hadn't seen in a long time. "Glad to see you're okay," he said.

"What's going on? Why do we need to leave?"

"I'll explain everything, I promise you that. But, we do have to leave. Now."

"What about Ally? Selig and his family? What about Mom, you, Enrik, Sindri, and his family?"

"Enrik is going, but our family and Sindri's are staying here, as am I."

I just stood there. Leaving my family was something I had never planned on doing. I wasn't about to abandon my family and friends. I wasn't ready to. "No," I said. "I'm not leaving them."

"You don't have a choice," my father snapped. "If you two stay here, you will be taken to Ashtan and put to death, or worse. Do you understand me?"

"Do I even want to know what could be worse?" Mihkel asked.

"Right now? No," Sayers said, checking his watch. "We need to go."

"Where are we supposed to be going?" I asked.

"Aion," Ballory said simply. I jumped slightly when he appeared right beside me.

I sat down next to Mihkel and looked at him. "How's your shoulder?"

"It hurts."

"Can we have a minute alone?" I looked at my father.

"One minute. Then, we start the preparations," my father said. He and Sayers left the wing. Sayers tugged on Ballory, who followed.

Mihkel cupped my cheeks in his hands. "Are you okay with leaving?" I asked, squeezing his wrists with my trembling hands.

"My family is gone. I've got nothing left here."

I sighed and closed my eyes. "I don't know if I can leave my family."

"Your father is making it sound like we don't have a choice."

"My father…" I opened my eyes, feeling the tears start to build up. "How bad do you think things are going to get?"

"I don't know," Mihkel said, looking me directly in my eyes. He leaned in and kissed me. It was a simple kiss, which I returned with the same amount of simplicity. This was enough to make me want to forget about everything, and just go back into the past. When the kiss was done, I threw my arms around his neck. Never wanting to let go.

We were interrupted by Ballory and Michael coming into the medical wing. "Elena, he needs to be taken to a cell," said Ballory.

"I thought we were leaving," Mihkel said, breaking the hug.

"Tonight," Michael said. "You're coming with me."

Mihkel and I looked at each. "Tonight," he said.

"Tonight."

"Come on," Michael said.

"Where are we going?" I asked.

Chapter 38

Michael didn't say anything until we got to my neighborhood. "You don't want to leave, do you?" he asked.

"Of course I don't," I said. "I don't want to leave my mother, Selig, or Ally. They will die if I'm gone and my father gets...punished for this."

"Don't sell your brother short. He may not be able to go from tree to tree, but the Captain taught him everything he taught you. Besides, he has a skill that CROSS finds very valuable." Michael put his hand on my shoulder. "You will see them again, this isn't permanent."

"How is it not permanent?" I shoved his hand off me. "It's not that I don't think my brother can provide for the family, it's what GUARD is going to do to them. My father can't save them, they won't have a chance." That made me think of Willow, and how she would be affected by all of this. She was considered a Hawthorne now, and that wasn't good for anyone.

Michael held up his hand. "You have no idea what your father has had to do to keep you out of Ashtan. Breaking all the rules you have broken...I don't believe in miracles, but the Captain has done a lot more for you than you realize. He's not going to be leaving us, he's going to be the one hunting us."

I stopped. My father was the best tracker I knew. I could track, but I wasn't anywhere as good as he was. I had a feeling if he had joined up with GUARD, he would be the lead tracker. "So, we're dead no matter what..."

"It's been a very long day for a lot of people. Say good bye to your family. I will do everything in my power to make sure you see them again."

That made me think of Mihkel and his father. "Craig's dead, isn't he?"

"No," said Michael. "That stunt Mihkel pulled just angered Bogdan even more. Craig won't be dead for a long time. If he's lucky, he'll be dead within a week. Bogdan's specialty is torture."

"Mihkel doesn't know, does he?"

"No, and your father doesn't want him to know. Craig doesn't want him to know, either."

* * *

"You spoke with him?"

That made Michael stop. He avoided eye contact with me and rubbed the back of his neck. "The serum I had to inject into your thigh so your body wouldn't reject the metal limb, it has two uses."

"You didn't—"

"Administered in the right amount, the serum allows the body to adapt to Shinar limbs. Anymore and it makes the person's nerves feel like they're on fire. It's used more for interrogation than it is for its intended purpose."

"What in the name of the Gods...none of this is happening. It can't be happening." I took in a deep breath, trying to keep myself from hyperventilating.

"Let's go see your family, you'll regret not saying goodbye to them."

"You're talking like you've been through this before."

Michael started walking, placing his arm around my shoulders. "You want to know where I'm from? Originally?"

"Where?"

"My mother is from Arcadia and my father is from Aion. I'm a half-breed."

"You say that like it's a good thing."

"The Aion part is," he said. I had been to Aion once in my life. The only thing I remembered was that it was covered in snow, and it wasn't Ashtan.

"That's what I thought."

++++

We stayed silent until we got to my house. Michael motioned for me to go inside. "I'm going to wait out here."

"I don't know what to say to them."

"Tell them you love them and you'll see them later, don't tell them anything else."

I nodded and went inside.

My mother was sitting at the table reading a book. She looked up at me and smiled. "Hey, sweetheart...everything okay?"

"Yeah..." I said sitting down. "Got caught up in the riot."

• • •

"When are you going to realize that you're not bulletproof?"

"I already know that," I said and stood up. "I'm going to see Ally for a minute."

I walked into the bedroom and saw Ally was fast asleep. I hesitated before sitting down on the bed. Watching her sleep, I brushed some hair out of her face. "I'll see you soon, okay?" I whispered.

Standing up, I walked out of the bedroom and saw Selig standing there in the kitchen cradling his hastily bandaged arm with Willow making tea. "What happened?" I asked, unable to stop staring.

"It's nothing," said Selig, a soft grin on his face. I noticed he had a silver wedding ring on. "It was just a very rough first day. Any reason Chief Engineer Crane is hanging around outside?"

"He's waiting for me," I said.

"Elena…" our mother said. "What have you gotten yourself into?"

"Nothing I can't handle."

Selig made a playful swing of his good arm at me and I ducked, causing us both to laugh. "Be still thy beating heart," our mother said. "My children are laughing."

"And, now we're done," Selig said.

Our mother closed her book and stood up. "I'm going to start dinner. Your father will actually be home for a family meal tonight."

Not being able to stop myself, I hugged her. "I love you," I said.

"I love you too, sweetheart. What's going on?"

I released her and smiled. "Nothing, I just don't say it enough."

The look on my mother's face said she didn't believe me, but I couldn't tell her what was going on. The less they knew, the better. I squeezed Selig's shoulder and walked out of the house.

Michael was leaning against the house with his arms crossed over his chest. "Ready?"

"They're going to figure it out eventually. Selig will be the first, being a part of CROSS."

● ● ●

195

"I wouldn't be surprised." Michael rotated his Shinar arm.

"Isn't that a bad thing?"

"Possibly, you know how it's going to happen tonight?"

"No."

Michael sighed and turned around. I turned to see Sayers and Ballory walking up to us. "Elena," Sayers said.

"What's going on, Captain?" Michael asked.

"You're dismissed, Engineer Crane," said Sayers, not looking at Michael as he said it. He kept his eyes on me. I was starting to feel uneasy from the way he was staring.

"Captain…" Michael started to protest.

"Engineer Crane, you're dismissed."

Michael looked at me briefly before he walked away. As I watched him walk away, Sayers' voice brought me back to reality. "You're under arrest," he said.

"What?" I asked, just staring at him.

"You're under arrest for a lot of rule breaking," Ballory took out restraints and motioned for me to turn around.

"Don't even think about running," said Sayers.

I slowly turned around and felt the metal go around my wrists. I couldn't tell if it was Ballory or Sayers that put his hand on my shoulder to lead me away.

Chapter 39

I was put into a holding cell that was right next to Mihkel's. He raised his head up from lying on the floor and looked at me. He didn't look surprised that I was being brought in here, so that meant he must have been told what was going to happen already.

Ballory opened the cell door and pushed me inside. Closing the door, he looked at me. "Give me your hands, I'll take the restraints off."

Taking a couple steps backwards, he unlocked the restraints. I massaged my wrists, trying to get rid of the feeling of the metal against my skin.

It wasn't until Ballory closed the door that Mihkel spoke up. "So, they arrested you too..." he said, propping his head up on his arm.

"I take it you know what's going on?" I asked, letting myself sink to the ground with my back up against the shared wall made of bars.

"They informed me," he laid his head back down on the floor and closed his eyes.

I looked at Mihkel, who still had his eyes closed. "I'm sorry about your parents."

"They weren't really my parents, were they?" he muttered.

I didn't blame him for thinking that. When I had first heard that Carter and Elise Hawthorne weren't my biological parents, I felt a sense of...anger toward them. For never telling me the truth, for keeping me in the dark about everything. "I know..."

"Know what?"

"I know my dad isn't dead," he said after five minutes of silence. "I know that what I did just angered Bogdan and it's my fault that my dad is going to be alive for at least a week or two."

Turning my head, I saw he had outstretched his hand on the floor. I adjusted myself to be lying on the floor like him and snaked my hand through the bars. When our fingertips touched, I started to relax slightly. I wasn't sure why, but in the midst of everything that was happening, the little moments that were happening between us made me feel better about. But, not

● ● ●

fooling myself, I had wished it was Sindri in the cell next to me, not Mihkel. Even with everything that has happened, he was still the boy who broke my heart. Although, whatever I was feeling when I was around him was slowly making me change my opinion of him.

++++

I shot awake with a very stiff neck. Slowly, I pulled my arm back to my side, attempting to rotate my shoulder slightly, trying to work the tightness out.

As I was just able to move my shoulder again, the door opened. I heard at least two pairs of footsteps.

"Long time no see, Elena," a recognizable voice said.

I felt my heart jump in my throat as I slowly looked up to see Crispin Frost standing there. He looked different, his long hair had been cut short and he was clean shaven. He was wearing something that resembled the CROSS uniform, but not quite. It looked like more of the uniform that the rookies wore when they were in training. "Frost?" I asked. "I thought you were—"

"All part of the plan," said Frost unlocking the door to the cell. He tossed the keys to Ballory, who unlocked the door to Mihkel's cell. "Come on." He motioned for the two of us to get up.

"It's time," said Ballory.

As Mihkel and I stood up, Ballory tossed us each a backpack. I slipped it on over my shoulders and clipped the latches together over my chest. Mihkel did the same, only his latches clipped together over his chest and abdomen. Looking up, I saw Ballory holding out two pairs of fingerless gloves. Tree jumping gloves. We both took a pair and pulled them on. It was then I suddenly remembered something. I had a black capsule in my pocket. "Can you get me to where Craig is being held?" I asked.

Mihkel, Ballory, and Frost all stared at me. "Are you aware of what you just asked?" Ballory asked with raised eyebrows.

I took the capsule out of my pocket and held it up so they could see it. "Aryen gave me this...before he died."

● ● ●

198

Frost took the capsule and looked at it. "I thought these were all destroyed."

"Aryen liked to keep a private stock of some things." Ballory took the capsule from Frost. "It's impossible to get to him, not without having to go through GUARD."

"Is there any way to get this to him?" Mihkel asked.

"No," said Ballory. "He's under strict watch of GUARD. We need to go now, we're already behind schedule."

Chapter 40

Ballory had given me my jacket back and one of my gloves to hide my Shinar arm seeing as I'm very easy to spot with metal limbs. I'm one of the few with Shinar limbs that isn't completely attached to CROSS.

Ballory led the way with me behind him, Mihkel and Frost bringing up the rear. I opened my mouth to ask where we were going, but then I realized we were going deeper into the Justice Building. "Why are we going deeper into the building?" Mihkel asked.

"There are a few more people coming with us," answered Ballory. "Two of them will already be at the meeting point when we get there. We have to...acquire the fourth person."

"Acquire?" I asked.

"We're going to break him out, like we have with the three of us," Frost said.

I stopped walking. "Drake?"

"She is smart," Ballory said, nudging me with his elbow. "We need to keep moving."

It wasn't until we reached two double doors that Ballory took out his sidearm. Frost did the same. Mihkel and I shared an uneasy look between us.

"Get by the wall," Ballory said motioning for the two of us to move. Ballory did the same. They looked at each other and threw the doors open.

Right as the door opened, we heard a screech that I had never heard before. From the expression on Mihkel's face, he hadn't heard it either. We had to cover our ears from the high pitch screech and didn't see Ballory or Frost when the noise finally died.

Slowly, we stood up and took a couple steps toward the doors. Peering inside, my heart skipped a beat at what I saw.

It was a beast of some sort, or a rather large lizard with the life slowly fading from its yellow eyes. Blood was seeping out of several gunshot wounds in its chest. The screech had been so loud that we hadn't heard the gunshots. Something told me that is what they were counting on. "I'd stay away from it if I

• • •

were you," said Ballory without looking at us. "Just because it has been shot, doesn't mean its dead."

Mihkel took a step in front of me and nudged me toward the wall. I let him, still in awe of the giant lizard that was staring at us, flicking its tongue out; smelling us. The look in its eyes showed us it wanted to rip everyone in this room apart. The blood pool was still getting bigger as we watched the dying creature. The blood wasn't red, it was black. "Don't touch the blood," Frost said, coming over to us.

Both of us jumped when he spoke. He pulled on black gloves that were similar to the ones Mihkel and I were wearing and took out a knife. He knelt down, making sure he didn't touch the blood pool, and stuck the knife into the back of the lizard's head. Its tail thrashed for a matter of seconds before it died completely. Frost took out his knife and wiped it on a piece of cloth he had taken out of his pocket.

It was then my attention was focused on something else. Ballory was helping a man walk toward us. It took me a minute before I realized it was Drake.

Drake looked like he had been used as a punching bag. His face was covered in a mix of fresh and dried blood, as was his clothing. He hung onto Ballory, seemingly unable to walk on his own. He gave me a weak smile with the eye he could see through. "Glad to see you're okay…"

"What happened to you?" Mihkel asked.

"I broke a rule," Drake said meekly.

Frost took out a piece of black cloth and tied it around Drake's bad eye. "Once we get out of the city, we may be able to heal some of your wounds. But, I don't think we'll be able to heal your eye."

"I knew what I was getting into when I agreed to this." Drake looked at the two of us with his working eye.

"Let's get moving," Ballory said. "GUARD will be back within half an hour."

It was then Frost held the knife he had used on the lizard out to me. "I need to help Ballory get Drake out of here. The three of us will feel better if one of you is armed."

"If you give him a bow and arrows, he'll be the best shot out of all of us," I said.

* * *

201

Ballory thought for a second. "The armory is on the way out of here. I'll see if there is something in there he can use."

++++

Just as we reached the armory, we heard a commotion. "Shit..." Ballory muttered under his breath. "I was hoping they wouldn't find the carcass so soon."

"It's GUARD, Bogdan is looking for any excuse to disband CROSS altogether," muttered Drake.

"He might just get his wish," Ballory said. He typed in a code on the keypad and the door opened. "Wait here." He disappeared into the armory.

Mihkel and I helped Drake lean against the wall as Frost drew his gun, turning his back to us. "Hurry up, Amon," Frost said.

Ballory came out with a black metal bow and quiver full of arrows. He gave the bow to Mihkel and strapped the quiver onto his back. Ballory then took out a syringe and injected it into Drake's neck. "Adrenaline. This should be enough to get you to the meeting point."

Almost instantly, Drake stood up and started to rotate his arms, wrists, and neck. "Thanks," he said.

"Traitors to the crown, do not move!" a man yelled.

We all turned to see Bogdan standing there with a shotgun trained on Frost's chest. There were at least six GUARD soldiers behind him. I stopped when I saw my father and General Nolan were also with them. But, I already knew it was going to be those two that were going to track us.

I noticed that Ballory had a small black device in his hand. Looking at it out of the corner of my eye, I saw it was detonator. He flicked back the cover on the switch with his finger.

"Lieutenant Amon Ballory...you're under arrest with the rest of the traitors," said Bogdan.

"Any time now, Amon..." Frost muttered.

"...Boom..." Ballory said hitting the switch.

Instantly, we were thrown from our feet, landing twenty feet behind us. Before Mihkel covered me with his body, I saw

• • •

that Frost had covered Drake and Ballory was shielding his face from the blast. I felt Mihkel tense up as the hallway fell down around us.

Chapter 41

When the dust started to settle, I slowly raised my head up. I could now see why Ballory was the head of demolitions for CROSS. He had just blown up a section of the hallway, but the rest was still standing. "That should give us enough time to get away," Ballory said, pushing himself up to his feet.

He held his hands out to Mihkel and me, and we took them. He pulled us to our feet and then helped Frost and Drake to their feet. "Everyone okay?" he asked.

"Yeah…" I said with a shaky voice, looking myself over.

"I can't believe you just blew up part of the Justice Building," said Drake. "Without much of a warning." He shot an irritated look at Ballory.

"Whatever gets us out here," Amon shot back.

"I suggest we keep moving and save the fighting till later," Drake said. He was still looking rather weak, though he was standing on his own.

Mihkel, who was pulling on a shooting glove, looked at me. "Are you okay?" he asked.

"Considering we were just in an explosion, I'm fine." I looked at the debris that separated us from GUARD, along with my father and General Nolan.

"Elena," Ballory said bringing me back to reality. "We need to go. Right now."

I felt liquid roll down the side of my face. Gingerly, I touched the spot on my head. My fingers came away with blood. Mihkel had a large gash on his shoulder, and when he turned, I saw he had one on his back as well. I opened my mouth to say something to him but Frost gave me a shove, to get me to move.

"Do you think any of them are dead?" Mihkel asked.

"We can only hope," Ballory said. He looked at me when he said it. I didn't meet his eyes. We didn't stop moving until we got to what looked like the back entrance to the Justice Building. "Once we leave, we are very much on our own until we get to where we're going. And, that's only if they're willing to help."

I wanted to ask where we were going, but I decided to keep my mouth shut. The look on Ballory and Frost's faces said that they weren't about to answer any more questions.

● ● ●

Ballory must have done more damage to the Justice Building than I had realized, for we didn't have any run-ins with GUARD or CROSS. Again, I wanted to ask about it, but Drake stopped me. "Hold all your questions until we're outside of the city," he said into my ear. The smell of blood on his breath made me sick to my stomach.

We stopped walking when we reached the wall. "Don't relax yet," Ballory said taking out another syringe from his bag. "We're just stopping so I can give Captain Fisher another adrenaline injection."

"Wasn't the first injection enough?" Mihkel asked.

It was then I realized we were going to be climbing the wall. I took off my black gloves and pulled out my tree jumping gloves. Since I had a feeling where this was going, I was going to want these on. Mihkel saw that I was putting on the gloves, so he did the same. He wasn't a natural at the tree jumping like I was, but he could keep up once he got into a pattern.

"We're going to split up for a little while," said Ballory. "Elena, Mihkel, and Frost, you will go up the wall and through the trees to the top of the water reservoir tower. Captain Fisher and I will be taking the ground."

If my father had been in the group and Ballory had said that, he would have pulled rank. Drake would have done the same thing, but I think he was too hurt and probably also exhausted to pull a power play.

"Which way are we going?" Mihkel asked.

"North," said Frost. "I'm sure you two have memorized every way to the water tower. Don't worry, I can keep up.'"

"I don't think they're worried about that," Drake said. "I think they might be worried about running into another airship. I wouldn't want to have four Shinar limbs." His eyes flicked to me when he said that.

"They would have to locate us before the airship could do anything. If Captain Fisher and I aren't there in an hour, go down into the water and follow the underwater path," Ballory said.

I knew what he was talking about, I had heard about the underwater path, but I had never gone through it. "That's usually closed off."

"It won't be tonight," Frost said, pulling on gloves. "Let's go."

++++

Frost, Mihkel, and I started climbing the wall. We made it up easily enough with me leading, Frost on my left and Mihkel on my right. At the top of the wall, I stood up and rotated my Shinar wrist. Mihkel stood next to me and sighed. "How long do you think it'll be before we'll see home again?"

I had a feeling we weren't going to see Ragnar City ever again, but I didn't want to say it out loud. "I don't know."

"As much as I hate breaking up this moment between the two of you, we need to keep moving," Frost said.

We watched as Frost threw himself to a tree and grabbed hold of a branch. "After you," Mihkel said.

I took my stance and jumped to the tree next to Frost. It was better to have one person per tree, if possible. Tree jumping was dangerous, so you had to be careful.

I grabbed the branch with my hands and was surprised I didn't feel any pain at all. "What's on your mind?" Frost called out to me from his tree.

"It didn't hurt at all when I grabbed the branch," I said, pulling myself up.

"Crane's a genius," Frost said. "I'm going to scout ahead a little bit, I want you to stay close behind me."

I watched Frost until he was out of sight and then turned my attention to Mihkel. He was currently pulling himself up onto a branch. He made his way over to me and I pulled him up onto my branch. "Where's Frost going?"

"We need to follow him."

Chapter 42

It had taken us about thirty minutes to get to the top of the tower. Frost had gotten there first and was waiting for us. Mihkel and I never stopped. Frost hadn't doubled back, so we took that as the coast was clear.

Frost took his pack off and sat down on the ground. Taking out a water skin, he took a drink and then held it out to me. I declined. "You're going to want to stay hydrated."

"Where are we going?" I asked.

"Aion, like it was said before," Frost responded.

"Aion is covered in snow year round. It's not like we're going to Solanum or Xing. Hell, even Banorae," Mihkel said.

"Your point?" Frost asked with his eyebrows raised. "Relax, do what you're told to do and you'll make it."

Mihkel didn't say anything. Frost opened up his pack and took out something wrapped in a piece of cloth. Opening it up, I saw he had several strips of dried meat. "Eat," he said.

"Aren't you just acting like a guardian to us both?" I said, taking a piece of the dried meat. Biting into it, I realized it was beef. "It's beef…"

"Thank Ballory for it," Frost said, tearing off a piece with his pointed teeth.

Mihkel took a piece and ate it rather quickly. He started to reach for another, but hesitated. "Go on," Frost said. "I brought this for you two. You need it more than I do."

I watched Mihkel eat three pieces in under five minutes. "How long has it been since you've eaten?"

"It's been over 24 hours," said Mihkel. He was like me and knew what it was like to go hungry. Being the son of a miner meant food was scarce.

++++

I must have fallen asleep again, for when I blinked a couple of times Ballory and Drake were there. Rubbing my eyes, my vision came back into focus. "How long was I asleep?" I asked.

"Not long," Frost said. "Maybe five minutes, get ready to move."

One of them held their hand out to me and I took it. He pulled me up and I saw it was Ballory. "Everyone can swim, right?" he asked.

When everyone nodded, Ballory looked a little relieved. "Frost, you're first, then Captain Fisher. Elena, Mihkel, you follow them. I'll be last, keeping an eye on the sensors," Ballory said as he injected another dose of adrenaline into Drake's neck.

"Would you stop injecting me in the neck?" he muttered rubbing the injection point. "Lieutenant."

"Fastest way to get it into the bloodstream," Ballory said. "Captain."

"Think there'll be any tree climber snakes this time?" Mihkel asked, adjusting his shooting glove, nudging me with a smile only I could see.

"Well, if there are, you'll be able to test out your new bow," I said to him.

Frost then took his pack off and dove into the reservoir, using his pack to break up the water. The rest of us just stared down at him, waiting for him to resurface.

When he shot above the water's surface, I relaxed only slightly. Frost gave us a small wave to show he was okay. "Contractors are always the crazy ones," Ballory muttered to himself, thinking that no one else heard him.

"Is that how you expect us to get down to the water?" Mihkel asked.

"If you want to," said Ballory. "Elena should be able to do it without any problem. You should be able to as well."

Mihkel just looked at me. Ballory knew something that we didn't and the feeling of being kept in the dark was getting on my nerves. "What is that supposed to mean?" I snapped at him. Drake patted me on the back and gave me the smile he had only saved for his wife. He followed Frost and dove into the water. Something told me the adrenaline was working overtime for that.

"Again, what is with the Contractors trying to kill themselves?" Ballory asked. "You two are next."

I looked at Mihkel and looked away before he could return the glance. It was then we heard the familiar sound again, an airship. "Not again..." said Mihkel.

"Time to go," Ballory said.

* * *

Mihkel dove into the reservoir without hesitation. I watched until he came above the water's surface. "Elena, you'll be fine, the snares were decommissioned a couple days ago to put new ones in," Ballory motioned with his head. "Go."

I didn't. The flashes were coming back to me, the pain was coming back, and I wasn't prepared for it. "How do you know the new ones haven't been put in?"

"I was told to rig something with your brother to have exploding snares." The next thing I knew, I was falling.

Ballory had pushed me and I was furious with him. Even though I knew that this was what it was going to come to. He was right beside me, a calm look in his eyes. For some reason, this was calming me.

We hit the water and I felt my feet touch the bottom of the reservoir. I pushed off the ground and felt my lungs burn as I lunged for the surface.

I gasped for air once I hit the surface. I felt someone grab the back of my jacket collar and pulled me up onto the crumbling tower in the middle of the reservoir. It was Frost. "You alright?" he asked.

I managed to nod when I learned how to breathe again. We stayed still. Mihkel, Drake, and Ballory were still in the water as the airship passed over. When it passed, Mihkel and I shot a look at Ballory. "How did they not see us?" he asked.

Ballory climbed up onto the metal island and peeled his jacket off. On his inner right forearm, I saw a raised red bump. "This little number throws off the trackers. We thought just about everything through."

"What didn't you think through?" I asked, helping Mihkel up onto the crumbling tower.

"I didn't think that you two would freeze about doing something to save yourselves," Ballory sighed. "Frost, do you want to lead or should I?"

"I think you should," Frost said, sneaking a look at me. I had a feeling I was going to have a bodyguard or a babysitter with me for the rest of the time, all because I froze at the top of the tower.

Ballory gave Drake another shot of adrenaline. Something told me that whiter he was getting shot up with

* * *

wasn't just adrenaline. It usually lasted longer than this. At least, the stuff created in the military labs should be lasting longer than this. I didn't get a chance to ask and I had a feeling they weren't going to tell me even if I did.

Ballory led the way through the underwater tunnel. Then it was me, Frost, Mihkel, and Drake was last. It was relatively light in the tunnel, which was surprising. I thought back to when Selig and I were around ten and our father taught us about various plant life. I was betting it was the lichen I couldn't remember the name of; it gave off a glow as a natural flashlight. This was probably one of the main reasons we were going this route. We had the way lit for us.

The swimming was easy with the current in our favor. The only problem was I had to go up for air quicker than Frost or anyone else did. So, when Ballory stopped for a rest, I had the nagging feeling that he stopped because of me. I hated being the weakest one in the group. But, then, I was the only female. Ballory, Frost, Drake are or were part of CROSS, so they had to be in top physical shape. Mihkel and I were in decent shape, but him being male meant he was automatically stronger than me.

Frost got out of the water first and held his hand out to me. I wanted to ignore it, but I was getting tired. He easily pulled me out of the water and took something out of his pack at the same time. I saw it was a waterproof flare. He lit it and set it on the cold stone in the middle of the group. "Hold your hands near the flame to keep them warm. Can't have your muscles cramping up in the middle of the escape."

Mihkel and I did as we were told. We looked at each other briefly until we heard a sharp coughing. I turned to see Drake was doubled over on all fours. He wasn't coughing, he was vomiting.

Chapter 43

I started to stand up and go over to Drake when Frost put his hand on my shoulder. "There isn't going to be anything you can do."

"What's happening?" Mihkel asked.

"A bad reaction to the adrenaline," said Frost. "Best to just stay out of the way."

We watched as Frost maneuvered his way over to Drake, who looked to be in twice amount of pain as he was in just thirty seconds ago. I could only stare as I saw him collapse on his side with Ballory frantically tossing a med kit to Frost. "What do you think it is?" Ballory asked.

"Allergic reaction," said Frost, taking out an empty syringe and a vial of clear medicine. He filled it up all the way and pushed the air out. "Turn him on his back. Mihkel, bring the flare over. I need to be able to see exactly what I'm doing."

Mihkel hesitated before he picked up the flare. "Mihkel, now!" Ballory yelled.

He snatched up the flare and brought it over to the other two. "Keep it steady by his chest," Frost said, taking out a knife and tearing open Drake's shirt.

I watched Frost's steady hand, even though I knew he had to be freezing like the rest of us. "Okay, Captain, this is going to hurt, but it's going to help you breathe."

"He's running out of time, Crispin," Ballory said.

"I'm not Doc Aryen. This isn't second nature to me," Frost snapped at him. He thought for a second and then looked at me. "Elena…do you know exactly what your ability is?"

I just stared at him. That was the last thing I thought he was going to ask me. "I'm not sure."

"Think," said Ballory. "What did Fisher tell you?"

Blinking a couple of times, a memory flash came to me. But, it wasn't when Drake was talking to me. It was before I lost my arm and leg. "I think I can see things and places in my head before my eyes do."

"S-Sensory Fib-Fibers…" Drake whispered.

Ballory leaned over, putting his ear to Drake's mouth. "Sensory Fiberfs?" he asked, looking at Drake. "Captain, is that what you said?" All Drake managed to do was nod.

"What are those?" I asked.

"Those are what are allowing you to see what you would normally can't," said Frost. "I need your help."

"Help with what?" Mihkel asked, looking at me. Both of us were so stressed we couldn't see the obvious.

"I don't have the tools that I need to do this without hesitating." Frost placed two fingers under my chin and forced me to look at him. "I need you to guide me to where the block is. If I hesitate and make a mistake, he will bleed out into his lungs and die."

"I can't use this ability on command," I said. "I don't know how."

"Elena, focus. Look at me," Frost said. "I could do this blind, but we would have to stop every twenty minutes at the most to make sure he's able to breathe. He won't be able to walk on his own."

"Frost, make a decision! We're going to lose him!" Ballory yelled.

"Elena!" Mihkel yelled.

Ballory suddenly whipped out his gun and put the barrel to my temple. "Make it work," he said through gritted teeth.

"Lieutenant, what the hell are you doing? There has to be another way!" Mihkel yelled, getting ready to throw the flare at Ballory.

Ballory pulled the hammer back. "You let him die because you're scared and I will put you down right here. I don't care who you are to this ill-fated cause."

I closed my eyes, knowing I didn't know how to use my ability on command. I was going to die.

All of a sudden, I was seeing inside of Drake's body. I scanned through his body and stopped at his lungs. It was at the base of his left lung, a large clot that was getting bigger by the second. "It's at the base of his left lung," I held my thumb and index finger about two centimeters apart. "It's about this big, but it's getting bigger by the second." I tentatively put two fingers on

Drake's chest where the clot was. At that time, Drake started seizing.

Frost raised the needle up to his shoulder and jabbed it into Drake's chest. Drake's whole body tensed up as Frost injected the medicine into him. "Again," Frost said.

I put my fingers in the same spot and I saw the clot was smaller. "It's smaller, but not gone."

Ballory started to fill up the syringe again when Drake vomited blood. "In the name of the Gods…" Frost said. "Turn him on his side and keep him still."

"Venom?" Ballory asked.

"That would be my guess."

Mihkel and Ballory turned Drake on his side and kept him still. As Frost filled up the syringe again, he injected it into the same spot. As soon as the liquid went into his lung, he stopped seizing and relaxed.

Chapter 44

I shot awake, gasping for air and finding that someone had put a coat over me. Sitting up, I saw Frost was checking on Drake. When he finished, he came over and sat down next to me. "Drake is too weak to move on with us."

"We're not leaving him to die," I said.

"That's not what I'm getting at, Elena," Frost said, holding up his hand. "What I'm saying is, we have to split the group up."

"So, what? Mihkel and I go on to Aion without you three?"

"You, Mihkel, and Ballory will go onto Aion. Drake and I will stay here," Frost turned his head and looked at Drake. "You'll have to send someone back for us with better medical supplies."

"What happens if GUARD catches up?" I looked at him. "If you can't move him…its suicide for you both." I hadn't known Frost long, but I did know that he wouldn't leave Drake to save himself.

"That is where I come in," Ballory said, coming over to us. "I'll do what I did in the Justice Building."

"You're going to blow the entrance of this water path?" I just stared at him. "That will block the water that goes to Xing and Aion; it would block the water that goes into Banorae. Aion and Xing would take it as an act of war from Arcadia or even Banorae."

"Is that a bad thing?" Ballory asked. "Aion carries almost as much military power as Arcadia does. Maybe even more if Banorae gets on the same side. If Xing were to back Aion, Arcadia wouldn't have a chance."

"Amon, stop," Frost said. "One man isn't going to start and finish a war."

Ballory sighed, looking at Frost and then me. "If we're splitting up, then we need to decide right now."

"I don't think we should," I said. "If he doesn't die from this illness, he'll die of hyperthermia. So will you." My Shinar leg was getting stiff from the cold temperatures.

Frost sighed and rubbed the back of his neck. "Is there any way to not obstruct the waterway?"

"If you want to be found. You know if has to be done or you'll be sitting ducks."

"You know if Xing were to ever find out it was CROSS that had something to do with the tunnel collapse, all of us will be hunted down like stray dogs," Frost said.

"We're not part of CROSS. Not anymore." Ballory looked at the two of us. "I need a decision, now."

Frost looked at Drake and Mihkel before he looked at us again. "May the Gods see us swiftly into chaos…"

"I'll take that as a yes," Ballory said, turning to me. "Go get him up and get ready to go."

"We're really going to leave them behind?"

"We're coming back for them," said Ballory. "Go get him up and get ready to move."

I opened my mouth to argue some more, but the look in Ballory's eyes made me hesitate. I had seen a similar look in my father's eyes before, but seeing it on Ballory made me uneasy.

I walked over to where Mihkel was sleeping and knelt down. Gently, I put my hand on his shoulder and shook him slightly. "We need to keep moving," I said when he stirred.

Mihkel rolled over and blinked a couple of times. Slowly, he raised his head and looked around as if he had forgotten where we were. "Is it a bad thing to hope that this was all a nightmare?" he asked, rubbing his eyes.

"You wouldn't be human if you didn't wish it," Ballory said.

"Are we human?" I asked.

"That's a story for another time," Frost said, coming over to check on Drake. He put two fingers on his neck. "His pulse is still weak. Damn it!"

"What's going on?" Mihkel asked.

"I'm betting this whole…plan Carter Hawthorne conceived wasn't as secret as he originally thought. I'm betting the adrenaline was altered. You three need to get going now, if he's going to survive this at all."

"He's dying?" I asked, my heart sinking.

"When you play this game…you win or die. There is no middle ground," Drake whispered.

"In a sense," said Ballory. "Let's go, we have a long way before we reach Aion."

I didn't want to leave Drake and Frost alone in here, but I knew we didn't have a choice. As Mihkel and I were pulling on our packs, we heard something. "Get down!" Ballory hissed urgently, taking out his sidearm.

Frost did the same and knelt down beside Drake. Ballory looked at the two of us and put a finger to his lips. Mihkel had taken out his bow and was readying an arrow. I took out my knife and flicked the blade open.

As the footsteps came closer, I could hear that there were only two people. I saw that Ballory noticed it as well. He held up two fingers and turned the safety off on his gun. He had started to move when he suddenly stopped. Motioning to me, he held his hand out. Handing him my knife, he gingerly put the gun in my hand.

We watched as Ballory disappeared. There was a brief amount of shuffling, then something that sounded like meat being split with a knife. I heard a gagging sound and then…nothing. I held my breath for a second when I felt someone's hand on my shoulder. I didn't have to look to know it was Mihkel.

Chapter 46

Michael

Create. Utter. Total. Chaos. That is what had to be done…and there was only one way I knew that it could be done. Balthar Fairbain. I was one of the three people that knew his true name. I was also one of the three who knew he was alive and rotting in a stone pit, instead of a dirt hole in the ground. There was only one problem…getting near that stone pit meant an automatic treason sentence. The poor or idiotic soul didn't even get last rites. Not that the ceremony existed anymore.

This was going to be the only time I was glad I had been reinstated into CROSS. It would have been impossible to do this on my own. Although, it would have helped if I didn't look like a punching bag. Though, it shouldn't raise suspicion seeing as there wasn't a CROSS member who hadn't been bloodied in the miners' revolt.

"Where do you think you're going?" a GUARD member said, pushing me away with his hand. "This area is restricted."

"I'm under orders to sweep this area for anything pertaining to my specialty," I said, having to fight the urge to bash his face in with my Shinar hand.

"What is your specialty?" the soldier asked.

"He's the best engineer the world has to offer," a familiar voice said.

We both turned to see Captain Sayers walking toward us. "We're both cleared to go through."

"I'll have to get authorization—" the soldier started to say.

"Captain Bogdan authorized us," Sayers snapped. "I don't know about you, but I wouldn't want to be the person who is openly questioning Captain Bogdan right now."

The two GUARD members looked at each other and then moved out of our way. I had to hide the look of surprise on my face until we were alone. I knew that Captain Sayers was one of the other two men that knew Fairbain was alive, but I didn't know who the third man was. I remembered Sayers told me it would be safer that way. "Captain Bogdan?" I hissed at him. "Bogdan is the third man who knows?"

"There is a whole lot of evil in the world. Sometimes the best choice is one of the worst choices. It was either Bogdan knowing about it or Cyrille Dorian. Bogdan may be ruthless, but Dorain would try to clone the son of a bitch before he was done." Sayers pushed me against the wall and had his hand on my throat. "If you're having second thoughts, then I will do this on my own."

"I'm not," I said.

"Good. We're going to need your Shinar limb to help control this guy. Something tells me he won't be too thrilled to see us again."

++++

The stone pit was isolated and barren of any guards. There was only one way out of the pit and Fairbain had his way cut off.

Sayers looked at me when we got to the door, the only thing separating us from one of the most dangerous men around. "This guy isn't a Contractor, is he?" he asked.

"You never read his file, did you?"

"We were in the middle of a rebellion with the Isolated Province. I was a little busy."

"No, he's not a Contractor. But, he's still dangerous. He has a hobby of killing officers on either side of the war. It doesn't matter to him."

"Something tells me I'm on the top of his list to kill."

"The three of us are. I'll go down and try to subdue him."

"Try? You're not giving me a whole lot of confidence here."

"You want to go down in there with a man who has been down there for ten years? Be my guest."

Sayers hesitated, but then took out a curved blade that was made to be worn like brass knuckles. "Use it if you need to, but try not to kill him."

Hesitating for a second, I took the blade and fitted it over my flesh hand. I then opened the door and walked in. At this moment, I wish I was on my way to Aion and not about to face one of the biggest fears someone in CROSS could have.

● ● ●

Adjusting the blade around my fingers, I took in a breath and closed the door behind me. "Crane, maybe it's a good thing you lost everything..." I muttered to myself.

"You haven't lost everything, you're still alive..." an all too familiar voice said.

"Why do I get the feeling that both Gods Valefor and Fenrir are laughing at me right now?"

"Maybe because you're about to ask me a favor, and if I refuse, then everything goes to hell?" Fairbain asked, making the hair on the back of my neck stand on end.

"Will you behave yourself for five minutes?" I asked, breaking a light stick and sticking it in my pocket. "I'd like to talk to you face-to-face about this favor."

"I'll give you three minutes."

"Is there somewhere you have to be?"

"You now have two."

The pit wasn't deep enough that if I jumped I would break my legs, but it was deep enough I would have a rather hard time getting out. I jumped down into the pit.

My landing sent shockwaves through my legs and I had to lean against the wall. "Well, well, well...look what the cat dragged in," Fairbain said, looking worse for wear.

"Balthar, just listen to me, you do what is asked of you and you can live out the rest of your life where there is sunlight," I said, holding up my hand with the blade on it.

"You say that like it's a good thing. I'm blind in any form of light. I've been in this cell for ten years. You think you're doing me a favor by offering me sunlight? You don't have the authority to give me what I want. Neither does Captain Dragan Sayers. There is only one man who can give me what I want."

"We may be talking about the same man then," I said, wishing this pit was a little bigger so I could have a little more space between us.

"You've got less than one minute, state your business before I grow bored..." Fairbain said through clenched teeth. He held up his hands showing the metal brace on his wrists, the thing keeping him from escaping.

"What would you say to killing the most powerful man alive?"

* * *

"You're going to have to be more specific."

"Create utter total chaos. There is only one way to do that," I said, fighting not to stab him in the gut. "You're always wanted to go down in history. I have a way you can do that."

"Speak in a riddle one more time, that little knife and metal arm won't save you."

"I am asking you to take part in killing the King."

Chapter 47

Fairbain just stared at me, his hands held up in the air close to my neck. He may have had the thought to strangle me, but from the look on his face he wasn't thinking anything at the moment. "Did I hear you right? Engineer Michael Crane wants the person he said he would kill with his bare hands if I took in someone else's air… to kill the King?" He put his hands down and leaned against the wall. "Michael Crane…" He started laughing.

"Come on, Fairbain. Somewhere in that twisted mind of yours you know you have always dreamed of doing something like this. I'm giving you that chance. Sayers is giving you that chance."

"What about the third man?"

"He knows as well, this wouldn't be able to happen if he didn't know about it."

"So, all three of you are asking me for a favor? I never thought this would ever happen." Fairbain raised his hands again and I saw just how ragged and rotted his skin was where the restraints were. "How about you do me a favor and remove these restraints?"

"Those will stay on until it's decided whether or not you're going to behave."

"Alright, I'm in."

++++

Fairbain was on his third plate of food while I warily wrapped his wrists. "Take it easy, you don't want to break his wrists," Sayers said, leaning against the wall with his arms crossed.

"So, what's this plan of yours for us to commit high treason against the crown?" Fairbain asked, finishing his third plate.

I didn't say anything as I finished wrapping up his wrists. "You're the most dangerous man alive. I think you can handle it," Sayers said.

"Are you sure about that? I'm just a man. I'm not one with abilities as some of the others I used to fight alongside," Fairbain started to stand up. Sayers put his hand on my sidearm and I gripped the blade in my hand. "Captain Sayers…you should know this as well as I do. Being a Reaper and all…" He started to reach for the cup of water.

Sayers beat him to it and held it up in front of him. "We may have carried the same title, but that doesn't mean we are anything alike." He spat in the cup and shoved it into the Fairbain's hands before walking out of the room, slamming the door behind him.

"I think I hurt his feelings."

I sighed heavily and pushed Fairbain back into his chair. "Don't do anything stupid."

I walked out of the office and saw that Sayers hadn't gone very far. "Captain!" I called out as I ran up to him. "What was that about?"

"This was an idiotic idea. A man who should have been executed ten years ago has the fate of this plan and this world in his hands? You know where the term Reaper came from? It came from him."

"What do you propose we do with him then?" I stopped as two CROSS soldiers walked by us. Sayers waved off their salutes. "We can't just kill him now."

"Why do you say that?" he asked.

"We kill him now and all eyes are on us, not just those who wish to see us in the ground. Fairbain won't go quietly, no matter how we take him out."

"Right now, I don't care. Seeing him alive and gaining his strength…things are only going to end badly for all involved. It doesn't matter what badge or rank we carry."

"Should I just make my escape now or is something going to happen?" Fairbain asked.

Sayers spat on the floor. "Get him ready to travel as a CROSS soldier and may the Gods give us pity when we need it."

++++

I had shaved off most of Fairbain's hair, leaving only a thin layer on his head. I only thinned out his beard since we didn't have the time to make him look completely presentable.

* * *

"Never thought I would be in a CROSS uniform again," Fairbain said, taking the gloves I held out to him.

"It'll be easier to get you into Arcadia and into the Royal Capitol with a CROSS uniform on, rather than a GUARD. That, and Captain Bogdan will not allow you to touch a GUARD uniform."

"I don't suppose I could trouble you to stop by a favorite brothel? Ten years is a long time..."

"This isn't a vacation for you," a dark voice said. "You are only out for one purpose."

Both of us turned to see Captain Bogdan walking over to us. He was dressed in his flashy GUARD dress uniform. Keeping with the image portrayed, his sunglasses were still on— as they always were.

"Killing the King..." Fairbain looked at Bogdan with raised eyebrows. "I understand where Crane here comes from and even Sayers, but why you? What do you get out of this?"

I had been thinking the same thing, Bogdan had always been loyal to the King. Why now?

"Captain...are you coming with us?"

"Yes," Bogdan said simply. "Keep in mind, Engineer Crane...if this goes south, everyone will be on their own. It doesn't matter whose blood flows through your veins."

"Just so we're clear, if everything goes to hell you will throw me under an airship to save yourself?"

"I will pull the trigger myself, just so we're clear."

Chapter 48

We had gotten on the bullet train easily enough, Captain Bogdan made sure of that. Captain Sayers wanted to restrain Fairbain, but it would have brought on too much suspicion. People had forgotten Fairbain's face, but it wasn't a permanent loss.

Captain Bogdan had gotten a private GUARD car for us so we wouldn't be disturbed for the three hour ride. I took the opportunity to change the bandages on his wrists. "How is it your wrists aren't completely rotted through?" I asked.

"Wasn't my idea," said Bogdan. "Sayers thought of it, I just wanted to put a bullet in his head."

"I thought it was the other way around..." Fairbain said, fighting not to show his anger. I wasn't using my good bedside manner with him. Frankly, I didn't think he deserved it at the moment.

"Who knew you would spend your one humanitarian choice on a mass murderer?" I asked with raised eyebrows.

"I chose you once, didn't I?" Sayers snapped. The anger in his eyes was bold, and he didn't make any effort to hide it. Clearly he was against this whole idea. Or at least, against the idea of using Fairbain.

"That's enough," said Bogdan. "Let's just get this done."

++++

I shot awake, grabbing someone's wrist when I felt their hand on my shoulder. It was Captain Sayers. "We're here," he said, keeping his contact short.

Sitting up, I saw that Fairbain had already gotten his shackles removed again and was looking at me with a face I hoped to never see again. "How long was I asleep?"

"About two thirds of the trip," said Bogdan. "Let's go, we're late."

"I didn't realize we had an appointment to keep," said Fairbain.

"Keep it up and I will gut you right now," Sayers shot at him.

"Knock it off, all of you," Bogdan said with a sigh.

• • •

The Royal Capitol Ashtan was still as vibrant as I remembered it. Most of the citizens living in the Capitol either had no idea or didn't care about the state of the rest of the world was in. As long as it didn't affect them, they didn't care. I used to have the same mentality growing up under my mother's roof. "Something on your mind, Chief Engineer?" Bogdan asked as we were walking the streets surrounded by the brightly colored buildings. While he had no problem getting through the crowds of endless people, I had a rather difficult time. I had to keep Fairbain in front of me, and no matter what he said, he had been in a hole for ten years. He was going to be out of place for a long time.

"I haven't been back here since…" I thought for a moment. "Since my mother abandoned me."

"We all have issues here," Bogdan muttered.

I raised my eyebrows and stopped walking. I've known Bogdan since I was young, but I've never heard him talk like this. "Keep it up, Chief," Sayers said, nudging me with his elbow as he kept a steady watch on Fairbain's every step.

The uneasy feeling I had was forming a pit in my stomach with every step that got us closer to the citadel of the Royal Family Kahler.

++++

By the time we had gotten to the middle of the city, where the citadel was, the sun was setting. We weren't going to see the King tonight. We were going to have to wait until morning. Sayers rubbed his mouth and looked around the area. "There's a tavern that caters to CROSS only."

"They won't ask questions?" Bogdan asked.

"No," said Sayers. "But I would get rid of the GUARD insignia or they won't allow you in."

"How is that even possible?" Fairbain asked.

"He called it a tavern," I said. "It'll be run down and somewhere GUARD wouldn't be caught dead in."

"You say that like it's a bad thing," Bogdan said.

The Resting Glass used to be a safe haven for those of us that were cursed to the CROSS emblem, especially when we were trapped in Ashtan. Sayers and Bogdan went to Bogdan's place so he could change. I was stuck with Fairbain. "How much do you want to bet Ostro remembers me?" Fairbain asked, looking at me.

"Since you're the one who blinded his daughter and robbed him of his right hand…I'm betting I'll have to…use my ability."

"The great Chief Engineer Michael Crane is willing to use alchemy for my sake?" Fairbain put his hand over his heart. "I'm speechless."

"Then how about you shut up?"

Pushing the door open, the crowd was pretty thin in the tavern. "Why do I get the feeling we're not supposed to be in here right now?" I asked no one in particular.

The old man himself was currently wiping down a glass, which probably hadn't been truly clean since he bought it. He did a double take of me and set the glass down. "Michael…I didn't think I'd ever see you here again. Not that I didn't wish to ever see you again."

"I come in peace, Ostro," I said, holding up my hands. "Just need a place to crash for the night, then we're gone."

"The last time you needed a place to crash my daughter ran off with—we're?" Ostro asked with a raised eyebrow.

"There are four of us all together," I said.

The old man sighed and stared at Fairbain. "Any trouble from him and you're both dead."

"Don't worry. There are three other men that want me dead before you. I don't think you'll get to do the actual killing of me," Fairbain said. "Besides, I think your daughter couldn't wait to get away from you."

"I will rip your tongue out of your head if you don't shut up," I said.

Ostro took out a shotgun from under the bar and cocked it. I didn't even want to ask what he had to do to get that seeing as guns have been outlawed to the public for over seventy years.

"Ostro…use your words," I said.

"There will be no more bloodshed in my place of business." He pointed the barrel at both of us.

"You may want to hear what we have to say before you pull that trigger," Sayers said, suddenly coming up beside me. "Ostro, just having that gun in your possession is an automatic twenty lashes."

"We're not in Blackwater," Ostro spat.

"I could blow his head off right now," said Bogdan, putting his handgun to the back of Ostro's head. I already knew how this was going to end.

"Bogdan don't—" Sayers started to say, holding up his hand. The anger had disappeared from his eyes and was replaced with desperation.

The gun went off, sending me to slam my hands against the ground. The floorboards shot up, catching most of the pellets from the shell. "Bogdan, I will gun you down if you don't put the gun away!" Sayers yelled when he looked up from diving to the ground. "Everyone okay?"

"Yeah..." I said. "Fairbain?" I looked around when I didn't get a response. He was lying on the ground clutching at his throat, gagging on blood.

"In the eyes of the Gods..." Sayers muttered, slowly standing up. "I will kill you if this plan happens."

I went to Fairbain and forced his hands away. He had been struck with a massive splinter from the floor. "I need towels," I said.

"We need to get out of here," said Bogdan. "That gunshot is going to bring in the wrong company."

"Whose fault is that?" I snapped. "Ostro! Towels!"

When Ostro didn't move fast enough, Sayers grabbed them from under the bar and tossed them to me. Putting one of the towels against Fainbain's neck, I looked at him. "Balthar, look at me...I will keep you alive, but you have to trust me. This will hurt."

"It's too late for him," Bogdan said.

"Says the man who got him shot," muttered Sayers.

"How about both of you stop showing your love for each other and help me out here? Captain, how about you keep GUARD from coming in here? Sayers, keep him steady or this won't work."

"It's too late," said Bogdan. "They're already here."

● ● ●

"You better hope the General isn't here," I said and then thought for a moment. "Ostro, do you still have the underground passage?"

"You're not pulling me into whatever it is you have planned."

"You were pulled into it as soon as you pulled that shotgun out from under the bar," I said through clenched teeth. "Dragan, get him up and into the underground passage, keep his neck steady."

"What are you going to do?" Sayers asked, hoisting a weak Fairbain up.

"I'm going to stop this before it begins," I slammed my hands against the floor, putting it back the way it was. Being an alchemist since I was created, I still didn't know where my ability actually came from. It was never explained to me, it wasn't explained to any of us.

"To those who dream…" said Sayers.

"To those who dream." I hadn't heard that in years.

Chapter 49

Elena

We had been walking through the tunnels for around an hour when we stopped for a short break. Ballory set Drake down with his back against the rock wall. He started to rotate his arm, working out the stiffness from carrying Drake. "Damn it. This is going to take its toll if we keep going like this."

"How else can we move him? Can't stay in one place too long," said Frost, kneeling down beside Drake.

"We're not leaving him here." I shot a look at Ballory.

Ballory just looked at me. "No one said that," he said. He sighed and knelt down, looking Drake in the eyes. "At least we haven't said it before now."

"I always knew you wanted to see my die..." Drake whispered with a weak smile.

"You were never one for my lifestyle..." Frost said.

"No one is going to die," Mihkel said suddenly.

I opened my mouth to say something, but Mihkel put his hand on my arm. He just shook his head slightly. The look in his eyes told me that we were going to have to leave Drake behind, but not permanently. "Think you could handle hanging out in a tree?" Ballory asked.

"I'm not the biggest fan of heights," said Drake. He looked like his eyelids were getting rather heavy.

"We need to get him out of the tunnel," said Ballory. He looked at Frost and held out his hand. "Give me another syringe of the adrenaline."

"That will kill him," I said.

"No, it won't. But, he will have to deal with dangerous side effects," Frost said.

"We don't have a choice, do we?" Mihkel asked. "We're getting to the part of the tunnel where we will have to go into the water. He won't be able to swim without the adrenaline."

"If we have to leave him behind, why can't we just leave him in the tunnel?" Mihkel asked. At this point, I knew exactly who had the medical knowledge and who didn't. Frost knew the most, but I was willing to bet Ballory was like Mihkel and I in not knowing much. Although I knew more than he did, something told me he didn't deal with someone infected with Stigma on an everyday personal basis.

"It's too cold to keep him here," I said. "What about getting him up a tree?"

I had spent many hours hiding in trees as part of the training my father had put me through. I knew exactly which trees were dense enough that Drake would be safe in, at least from airships. But, my father was tracking us and he had to get some results or they would suspect something.

"Then, it's back to the original plan," said Ballory. "We split up."

"Okay…" Frost said, wringing his hands together. "You three will go on ahead, Fisher and I will hang out in a tree."

There had been a question nagging at me in the back of my mind for some time now. I couldn't ignore it any longer. "Where is Michael?"

Frost, Ballory, and even Drake just looked at each other. "Why do you insist on keeping things from us?" Mihkel asked. I could hear the tension in his voice.

"They need to know. After all, their faces will be plastered all over it," Drake said, sounding very out of breath.

Ballory looked like he was about to respond when the ground suddenly started to vibrate. "Terrific…" Frost muttered.

"What's going on?" I asked.

"They're flooding the tunnels," said Mihkel.

Frost pulled part of Drake's shirt down at the collar. "This is going to hurt."

"You're going to kill him!" I shouted.

"The tunnel is getting flooded, we don't have time! There is no point to any of this if Fisher dies in the damn tunnel. There is a very slim chance that any of this will work if we leave him behind." He jammed the needle into Drake's heart.

Mihkel and I looked at each other before I spoke again. "When will all of you stop hiding things from us?"

"As much as I would love to continue this conversation…" Ballory motioned to the tunnel. "We need to move, now!"

• • •

I turned in time to see the water level starting to rise. Drake suddenly got to his feet and looked like he did when I saw him a few months ago.

We started running. Ballory was first and then Mihkel, helping me keep up by holding onto my hand. Frost and Drake were right behind us, but we weren't going fast enough. The water was reaching our heels faster than we could move.

"The water!" Frost yelled. "Dive into the water!"

Without hesitation, we all dove into the water, packs and all. I had to fight not to swim up to the water's surface. As the force of the water spun us around, the more I wanted to get up to the surface.

Under the water, I saw I wasn't the only one struggling to stay under. Mihkel wasn't doing so well, but Ballory, Frost, and Drake seemed to be almost at ease.

As we were being tossed through the water, I felt the force of the water start to weaken. As my vision was getting clearer and clearer under the water, I saw Ballory motioning for me to go to the surface.

I shot above the water's edge and I tried to take in a breath of air, but I hit my head on the top of the tunnel. Clutching my head, I felt as if someone was in front of me, it was Ballory. "Take a breath and start swimming. The tunnel will be completely flooded in less than two minutes. Don't worry, the current is fast enough you won't drown, if you don't panic."

"That's easy for you to say," I said. I felt at ease in the trees, not the water.

"Take a breath, Elena, and start swimming. If there is an air pocket, I'll direct you to it," he said as he put his hand on top of my head and pushed me under the water.

Ballory was right; the current was strong enough that we would make it through with one breath, as long as we didn't panic.

I kept my eyes on Ballory and Mihkel as they were leading the way, even though it was rather difficult. I hadn't spent a lot of time swimming, so I had to really focus. Which, in turn, was making me use up my air quicker. I about jumped out of my skin when I felt a hand clasp around my shoulder. They were pulling me up to the top of the tunnel.

● ● ●

While I was being pulled out of the water, I saw that it was Ballory. Then, I saw the air pocket. Slowly, I took in air when my face went above the water. Frost was also taking a breath and so was Mihkel. When Frost went back under, Drake took his turn.

Drake and I were about to go back under when the light the lichen was giving off suddenly died. "What's happening?" I asked.

"Whatever it is, it's not good," Drake said. "Something is coming. Whatever it is, it's scaring the lichen."

I wanted to ask what could scare plant life, but I didn't get the chance. Massive vibrations suddenly shot through the water. "Oh, yeah, this just keeps getting better and better..." Drake said.

"What was that?" I suddenly felt very heavy in the water. "Drake, what was that?"

"I suggest you keep going," said Ballory coming to the surface. "The others have already gone ahead."

As I was about to take it another breath, another massive vibration shot through the water. Ballory looked at me. "Go..." he whispered. "Go." We started swimming.

The current was getting stronger as we swam, but we were still far enough behind the others that we weren't catching up to them. I concentrated on holding my breath since I didn't know if the tunnel had been completely flooded or not. I wasn't about to go to the surface and find out.

Suddenly the current was too strong and we were being tossed around the water like rag dolls. Then, we were falling.

Chapter 50

The waterfall meant we had reached the end of the underwater tunnel in Blackwater. We were in Aion's water territory now, but I didn't know how much longer before we got to the actual reservoir.

Landing in the water, I was almost able to touch the bottom before the water slowed my descent. Swimming up to the surface, there was an outstretched hand. I grabbed it to see it was Mihkel. He pulled me easily out of the water and onto lichen covered rocks. The lichen was brighter in this part of the tunnel than it was in Blackwater. It took a couple minutes for my eyes to adjust.

When I could see clearly, I sat down on the rock next to Mihkel and sighed heavily. He looked just as exhausted as I was. "Where are we?" he asked

"We're about halfway to Aion. We're in their water supply now," Ballory said. Opening up his pack, he took out a package and tossed it to Mihkel. "You two, eat that. Get some energy back."

I didn't wait for Mihkel to open the package; I had more on my mind than food. I slowly stood up, hoping I wasn't going to get dizzy from being thrown around like I weighed nothing just a few minutes ago. "What was that in the water? What made those shockwaves?"

Ballory and Frost look at each other while Frost was tending to Drake. "It's better to wait till we get past the Aion walls than spill secrets now," said Frost.

"No!" I said sharply. "Stop hiding things from us, what was in that water? Who has a grip so tight over my dad that he is the one tracking us?"

Frost sighed and rubbed the back of his neck. "Eat your share of that food, get some rest, and we'll talk later."

"You sure about that?" Ballory asked.

"Something tells me they'll find out either way, with or without us telling them." Frost walked over to us and sat down. "We've got a long way to go before we get to Aion."

· · ·

Mihkel stood up. "How about you tell us now? I've lost everything for whatever this…cause is. I don't even know if I believe in it or not."

Suddenly, Ballory charged at Mihkel, sending them both flying into the water. "Amon is going to get himself shot…" Frost muttered.

I started to move toward the water when Drake put his hand on my wrist. "I wouldn't interrupt this," he said.

"You're just going to let him drown Mihkel?"

"He won't drown him, not his own kin," Frost said.

I did a double take. "Kin? As in family?"

"Nephew," said Drake.

"You were just planning on keeping this from us?" I pushed Drake's hand off my wrist and made my way toward the water when someone grabbed the back of my jacket. It was Frost.

"Leave them be, Ballory's older brother is Mihkel's biological father."

Mihkel suddenly shot out of the water, trying to get away from Ballory. Because he was taken by surprise, he was no match for Ballory. "You think Craig died for nothing? That he didn't know the risks when he took you in as his own?" He grabbed hold of Mihkel and forced him to look directly at him. "Did you think that your blood relatives just abandoned you to a total stranger? I wanted to take you in as my own son, but it would have been too dangerous for you."

"Amon!" Frost yelled. "That's enough! Let him out of the water, we need to talk to them about everything."

"So, Ballory tries to drown one of us and that makes you want to open up about everything?" I frowned.

Frost gave me warning look. "I suggest you watch your tone, Elena." The looked reminded me of my father. He stood up and pulled Mihkel and then Ballory out of the water.

Mihkel started to sit down next to me when Drake stopped him. "It's going to get dark soon, I suggest everyone change into dry clothes. The temperature is going to drop drastically and no one needs to get sick and die of pneumonia."

After we changed clothes, Frost forced everyone to eat something. "I appreciate all of this, but why are you becoming mother of the year?" Drake asked, tearing a piece of bread off the loaf and sticking it in his mouth. "Lieutenant."

"I won't be held responsible for some stupid decisions made by certain people in this group," said Frost. "As much as I fought your father on this, I still got saddled with the responsibility of the most dangerous job around. There is a very good chance that there will be blood because of all this. I was actually looking forward to living till I was in my sixties and retiring to some province that isn't Arcadia or Blackwater to die."

"How bad is it going to get?" Mihkel asked, placing his hand on top of mine.

"You have no idea," said Ballory.

"Let's not scare them before anything even happens," Drake said.

"How about you tell us what's going on? I, for one, would like to know in case I die," I snapped. "Lieutenant Ballory, here, almost drowned Mihkel not twenty minutes ago."

"Welcome to the family," Ballory said, shoving a container of water under Mihkel's nose.

"That's enough," Drake said. He was still looking rather weak, but I was glad to see he was on his feet. He took something out of Ballory's pack. "Do either of you know who this man is?"

Mihkel and I looked at what was in Drake's hand. It was a black and white photo of a single man. He was in a uniform that was similar to CROSS and GUARD, but not quite. His hair was short and he was clean shaven, but what caught my attention was the emptiness in his eyes. There wasn't coldness or hatred in them like my father, or Sayers, just emptiness.

"No," I said.

"Jon Lucis," Mihkel said, causing me to stare at him.

"How do you know who he is?" I asked.

"Craig," Mihkel said simply, causing Ballory to smack him upside the head.

"Show some respect," Ballory said. "Even though he wasn't your biological father, he was still your father."

Ballory had a point, I still thought of Carter and Elise Hawthorne as my parents, and I was going to keep Elena

* * *

Hawthorne as my name. Then, it hit me. Mihkel didn't know his true name. I was quite curious myself. "Your birth name," I said.

"What?" Mihkel asked with raised eyebrows.

"Do you want to know what your birth name is?"

Ballory, Frost, Mihkel, and Drake just looked at me. "You know what my real name is?" he asked. "Why didn't you tell me earlier?"

"I don't know your birth name, but Ballory does," I said.

"Simon Redfield," said Ballory. "I told you, we're family, by blood."

"Why would your name be Ballory if you are my father's younger brother?" Mihkel asked.

"Save the family drama story for another time," said Frost. "Get back to explaining Jon Lucis to them, they need to know about him and The Order more than anything."

"Who is Jon Lucis," I asked.

"What is The Order?" Mihkel asked.

"The Order is a group of people who decided to give one man so much power that he created something that could destroy the entire world," Drake said. He had laid down, putting his head in my lap, the adrenaline was wearing off. "A relative of yours."

"Mine?" I asked. "I'm related to Jon Lucis?"

"No," Drake said keeping his eyes closed. "I'm really glad he isn't here to hear that. That would really rub him the wrong way. This relative goes by the name of Aleksandar Cedomir."

My heart started swimming. All this new information was finally taking its toll. Closing my eyes, I took in a breath. "I know this is a lot for both of you," said Ballory. "Things haven't been going to plan."

"Plan?" Mihkel asked.

"The group going to Aion was supposed to be bigger than five," Frost said.

"Who else was supposed to be coming with us?"

"Captain Sayers, Chief Engineer Crane and…a woman," said Ballory turning slightly red. When Ballory mentioned the woman, Frost shook his head and Drake let out a heavy sigh in my lap.

Mihkel spoke before I could, "Who is she?"

"You will either find her to be an ally or a thorn in your side," Drake said.

"That doesn't answer the question," I said.

"Morgan Thrace. She's originally from Solanum, but she's been a nomad since she turned sixteen. Taking any job that would have her, she did work for both CROSS and GUARD, along with the Soli rebels. You pay her and she'll work for you."

"So, she's a neutral thorn in everyone's side?" Mihkel asked.

"More like a greedy bitch…" Frost muttered.

Ballory made a move toward Frost, baring his pointed teeth. Mihkel started to stand when I put my hand on his wrist and slowly shook my head. Drake didn't make any sort of movement, like he had seen this before. "Remember what I told you the next time you insult her?"

"I'd like to see you try…you're not even a Contractor," Frost said.

"And you're an abomination," Ballory snapped.

"Easy there, boys…" a woman suddenly said, making us all jump.

We looked behind us to see a woman wearing black pants, a black long sleeve shirt, and a dark brown jacket. Her long, dark brown hair was in a braid and she had tree jumping gloves on that were similar to the ones Mihkel and I had. She was armed with a knife and two long, thin swords. Mihkel and I helped Drake sit up.

"Morgan Thrace…" Drake said.

"Hi, Drake, you're looking a little worse for wear," she said, standing just out of everyone's reach.

"You look pretty good for someone that wants people to think she's dead." Drake was trying to force himself up on his feet.

"Sit down, Drake…before you hurt yourself," Morgan said, sitting down on the rock. She eyed Frost who had been staring at her this entire time. "Come on, Amon…it hasn't been that long. Down, Frost, I'm here as an ally."

"Forced ally," Frost muttered.

"You haven't aged a day," Amon said. "It's been six years." I watched as he unconsciously rubbed his left ring finger where a wedding ring would have been.

"The gift of being a descendent of the Erathis."

"Of a curse—" Frost was cut off by Drake doubling over and vomiting blood.

"Lay him on his side," said Morgan, taking her pack off and coming over to Drake.

"What are you going to do?" Frost asked, grabbing her wrist.

"I'm going to save him, if you'll release me?"

"How do we know you're not going to kill him? The majority of us know your history with CROSS."

"She's an Erathis," Ballory said. "She is unable to hurt those who have not wronged her."

"He's dying!" I yelled. "Let go of her!"

Frost let go of Morgan's wrist and she went to work.

++++

That night I woke up to find that Mihkel was awake. He was sitting on the ledge with his legs hanging over the side. I picked up the blanket and walked over to him. "Can't sleep?" I asked, sitting down next to him.

"No, I was just thinking."

"What about?"

"About if we hadn't gone to the reservoir that day…maybe none of this would have happened."

I wrapped the blanket around us. "I wouldn't have this Shinar leg, we wouldn't have been forced into CROSS."

"Well, I think there is one good thing about all this." Mihkel looked at me with his dark blue eyes. It was then I realized they weren't blue anymore. They were jade green, just like Frost and Drake's.

"What's that?"

"You may not have forgiven me, but you're talking to me again." He took hold of my hand, squeezing it gently. "I never wanted to hurt you…"

"I know…I'm not the forgiving type. It's a fault of mine."

On a normal afternoon with Selig, and Mihkel, the rain was falling in relentless waves. We had been in town, trying to trade old chunks of paraffin for medicinal herbs, but the apothecary wasn't feeling generous. We would have gone to the Lore, but CROSS had been swarming the place all morning. It didn't help we were all quite hungry and getting weaker with every step we took. For two days, Selig and I had been trying to ease Ally's pain with boiled water and pine needles. We had come out on this futile errand because we couldn't take her crying anymore on that day.

Mihkel had gone home to see if he could scrounge up some spare coal for a trade. But by the time he would have gotten back, the market would be closed. Selig and I had found ourselves staggering along in the rain, trying to find a place to wait out the rain. My jacket had been soaked through, chilling me to the bone. Selig couldn't stop shaking; his jacket had been ruined and we hadn't scraped enough together to get him a new one.

Unable to take it anymore, Selig led us to the Lore hoping someone would take pity on us. Usually we were accepted there because of our grandfather. He had been one of the ones who started the Lore, and anyone carrying the Hawthorne name was generally accepted. It took some coaxing out of the traders, but Selig and I had been welcomed in. Our father had made them all nervous but there were a couple of times in which he accompanied us. It had been strange to see him out of his uniform.

I had gone into the Lore by myself when Selig got distracted by someone. I hadn't made it seven steps inside, when I was slammed to the ground. I didn't have any idea who it was, but I knew they were part of CROSS. I could tell from the scent left behind from the soap he used. My lungs were screaming for air as a boot was pressing down on my back, sinking me deeper and deeper into the mud. It wasn't until the weight was suddenly removed from my back, I managed to look up and see my brother had tackled the CROSS soldier into the mud.

Selig had lost it, repeatedly punching the young soldier who was only a Private. This couldn't have been more than his first month on the job, his uniform was still crisp. I sat there in the mud, just watching my brother dig his grave, deeper and deeper. Unable to do anything about it.

The next moment would have been the end of both our lives, if it hadn't been for Mihkel. General Nolan himself had snapped a whip, catching Selig by his neck, instantly making him stop, as he was pulled to his knees, gagging while trying to breathe at the same time. It was Sayers who had pulled me to my feet and forced me to watch Selig getting dragged out into the square where his lashings until death would happen. It would have been my turn next. Our desperation had made Selig snap, and had made me weak enough I couldn't have done anything to help him. Selig had to endure six lashings before Mihkel had returned with my father behind him. Both Selig and I gotten ten lashings each and I didn't speak to Mihkel for a year. I was so far gone, I couldn't see past what he had done as a betrayal.

Our conversation took me by surprise, making me realize something. The boy that irritated me had become the boy I loved again. "It's always the little things."

"Do you think you're going to go by your birth name when this is all over? If we survive this?"

I shook my head. I remembered when Michael told me what it was and I was glad to know, but I wasn't going to change who I was now. "What about you?"

"Thinking about it," Mihkel sighed and noticed I was shivering slightly. The temperature had dropped drastically. He opened the blanket and motioned for me to scoot closer to him "I'm not going to bite."

I sighed and moved closer to Mihkel as he wrapped the blanket around both of us. Feeling tired, I laid my head on his shoulder and closed my eyes for a minute. "I forgave you a long time ago."

"Thanks for letting me know."

We looked at each other and he put his fingers on my cheek. "I never stopped loving you," he whispered, putting his forehead to mine. He kissed me and it was the same kiss he had given me two years ago. Before everything happened. I kissed him back, welcoming the heat rising up my face. Breaking the kiss, I looked at him.

"What's wrong?"

"Give me your hand."

He raised his eyebrows at me, but held out his hand, intertwining our fingers.

The building was mostly made up of tinted glass. Something told me from the layout you didn't want to know what was going on behind most doors.

I stood there, in white colored scrubs, with no shoes or socks on. My hair was done in a side braid and I had a black metal band on my right wrist. The band had to have been made of something created by Ashtan, for I couldn't break it off. Mihkel was next to me, looking as confused as I used to be with these…flashes. He was dressed identically to me, with his coal-colored hair neatly combed and he was wearing the same metal band as I was.

It wasn't until we heard footsteps that I felt my chest tighten. I start to look for a place to hide when someone put their hand on my shoulder. We turned to see it was Captain Sayers. "Do you have abilities?" I asked.

"Wait a minute…what's going on?" Mihkel asked, turning his head, trying to take everything in. "What is this?"

Sayers just ignored him. "No, but your sensory fibers, your…deep connection with Tiitus, and because of his ability, we are bound in some way, allowing you to see me here," Sayers said. "You've got a lot to learn, Elena. And both of you will learn in due time."

I had never seen Sayers this way before. He was dressed in clothing I had never seen him in before and he looked disheveled. He even looked—ashamed.

"What's going on?" I asked.

"I second that question," Mihkel stated.

"It's the day when you and Mihkel were rescued from the Ashtan Capitol."

I wanted to ask him something but my attention was directed elsewhere; toward a younger Frost and Sayers. They were both armed with guns and had blank looks on their faces. I took hold of Mihkel's hand and squeezed it. Hoping he took that as I would explain everything as soon as I could.

"You two aren't the ones…who executed everyone? Are you? Tell me you're not the one who carried out the orders to kill

● ● ●

innocent children because someone got bored with the PULSE program in the Capitol." I let go of Mihkel's hand and shoved Sayers against the wall. I hesitated for a moment, forgetting how real all this felt; my hands shoving Sayers, the familiar touch of Mihkel's hand, and the rage I had building up inside me. All of it was real. We just had the misfortune of it being in a memory flash. So, whatever I did here, wouldn't translate to Sayers in present time. Unfortunately for Sayers, I still had my Shinar leg.

"Elena…" Mihkel said.

Sayers took the moment to speak. "It wasn't just the two of us. Somehow, I don't think you'll find it surprising."

My heart was in my throat as I watched Sayers motion for me to look back where the younger him and Frost came out. There were two young men I didn't recognize, but I was willing to bet one was Aleksandar Cedomir. It was then I saw the last person I was expecting to see.

My father.

I was suddenly back on the rock, next to Mihkel, who had a very confused look on his face. "Elena?" he asked. "What was…?"

"It was them…" I said, unable to catch my breath. I stood up as did Mihkel, slowly watching me.

"Elena, what did you see?"

I walked over to where Frost and Ballory were sleeping. I kicked Frost and then I kicked Ballory as hard as I could. "What in the Gods names?" Ballory muttered, clutching his abdomen.

"Is there something bothering you, Elena?" Frost asked, forcing himself to sit up. I had kicked him in his shoulder and, right now, I hoped I dislocated it.

"How could you?" I managed to get out before I felt my body start to shake. If I didn't calm down, I was going to hyperventilate.

"She saw something…" Morgan said, slowly sitting up. She had been sleeping next to Drake, in case something else went wrong.

"Elena…calm down," Mihkel said, coming over to me. He put his hands on my face. "You need to slow your breathing. Breathe."

• • •

Looking at Mihkel's face, I started to calm. "Want to let everyone know what you saw?" Frost asked, looking very irritated.

"She saw the truth," Morgan said. "What CROSS did, what GUARD did, what we all did."

"That was a mistake," Drake said suddenly, causing all of us to stare at him.

"No one said the truth was easy to hear," Ballory said. "You both need to understand this, The Order will be aware if they aren't already. The two of you have awakened. Completely. Disabling your trackers isn't going to keep you safe; it was just to get us a little bit of a head start. Understand this: life was hard before this happened. It's going to be close to impossible once they get a lead on you. So stop acting like children, and trust that we know what we're doing!"

"Then, how about you tell us the whole truth?" Mihkel asked, keeping his arm around my shoulders. "You want us to stop acting like children, then stop treating us like children."

"There are four men in the Ashtan Capitol of Arcadia right now and there is only one purpose for them to be there," Frost said.

"What's that?" I asked.

"To kill the King."

Chapter 51

Ballory and Frost made everyone eat something and rest till morning. Once again, they said everything will be explained, we would just have to wait. When it started to grow light, I sat up, unable to get more than an hour of sleep. I looked around to see Mihkel was unable to sleep as well.

I got up and walked over to where he was sitting. I sat down next to him and he looked at me. "Can't sleep again?" he asked.

"No," I said, sighing. "Did you get any sleep?"

"Maybe an hour." Mihkel held up a piece of bread and tore it in half. Holding up a piece to me, I took it. "I'm still hoping this isn't real, does that make me a coward?"

I shook my head. "You've been through more than I have in this short period of time."

"You lost a leg in a very painful way."

"You lost both your parents."

"They weren't my parents," said Mihkel. "Feel free to kiss me again, that whole memory flash thing...kind of interrupted us."

Not being able to control myself, I smiled. I kissed him, wanting to go back to before. Before we learned what they did. Before I had such a rage inside me, I was willing... no, wanting to inflict pain on those trying to protect me. The kiss was brief, but it put a smile on both our faces. What I had left of home, was Mihkel. As I was home to Mihkel.

"As much as I love young love, you may want to wait for a more appropriate time for that."

I broke the kiss to see Morgan was walking over. "You two need to get some rest," she said, sitting down next to us.

"I don't know if that's possible right now," Mihkel said, rubbing the back of his neck.

"Their intent on telling you everything wasn't meant to scare you, it was to make you aware. Blood was spilled, and more blood will be spilled before the end."

"Aware that everyone is going to be looking for us?" I asked.

"That and other things," said Morgan. "If you two can't sleep, then I suggest we keep moving."

"What about the others?" Mihkel asked.

"They can sleep anywhere and anytime, they were trained for it. You two will have more energy now than if we wait a couple more hours." Morgan stood up. "Get your stuff together, we're moving out in ten."

"How many more days do we have until we get to Aion?" I looked at Morgan.

"We have a day before it starts to get colder than you've ever experienced. Then it's another half a day if there isn't a blizzard," Ballory said, pulling on his pack.

I stood up, as did Mihkel. It was then the water started to seem like it was vibrating before moving into the ground. "What the hell is that?" asked Mihkel.

Ballory pulled his pack off and took out a pair of clear glasses; the ones all the CROSS soldiers of rank Lieutenant and Captain wore. He slipped them on and started to scan the sky. "Son of a bitch..." he said. "Everyone up! Now!"

"What's going on?" Frost asked, the first on his feet. He didn't say anything when he saw the glasses on Ballory. He took out a pair and put them on. "Time to go."

"What has you two freaked out?" Mihkel had a shaky voice.

"No time to explain." Ballory tossed us our packs. "When I say now, you two dive into the water and stay completely submerged."

"For how long?" I asked.

"Not sure," Frost replied.

Drake was up, but he was still looking rather weak. Morgan took out a syringe out of her pack and injected it into his neck. "I'm just letting all of you know, when this is over, I will repay you this pain you're putting me through," Drake said, rubbing his neck.

Now, everyone but Mihkel and I had on a pair of those glasses. "What are those?" he asked.

"I know you two have issues trusting us right now, but everything will be fully explained later," Ballory said. "Captain Fisher and I will be going in the water with you. No one goes anywhere alone. Morgan, you and Frost are going toward the trees. Feel up to being a distraction?"

"Distraction? For what?"

"It's The Order," Frost said. "This is imperative, do not disturb the water in any way once you're under."

"How the hell is that even possible?" Mihkel snapped.

"Follow my lead," said Ballory. "Use your packs to break the water surface."

"Maybe I should have learned how to cliff dive properly…" I glared at the water.

"Glad to see you can find humor in this situation," Drake had a dark smirk on his face.

"Dive or die by what is coming to kill us," Ballory said.

Without another word, Ballory dove off the cliff using his pack as a lead. Mihkel and I looked at each other briefly and then took our packs off. "Did I ever mention I hate heights?" Mihkel asked.

"Says the boy who climbed down the reservoir multiple times," I said, looking at him. I saw he was showing a nervous smile.

"If you two don't go now, I will shove you off this cliff," snapped Drake.

Mihkel dove first, mimicking the form Ballory used. I followed.

I landed in the water, feeling like my lungs were going to explode. The cliff wasn't any higher than the tower at the Ragnar City reservoir, but the temperature of the water was drastically different. It was freezing.

Right as I managed to gather my bearings, there was another splash beside me. It had to be Drake. Slowly, I swam up to the surface and stuck my head up enough so my chin was just touching the water. "Take a deep breath and follow me," whispered Ballory. "Elena, right behind me. Mihkel, you follow her. Fisher will follow a yard or two behind, ensuring we're not followed."

"I take it you know where you're going?" I asked.

"Of course I do," said Drake. "Get going."

Ballory took in a breath; Mihkel and I did as well. We sunk under the water and it only took about ten seconds for my eyes to get used to the water.

As I swam through the water, it was easy to follow Ballory. He wasn't using his full strength, which I knew was because of me. I was the weakest swimmer out of everyone due to my Shinar leg. I should have taken Michael's word that it was going to take longer than I thought to get used to this leg.

While we were swimming, I felt the pressure start to build up. Especially in my ears. I must have started to slow down, for Mihkel was suddenly beside me. As we were swimming, he gave me what looked like a wink.

Abruptly, Ballory stopped swimming. We caught up to him and he held his arm out, motioning for us to stop. I saw he had a knife in his hand. At that moment, I felt a sharp pain in my side. I let out the rest of the air in my lungs from the surprise pain. Almost instantly, I started to feel heavy. Someone with strong hands pulled me to them and put their lips to mine, blowing air into me. The facial hair told me it was either Drake or Ballory but my head was getting foggy too quickly. Whatever had bitten me must have poisonous teeth; I was being affected by it too fast.

I must have been drifting in and out of consciousness, for I couldn't remember getting out of the water. My vision was blurry, but my hearing was fine. "What's happening to her?" Mihkel asked sounding frantic.

"She was bitten by a ciclid, a highly poisonous fish. She doesn't have a lot of time," Ballory said. "Fisher!"

After that, I blacked out completely.

Chapter 52

I woke up in a lichen filled underwater cave covered in a blanket. I slowly started to sit up, only to realize I wasn't wearing anything. Clutching the blanket to my chest, I looked around. I only saw Mihkel. He did a double take, looking relieved to see me awake. He came over to me holding a canteen of water. "Amon said you need to drink plenty of water," he said, a gentle tone in his voice.

"What happened?"

"You were bitten by a poisonous fish of some kind, which was why Ballory had stopped swimming. We were going straight into a pool of them."

"Where's Drake and Ballory?"

Mihkel didn't answer right away. He gently placed his hand on my bare back, making the heat rise in my entire body. As if noticing my reaction, he turned his head as he wrapped the blanket completely around my torso and let me hold the corners of it. "Drink this."

I took a sip and tried to swallow but I couldn't. "I can't."

"Keep trying," said Mihkel. "Amon said it might take a couple of tries, but you have to drink."

He started to put the canteen to my lips again and I managed to take a couple of sips, my throat still feeling raw. Frowning, I tried to push the canteen away, but he wouldn't let me. Keep drinking."

When I managed to take another three or four sips, he let me stop for a minute. "Where are Drake and Ballory?" I asked again.

"They went to meet up with the others. They stopped the poison from spreading, but's still in your bloodstream."

"Did they ever tell you what was coming toward us?" I asked, able to hang onto the water canteen myself.

"Some type of bird that The Order created back when PULSE was created. If they had caught sight of us, they would have gone straight back to the tracking team." He stopped when he said that. "Sorry…"

"Not your fault."

Mihkel picked up some clothes and set them in my lap. "Ballory had to get rid of the clothes you were wearing. I'll leave you to get dressed." With that, he got up and walked over to the far side of the cave with his back turned to me.

Turning my back to him, I let the blanket fall to my waist and pulled on my underwear. The pants were a dark green and similar to the ones I had been wearing. The shirt was long sleeved and black. My boots were the same and so was my jacket. Pulling those on, I pulled my hair back into a messy knot. "I'm dressed," I said.

Mihkel turned around and came back over to me. "Think you're able to eat something?" He pulled out some more bread and started to tear it in half. I took a piece and took a small bite of it. Chewing, I saw Mihkel watching me intently, seeming to forget that he had the other half in his hand. I swallowed the bite of bread and took another drink of water. When he was satisfied, he started to eat his piece.

"How long was I out?"

"A few hours. Amon wanted me to tell you we're going to be reaching the beginning of the terrain that is covered in snow soon. As soon as they get back, we're going to leave."

I suddenly realized that I was shaking. I didn't know if I was cold, scared, or if it was a side effect from the poison. Mihkel sat down beside me and put his arms around me. "We should probably try and get some rest, they'll be back in a couple of hours."

"I don't think I can sleep." I was so wired, but I was also exhausted.

"Just try," he said, kissing my cheek lightly. "I will if you will."

We both must have fallen asleep, for neither of us heard Drake and Ballory come back. I shot awake when I felt someone shake me. "It's time to go," Ballory said, kneeling down. "Think you can stand?" He stood up and offered his hand.

I took it and he pulled me to my feet. I was a little unsteady at first, but after a couple of seconds, I was fine. "Water, bread, and sleep did you well," Drake squeezed my shoulder.

"You're looking better, too."

* * *

"Thrace gave me another injection of whatever it was," said Drake. "I'm on even more borrowed time."

I stayed silent, not knowing what to say to that. Watching as Drake pulled Mihkel to his feet, we picked up our packs without looking at each other. "Where are the others?" Mihkel asked.

"Depending on how fast they're going, I would say they're almost at the border of the snow region," said Ballory. "After all, Frost is from Aion, but I would have to say Crane knows the land better than anyone else."

"Both Frost and Crane are from Aion?" Mihkel asked.

"Not exactly, Frost came from the tracking surveying unit of CROSS which originated in Aion," said Drake.

"Things are going to get harder from here," said Ballory. "Because we're so close to the snow region, we'll have to avoid getting wet at all costs. There are plenty of people who have frozen to death on the way to Aion by taking shortcuts."

"What we're wearing isn't going to be warm enough," said Mihkel.

"Don't worry about that now," said Drake. "It's been taken care of."

As I was about to pull my pack on, Ballory stopped me. "I don't want you carrying anything for the first mile. Just to make sure you're well enough to walk."

It must have been showing on my face that I was going to protest because Drake spoke up first. "Let her have the pack, she'll be going up in trees anyway." He looked at me. "She's the best climber and a natural at tree jumping. The color is already coming back in her face. If she can climb a tree without a problem, then she can carry her pack, Lieutenant."

"Yes, sir." Ballory let go of my pack.

Pulling it on, I latched it across my chest and abdomen so it would be snug against my back for the climb. When I had first started to learn how to climb and jump through trees, I would have my pack loose and most of the time it would fall to the ground, defeating the purpose of staying up in the trees.

"Climb up a tree," said Drake. "Let's see how well you really are."

"We should probably get out of the cave first," said Mihkel.

The cave was smaller than the one in Ragnar City. It took only minutes to get through it. We were able to avoid the water without much trouble. Once we reached the end of the cave, the temperature dropped at least twenty degrees. "We have maybe another mile before we reach the snow region," Drake said. "We'll meet up with the others there and get some warmer clothes."

I took the opportunity to pull on my grip gloves. Flexing my fingers, I felt the gloves mold to my hands again. Thinking for a brief moment, I decided to keep my pack with me. It was because I was used to climbing with the extra weight. For whatever reason, I climbed better that way.

"I'll be back in ten minutes," I said.

Finding a branch, I reached up. When my fingers were wrapped around it, I put my foot on the trunk and did a mix of pulling and pushing myself up the tree. I had chosen a good tree; there were a plentiful amount of branches that I could just climb up normally. I wouldn't have to use my jumping skills, which always takes more energy.

As I climbed, the air was getting stiff, making me uneasy. The oxygen was lessening faster than I had hoped. I stopped climbing when I was two-thirds up. Looking down, I could barely see the others on the ground, so I decided to climb down.

When I reached one of the beginning branches, I let go of the branch I was holding onto and landed easily on my feet. "I think you're doing okay," Ballory said.

"Why is the air so thin already?" I asked.

"The trees are different in this area. That, and we're very close to Ishalgen, the tallest mountain. So, we're on a steady uphill climb," Drake said.

Chapter 53

The air seemed to have a thin sheet of ice over it as we moved. I wasn't the only one who was being slowed down by this. Though, I figured Drake was having trouble because he was in need of medical attention. I didn't know if Mihkel had ever been to Aion, but I knew that he and Ballory were related, so it could be something as simple as genetics giving Mihkel his edge. Someone noticed I was having trouble, for we suddenly stopped. "We're taking a break," said Ballory. He didn't look at me when he spoke, keeping his eyes trained on Drake. "Drink some water and catch your breath."

Ballory shrugged off his pack and opened it. He took out a small metal case and then a syringe that was already filled with some sort of medicine. Kneeling down, he injected the medicine into Drake's neck, causing him to stiffen as the medicine coursed through his bloodstream. "When we're in Aion, I'm going to do this to you. We'll see how you like it," Drake snapped at Ballory, rubbing the injection site on his neck.

"It's not my problem that you were unable to handle the repercussions of being sloppy in Ragnar," said Ballory. "Captain." The sarcasm was thick and gritty as he spoke. Something told me that these two never got along and it wasn't a good idea to have them work together.

We all stopped when we heard rustling coming from the trees and brush on my left side. Mihkel took out his bow and armed it with an arrow. Ballory took out a gun and tossed me a hunting knife, Drake also had a gun out.

As we waited for our opponent to appear, I was the first to realize who it was. "Enrik?" I asked.

Enrik jumped into view, his beautiful coat covered in a mix of mud and blood. He came up to me and nudged my leg with his nose. "Well, that wasn't what I was expecting to come through the brush..." said Drake, holstering his gun. Mihkel put his arrow back in the quiver and relaxed. Ballory was the last to put his weapon up.

"Do I even want to know how he found us?" he asked.

"He's a wolf," I said, kneeling down and letting Enrik lick my hand as I checked him over. It seemed that half the blood was his and the other half belonged to something else. He must have hunted on his way to find us. "My…dad used to take him hunting. He's a natural at it, and he always follows Selig or myself."

When I was satisfied that the blood belonging to Enrik had dried and the wounds were clotting, I relaxed. I stood up and scratched him behind his ears. "Glad you're here…" I said. I needed a familiar face with me and Enrik was it. Yes, I've known Mihkel and Drake for years, but Enrik was immediate family.

After we all drank some water, we started walking again. Enrik led the way, Drake right behind him. Mihkel and I were following with Ballory watching the back. After whatever had come to track us before I had gotten bit by the fish, we were being even more cautious. Now, everyone had a weapon at arm's length. Since Mihkel had the most work to ready his, he kept an arrow partly ready to shoot. I had never seen him shoot in a situation like this before, but I wasn't worried. He was the best shot I had ever seen. Though, I had never seen Ballory or Mihkel's biological father shoot. Something told me his abilities came from one of those two.

"Something on your mind?" Mihkel asked, snapping me back to reality so quickly I tripped over a root and had to catch myself by slamming my hand against a tree. "I'll take that as a yes. You normally have better balance than that."

"Just thinking about pointless things," I said, adjusting the glasses Ballory had given me. "It's not important."

"If it's making you lose focus then I'd think it would be." He looked at me with raised eyebrows.

"Keep quiet," Ballory said from behind us. "We're getting close to the region which means we'll have to avoid tracking on both sides."

"Aion is aware we're coming? Right?" Mihkel asked.

"No," said Drake. "The man in charge of security for Aion doesn't keep it a secret that he hates Arcadia. He was also openly against the creation of PULSE. It was the reason he left Ashtan and went to Aion."

"A traitor?" I looked back at Ballory. "To Arcadia?"

"Something like that, but the head family of Aion hates Arcadia just as much as the General does," said Drake.

* * *

"Brigadier General," replied Ballory. "He's not the man in charge. Not yet, anyway."

We walked for another twenty yards or so when Drake stopped. He held up his hand and Ballory shoved Mihkel and me to the ground. Enrik came over to where Ballory was with his fangs bared, the fur on the back of his neck standing tall. He raised his eyes when he heard something. As he sniffed the air, he started growling and bared his fangs again. The only time I had seen him like this was when two GUARD members came into the house and took my father away. He had the look of wanting to kill in his eyes.

Ballory and Drake took out their guns. One of them aimed their gun toward the direction Enrik was focusing on while the other scanned the area. Looking around, I saw there was a tree that was easy to climb. I started to stand up, reaching for the nearest branch. As soon as I felt the bark beneath my fingers I jumped, grabbing the branch with both hands and swinging my legs up.

I had gotten up a few feet in the air when I stopped. Looking around, I relaxed when I saw who it was. I took a roll from my pack and dropped it on Ballory's head. He responded by pointing his gun at me. "It's the others," I said. "Frost and Morgan." It was then that Enrik lunged and we heard a woman scream. What sounded like another wolf growling ensued.

Jumping down from the tree, I ran over to the screams and pulled Enrik away from Frost, who was now in wolf form. "I would say you guys are really loud, but I think we've both broken that rule," Morgan said, coming over to us. She put her hand on top of Frost's head. "He seems to be okay."

Frost nipped at her, causing her to flick him on his nose. "Fisher, how are you feeling?" she asked.

"Like my neck is the bend of a junkie's arm," he said.

After much protesting from Drake, Morgan gave him another dose of whatever she had been giving him. When everyone had their fill of water, we started to move again.

It seemed like it was getting colder with every step we took. The only one of us who wasn't having any difficulties was Enrik. His thick coat and fur between his paws made this environment ideal for him.

• • •

Enrik had disappeared from our sight for about ten minutes before suddenly coming back to us. "I'm betting he found the cliff," said Ballory.

"I almost forgot about the cliff," muttered Drake.

"We're going to have to tag team this," said Ballory. "Elena, you're with Drake, Mihkel, and I. Morgan, you and the wolves won't have too much of an issue getting up there. Mihkel and I will go up first; we'll be the spotters. Last thing we need is to be ambushed while we're climbing up the cliff."

When we made it to the cliff, my heart went into my throat. The cliff was a mix of rock, mud, and massive tree roots. It also looked very slick, covered in snow and probably ice. I could see why it was going to take two people to get up the cliff, even being experienced.

"As much as I love your take charge attitude…" Morgan said. "If the wolves and I can get up there without any help, then we're going first."

"Be my guest," Drake said. Morgan injected him with another dose of medicine. "Again? I'm going to get addicted at this rate."

"Wouldn't that just be too bad for you?" Morgan asked.

Mihkel and I exchanged looks. Right now, it seemed to be more dangerous to be around everyone here for their past.

Morgan opened her pack and took out two metal hooks. "See you up there." I had to admit, Morgan Thrace had me very curious.

The rest of us watched as Mihkel and Ballory struggled to get up the cliff. Ballory went first, trying to find just a bit of stable ground so he could pull Mihkel up.

It took them about half an hour to get halfway up. "Okay, Elena, we're next," Drake said. "This is going to take a while, so we need to start."

"I'll go first," I said.

"You sure about that?" Drake asked. "I'm aware you're the best climber, but trees are a lot different than a cliff."

I scanned the cliff and found a spot that was going to be easy for me to start the climb up. As I started to climb, I utilized my Shinar leg, making it easier to move.

Pulling myself up by a tree root, I looked to see Mihkel and Ballory had made it to the top of the cliff. Drake had caught up to me, for it was getting harder to climb. "Follow the path I take," he said.

Waiting for Drake to get a foot or two ahead of me, I started to mimic his movements. We had to stop and wait for Ballory and Mihkel to get their footing so they could help us up. The cliff was too steep for me to try to get over the gap in front of us by jumping. Ballory took the long metal hooks from Morgan and held them out with an outstretched arm. "Watch your head," said Drake, holding his hand open. He caught the first one as it was dropped and caught the second one just as easily. He wrapped the leather straps around his wrist. "Want to go for a ride?"

"I can get up to the top on my own," I said, even though he and I both knew I was lying.

"Elena…" Drake said, looking at me as he did when I was a child. "Come on, just until we get over this ridge, then you can continue to climb."

Knowing I was beat, I made my way over to Drake and wrapped my arms around his chest so I didn't choke him. He used the hooks and started to climb just as Morgan had. "What's on your mind, Elena?" he asked.

"I hate being weak."

"You're not a weak person, Elena," Drake said, as he continued to pull us up another couple inches. "Your sister would be in recovery if she had gotten a Shinar limb. Even your brother would still be in recovery. As much as you might hate to hear it, you are the kind of person that will be able to…embrace the limbs. Use them to your advantage." I didn't say anything else for the rest of the climb.

At the top of the ridge, there was a slab of stone that Mihkel and Ballory were standing on. Ballory pulled me up and then Drake. "You were carried, too?" Mihkel asked.

"Apparently I didn't have a choice," I said.

"Save your energy, we have to keep moving."

While climbing the cliff, the temperature had dropped again. "Is the temperature supposed to drop this fast?" I asked.

● ● ●

256

"No," Ballory said. "A storm's coming. We maybe have half an hour before it hits."

"We need to keep moving," Morgan said. "It won't matter how prepared we are if we get caught in the snowstorm."

"This just keep getting better and better," groaned Drake. "How is your leg holding up?"

"They may need to change it once we're in Aion," Morgan said. "Depending on your mechanic."

"Wait? What?" I asked.

"Shinar limbs made of iron that function well in the moderate to warmer areas will freeze and break in this climate. Most of them will, anyway," said Ballory.

"How do all of you know this and I don't? I'm the one with a metal leg," I snapped. "Why wouldn't have Michael told me?"

"He's the best engineer, but not always the best when it comes to his clients." Morgan took the metal hooks from Drake and put them back in her pack.

"Anything else I need to know?" I was feeling rather irritated.

"He probably made some altercations, so you should be fine," Drake said.

Enrik suddenly came trotting up to us, acting as if climbing the cliff was a breeze. "Show off..." I said, scratching him behind his ears.

"Let's go," Drake said.

Chapter 54

I could see why they called it the Snow Region or the Snow Covered Province. One step, we were walking on rocks and dirt. Now, we were walking in snow a foot deep. Even Enrik was halving a little trouble getting through the snow.

Ballory stayed beside me, acting like he was ready to catch me at any time. "We'll be there in around half a day, if the storm isn't too long…" Drake said. "How're you doing?" He looked at me.

"It's getting harder to move my leg," I said.

"That's normal," Morgan said. "Don't keep it to yourself when you can barely move it without a great amount of force. You'll have to stop or you'll damage your leg."

"How bad?"

"Bad enough to either need an enhancement or a whole new leg."

"Great…" I muttered to myself. I wasn't about to jump in line to get a new leg, the first procedure was painful enough.

It was getting harder to move as we kept walking, but it wasn't just because my leg was freezing; it was because my entire body was freezing. My jacket was soaked through with the snow that had started to fall and my hair was freezing from the contact with the snow.

"There's some shelter up ahead! We'll camp there for the night!" Drake yelled. I could barely hear him over the wind that was smacking us in the face constantly.

We made it into the shelter, which was an empty cave, and I was grateful for it. Sitting down, I couldn't stop shaking. My teeth were chattering so hard and loud, they were going to crack. "Captain," Ballory said. "A little help with a fire?"

"Is that wise?" Morgan asked, coming over to me and draping a blanket around the two of us. "In this condition?"

"Either that, or we all freeze," said Ballory. "Your choice."

Drake slowly peeled his gloves away and held his hand over the pieces of wood Ballory had produced from his pack. Holding his left hand over the wood, I couldn't help but stare. I had no idea what he was doing, but I knew exactly what was going to happen. Michael had said there was a Contractor who could create and manipulate fire. Then it happened.

A sliver of flame appeared out of nowhere, right under his palm. "If I was a religious person, I would be accusing him of being a Chaos Follower instead of a Cosmos Follower," Mihkel whispered.

The two of us watched, almost dumbfounded, as the flame slowly grew into a sphere. It wasn't until I noticed Drake's face that I managed to take my eyes away from the growing fireball. He was sweating and looked to be in an intense amount of pain. There was a puff of smoke and the fire was going.

Drake shook his hand as if extinguishing the flame and leaned against the cave wall, cradling his hand. Morgan got up and I wrapped the blanket tightly around myself. She opened up her pack, took out what looked like a first aid kit, and went over to Drake. She said something to him in a language I didn't understand and he responded in like. She applied some sort of off-white ointment all over his hand and wrist before wrapping a thick bandage around it. "The ointment will heal the burn. But, with your lingering condition, I want to take double precautions," she said.

"Thanks," he whispered, closing his eyes.

"What was that?" Mihkel asked.

"His Contractor ability," Ballory said, shrugging out of his coat and laying it by the fire to help it dry. The cave was getting warm rather quickly as he and Morgan worked to make it so the heat in the cave and the smoke left. My hair and body were thawing so quickly, I had to remove the blanket so it didn't get soaked.

"Come sit by the fire, you'll catch cold if you don't get your hair dry," Morgan said, undoing the long braid she had her hair in and combing her fingers through it.

"I want to go hunting," said Mihkel. "Tomorrow."

"We'll see," Ballory answered. "Morgan and I will go out when the storm stops to see just how far we have left to go. If it's going to be less than half a day, then we'll have enough food. If it's more than that, then you'll go hunting with me."

Ballory must have known what was going to come out of my mouth before I opened it. "Elena, you're staying here. You need to keep your metals limbs warm." The look on his face conveyed that I better not try to argue with him.

++++

The wind was keeping me awake. Usually, I could sleep through almost anything, storm or no storm. But, right now, my eyelids refused to get heavy. Rolling over, I saw I wasn't the only one who wasn't sleeping. Morgan was awake as well. When she noticed I was awake, she sat up and shifted so I could come join her.

 We sat away from the fire to not wake the others, but close enough to the heat that we didn't need a blanket. "Can't sleep?" she asked.

 "For some reason, the wind is keeping me awake," I said. "Usually it doesn't."

 "You're from Ragnar City. The storms are different in Aion than they are in the Forest Realm," she said.

 "Forest Realm?"

 "That's what my people call Blackwater Province. Aion is the Snow Realm, Xing is the Merchant Country, Banorae is the Desert Region, and Arcadia is also called the Valley of Death," she said, putting her long, black hair into a braid.

 "What about Kouros or Solanum?"

 "Kouros is Idle Hand for Arcadia, and Solanum is the Holy Land," she said without looking at me. "What do you know about the history of the Soli people?"

 I thought for a moment. I didn't know much, school was mostly just the basics and the history of the world. It was a rare thing that the teacher talked about Solanum. "I know they are easy to spot because of their different appearance," I was careful with choosing my words. "I know their religion is different from the religion the King pushes on everyone."

 "Do you know how it differs?"

 I had to think again. The religion that was followed in Ragnar City and the majority of the other provinces was simply known as 'the Fayth'. There are two gods; God of Cosmos, Valefor, and God of Chaos, Fenrir. Valefor rules over the heavens and Fenrir rules over the underworld. I had never put a lot of thought into religion. From the comment Mihkel made earlier, he hadn't either. It wasn't the most important task on people's minds in Ragnar City. Surviving day to day was more important. My family had adopted the philosophy of if you help others, they'll help you in return. It was getting harder and harder for that to work as an efficient system. The Fayth was more of an Arcadian thing, where the citizens didn't have to worry about where their next meal was coming from.

"The Soli believe in one God, not two," I said.

"You are smart, in more ways than survival," Morgan said. I think she meant that as a compliment, but I was too tired from the day to ponder it. "Firion is my people's God. The God of life and death. The story is that he takes the form of a large dog or wolf. He would walk through the land to personally witness the suffering his people were undergoing."

"After everything you've been through, you still believe in your God?" Drake asked, suddenly appearing beside us.

"It gives me something to hold some sort of faith in," Morgan said. "Lost it in the human race a long time ago."

"How bad was it?" I asked. "When you were in PULSE?"

"They own whatever piece of your soul you have left when they train you. You're a dog to them," said Drake. "Doing whatever they command you to do, proving you're helpful even though you have the skills you've acquired and the ability that made you special...or cursed." He ran his non-bandaged hand through his hair and sighed.

"Then why did you join CROSS?" I asked.

"I had the naive dream of wanting to change the world."

"Did you?"

Drake shook his head. "In the end, nothing will change. Besides, a person would have been a fool not to follow your father...your adoptive father."

"I think she still thinks of Carter as her father, unlike Mihkel," Morgan said.

That was true, even though my parents had lied to me for around eighteen years, or more like fourteen years, I still wanted to know who my biological parents were. Something told me I wasn't going to find out that easily.

* * *

Chapter 55

The storm died down in around four hours. Ballory and Morgan went out as they said they would, leaving the rest of us in the cave. I made tea while Mihkel checked the burn on Drake's and wrist. "This isn't healing as quickly as it should be, even with the ointment. That worries me."

"How about you just say it?" Drake asked. "I'm going to die."

"If you wanted to give up, why did you come?" Mihkel asked. "You could have just stayed in custody. They would have killed you quicker than what's happening to you now."

Drake looked at me briefly before he answered, "I'm not doing this for me."

Mihkel didn't say anything as he cleared off his hand and applied fresh ointment before placing a clean bandage on it. "You better hope they don't try to shoot you on sight when we get to the gate. They'll have better medical resources than what we have here."

"What's going on?" I asked.

Drake rubbed his mouth with his good hand and avoided eye contact with me. "You know that before one King was named...there was a treaty of peace between Aion, Arcadia, Kouros, and Xing?"

"Yes."

"The people in charge made it seem like everything was good and stable. But, it wasn't then and it isn't now. The once royal family of Aion...the history between the King of Aion and King Kahler was volatile and is still bad blood. One wrong move when we get there, and a war could start because the Regent Leven thinks we were sent as a decoy. The only reason they haven't blown each other up is because of Xing; they're the middle ground where all of the necessary meet-ups take place. Chancellor Luciar is traditional, but, unfortunately for the world, neither of his sons are like their father."

"The point of all of this is, right after PULSE was dissolved, some of them were sent to Aion."

It didn't go over well?" Mihkel asked.

• • •

"That's an understatement," muttered Drake. "We were used and then disposed of.'"

"Why wouldn't Arcadia look into it?"

"PULSE was looked at by the crown as an embarrassment. Some of us still work for Arcadia because your biological father was too proud of his accomplishments to have it completely erased.'"

"My father is one of the ones presumed dead?" Mihkel asked, sitting down next to me.

"Yes. Mathias Redfield. But, the last time I checked in on him, he was living in Solanum with his wife, your stepmother."

Mihkel and I looked at each other, unable to find words. The awkward silence didn't last long; Ballory and Morgan came back into the cave with a giant white wolf behind them. "That was fast," Drake said.

"We've got problems," Morgan said. "We need to go. Now."

"What's going on?" Mihkel asked.

"There isn't any time to explain, we need to be out of here in the next two minutes." Ballory picked up his and Morgan's pack. He tossed Morgan hers and pulled his on. "Come on."

Ballory pulled Drake to his feet and looked at Morgan. "We're going to have to split up again."

"In the next thirty seconds, it won't matter," Morgan said. "Elena, you and Mihkel go northwest with Ballory. You'll be getting close to the wall when you smell something like a chemical fire."

I knew what she was talking about; Mihkel also knew. The chemical fire was going to be whatever type of fuel Aion used the majority of the time. It was probably going to be coal since they were so high up in the mountains. "What are you waiting for?" Ballory asked. "Go!"

Mihkel and I picked up our packs as Enrik trotted out of the cave. The three of us followed after him.

Enrik stayed a couple feet in front of us, trotting some then stopping and sniffing the air. Then, he would watch us walk

* * *

toward him a few steps before starting to trot again. "Think he's doing that to make sure nothing ambushes us?" Ballory asked.

"No. He's either bored or he's hungry," I said. "He's loyal, but, like some of the people I know, he's a survivor."

"Only some?" Mihkel asked.

"Not everyone in Ragnar City is a survivor." I looked at him. "My mother and sister aren't survivors, neither is Selig's new wife. The only reason they're still alive is because of Selig, my father, and me. You and Sindri are a big part in keeping my family alive as—" I stopped when I felt something land on my face. Looking up, I saw it was snowing again.

"This will actually help our case," said Ballory.

"What's tracking us?" I asked.

"To be honest, it's something I've never seen before."

"Is it okay to be walking this pace?"

"Can't you smell that?" Ballory asked.

I stopped and breathed in some of the air. "Coal…we're already that close?"

"Yes and no," said Ballory. "We're almost at the wall, but we've still got a way to go to the main city."

"Are the others going to meet us at the wall?" Mihkel asked.

"Yes," said Ballory. "They went the other way around the cave. We'll meet up with them pretty soon."

"Then why did we split up again?"

"Just precaution." Ballory looked at the two of us. "You guys will be fine."

"You so sure about that?" Mihkel looked at me as he asked.

"I fear your fathers more than I fear CROSS or GUARD," said Ballory. "Elena, in your case, I fear your adoptive and biological father."

We found a well hidden spot to rest. Sitting under a thick row of trees, we ate a little more of the bread we had, waiting for the others to meet up with us. "Will they let us through the gate or will they try to kill us on sight?" Mihkel asked.

"It depends," Ballory said.

"On what?" I asked.

• • •

"On the mood of the man in charge of keeping Aion safe. Sometimes I wonder if your father modeled himself after the Brigadier General. They are the same in many ways."

"Brigadier General?" I raised my eyebrows.

"Aion has a standard military, they didn't want any part of CROSS, GUARD, or PULSE," Ballory said. "They have really gotten lazy when it comes to history."

"Actually, we learn a lot of history. It's just Arcadian history," Mihkel said.

"Touché…"

Ballory and Mihkel stood up instantly when we heard a branch snap. Enrik was on high alert as well. I slowly started to stand up, reaching for my knife. He was readying an arrow and I saw Ballory taking out his gun. I was going to need to learn how to shoot a gun or get a bigger knife.

Ballory turned the safety off on his gun and held his hand out to Mihkel and me. He motioned for Mihkel to move right as he went left. As Ballory had taken a couple steps, someone put a gun to the back of his head. "You should stick to what you know…" Drake said.

"Do you always have to use your gun or ability to make your presence known?" Ballory asked. "Captain?"

"The branch snapping didn't alert you enough it seemed." Drake holstered his gun. "Besides, I would never shoot Helo's brother."

"There is a call sign I haven't heard in a long time," said Ballory.

"The tone in your voice makes you seem so sincere," Morgan said, coming into view with Frost still in wolf form. "How about we get to the wall before we all freeze?"

"Sounds like a plan."

Frost had shifted back to his human form and dressed quickly. He led the way with Enrik this time. He had been so quiet and out of the way, I had almost forgotten he had been with us in the journey. As we trekked up the hill, the air continued to get colder and stiffer. As was my Shinar leg. Ballory had put his hand around my arm, which made me try to pull away. "This is just to help you get up the hill," said Ballory. "It's easy to see your limb is bothering you. Besides, another storm is coming."

"How can you tell?"

"The air," he answered.

At the top of the hill, my breath was taken away. The wall was truly a magnificent sight. Or, an intimidating one, depending on your point of view. Me, I wasn't so sure yet. But, I had a feeling I was going to form an opinion real soon. "Welcome to Aion…" Drake said. "A military power that rivals Arcadia, watch your step."

"Watch our step as in where we walk?" Mihkel asked, taking hold of my hand.

"In so many ways," Frost said, smirking.

The wall was made entirely of some form of metal. There were numerous guard posts and it was apparent a lot of their electricity went into powering the wall. "This is important, do not draw any weapon. They will see that as aggression and will open fire," Ballory said.

"A little paranoid this time," said Morgan.

"More like extremely cautious." Frost looked at Morgan with his still wolf-like eyes. "Hands visible, Elena, put this around Enrik's neck." He handed me a leather lead.

We started walking again, Enrik fighting the lead I had put around his neck. "It's temporary," I said.

"You don't ever have him on a lead, do you?" Drake asked.

"No," I said. "He's never needed one."

"It's just so they don't put him down on the spot." Drake rubbed the back of his neck. "He's intimidating if you don't know his manner."

We were about thirty feet away when Mihkel suddenly jumped in front of me and knocked something away by shooting an arrow. "How did you do that?" I asked after the shock wore off. I looked around to see it was a spear.

"I Think Mihkel's power just completely awakened…in the sense of true love," Ballory said. "Remarkable…from both parents."

"Well, well, well…if it isn't the dogs of CROSS," someone said. The man was dressed in a military uniform and had green eyes with a black streak in one. He was young,

266

couldn't be more than a year or two older than Mihkel and myself.

"Well I'll be damned…" Drake said, his voice full of mockery. "Look who's all grown up. That's an impressive trick."

I looked up to see another figure standing on top of the wall. Just from the way he carried himself, I could tell he was the Brigadier General. "There is only one explanation as to why you're missing Michael Crane and Dragan Sayers. The King is not dead. So…we have a problem."

Epilogue

Michael

There was a reason why I had decided to never return to this hell-in-disguise. It became apparent not six hours since I set foot in this place. Death followed me. Not that I was complaining, it meant that I was going to die sooner rather than later. But, I didn't want to go out the way I was dragging myself toward.

I kept the door barricaded until I heard the trap door latch shut. "I honestly thought I would last longer than this…" I said as I took a couple steps away from the door. I wasn't going all out on this…hero thing, but I wasn't going to bend over the table either.

Two GUARD soldiers broke down the door. As they filed in, they just stared at me. As I was scanning the unknown faces, my heart skipped a beat when I saw—him. "Faust…" I said, breathlessly.

Faust. The assassin who could bring even the God of Chaos to his knees. Parting the GUARD soldiers like they were water, I saw the familiar mask. The thin sheet of metal molded to his face, the facade that hid the one supposed weakness he had. Of course no one knew what his weakness was; at last anyone alive. He kept the hood of his cloak up and I already knew he wasn't going to remove his mask. He never took the mask off and he never spoke. Not that he needed to…he carries an unknown force with him. He was one of the few I actually feared. I had greatly underestimated the force behind the King. And, now—we were all going to pay for it.

My guardian's words seeped into my mind as I was raising my hands in surrender. *There will always be blood…*

"Faust…I'm surprised it took you this long."

Faust simply walked up to me and head-butted me. Everything went black.

Acknowledgements

I want to thank the person who pushed me to follow the hidden dream of being a writer. My Creative Writing and Composition Instructor Mike. I thank you with the love and respect I have for you. For the support you gave me when times were tough and letting me know I'll have at least one loyal fan throughout the writing career I'm so ever hopeful for.

I also want to thank my editor Monica for the amazing job you did, and for making the process go smoothly.

To Krystle Wright for the amazing book cover you created for this book. I hope it's the start of a long and eventful business relationship.

To fellow author Mark O'Brien, the encouragement and feedback you have given me through Facebook, Wattpad, and Twitter always made my day if not my week. Here is to both a long journey when it comes to writing, and know that I will be one of the first to read whatever you put out for the world.

And to my parents, words aren't needed.